WHITCHURCH-STOUFFVILLE PUBLIC LIBRARY

W9-ACZ-432

MINA'S CHILD

DEC 0 4 2020

Copyright © 2020 Paul Butler

Except for the use of short passages for review purposes, no part of this book may be reproduced, in part or in whole, or transmitted in any form or by any means, electronically or mechanically, including photocopying, recording, or any information or storage retrieval system, without prior permission in writing from the publisher or a licence from the Canadian Copyright Collective Agency (Access Copyright).

We gratefully acknowledge the support of the Canada Council for the Arts and the Ontario Arts Council for our publishing program. We also acknowledge the financial support of the Government of Canada.

Cover design: Val Fullard

Mina's Child is a work of fiction. All the characters portrayed in this book are fictitious and any resemblance to persons living or dead is purely coincidental.

Library and Archives Canada Cataloguing in Publication

Title: Mina's child : a novel / Paul Butler.
Names: Butler, Paul, 1964– author.
Series: Inanna poetry & fiction series.
Description: Series statement: Inanna poetry & fiction series
Identifiers: Canadiana (print) 20200203495 |
Canadiana (ebook) 20200203746 | ISBN 9781771337212 (softcover)
| ISBN 9781771337229 (epub) | ISBN 9781771337236 (Kindle)
| ISBN 9781771337243 (pdf)
Classification: LCC PS8553.U735 M56 2020 | DDC C813/.6—dc23

Printed and bound in Canada

Inanna Publications and Education Inc.
210 Founders College, York University
4700 Keele Street, Toronto, Ontario, Canada M3J 1P3
Telephone: (416) 736-5356 Fax: (416) 736-5765
Email: inanna.publications@inanna.ca   Website: www.inanna.ca

MINA'S CHILD

PAUL BUTLER

inanna poetry & fiction series

INANNA PUBLICATIONS AND EDUCATION INC.
TORONTO, CANADA

WITHDRAWN

WHITCHURCH-STOUFFVILLE PUBLIC LIBRARY

For Maura and Jemma

ALSO BY PAUL BUTLER

FICTION
The Widow's Fire
The Good Doctor
Titanic Ashes
Cupids
Hero
1982
NaGeira
Easton's Gold
Easton
Stoker's Shadow
The Surrogate Spirit

NON-FICTION
St. John's: City of Fire

Seven years ago, we all went through the flames; and the happiness of some of us since then is, we think, well worth the pain we endured. It is an added joy to Mina and to me that our boy's birthday is the same day as that on which Quincey Morris died. His mother holds, I know, the secret belief that some of our brave friend's spirit has passed into him. His bundle of names links all our little band of men together; but we call him Quincey.

—Jonathan Harker, *Dracula*, 1897

1. ABREE HARKER

FATHER'S SHRIEK WAS MUCH LOUDER than usual. This time it had formed a name: "Quincey!" As Abree hauled herself from her dream, luminous tadpoles swam around her, trailing their comet tails.

Abree's dream had been luscious, all enveloping, but this awakening was violent. She shrugged off her bedsheet and switched on her bedside lamp. Then she waited. Fear flooded around her like a rising moat. Huddled in the light's milky halo, Abree heard a far-off click, then Mother's soft voice, soothing like clear honey stirring in a pot. Mother had become adept at soothing of late. Her new skill had come from necessity. She obviously didn't want Jenny or Mrs. Rogers to come running, although the shriek, a lung-tearing sound, had surely awakened them. Abree knew the same discretion applied to her. If his daughter burst into his room, Father would be shamed. Even hearing her creak on the floorboards would be too much. So she remained motionless, head half raised from her pillow. The tadpoles swam for a few moments more before fading into sparks and then nothing. A moth, small and white like a paper scrap, battered its way around her lampshade.

Mother had dealt with the situation successfully, it seemed. She was talking softly. Whether responding or not, Father was obviously calm. Abree chased a desire to sink back into the same dream. But she knew it didn't work that way. The dream's details, so magical while she was experiencing them, were reconstituting themselves into waking thoughts; the scenario no longer seemed sublime but merely absurd. Abree had been the back end of a pantomime horse; the front end—a girl who seemed to know her but who Abree couldn't place—had been rhapsodizing about the stars. It had been weird enough but supremely enticing. A glorious cornucopia of flavours, textures, and colours had dwelt within her friend's descriptions. Stardust had tingled on Abree's tongue like some impossible combination of childhood sherbet and champagne. The friend had promised they would soon change places. Abree would have her turn to gaze at the heavens and absorb the wonder.

And then, Father's shriek.

She couldn't be mistaken about the word. *Quincey!* still echoed in the hiss of the bedsheet against her nightdress. She'd already known the nightmares were about Quincey, of course; it made sense that the dead son should haunt his father's dreams. What had never made sense was the fact that his son's name never passed through his lips during the day. Father *not* talking about Quincey had created a forbidden space in the house, a dangerous vacuum. Mother and Abree had stopped talking about him too. Quincey existed only in the silence. He nestled between the ticks of the grandfather clock.

Abree wondered about Mother, that she should have taken on her husband's taboo. She had winced last week, Abree noticed, when Jenny dusted around Quincey's picture.

"That's enough, Jenny," she'd said abruptly. "You can go and help Mrs. Rogers with lunch."

Jenny had curtsied and blushed before leaving the room. It was as though in that instant she too had taken on the family secret of Quincey, the dead one nobody was allowed to mention.

Mother knew how to share the language of emotion with the minimum of words. It was something in her pauses and the subtleties of her looks. Mother contrived to make children and servants feel as though they were in some undefined, permanent debt. Everyone watched her closely.

To the outside world, Abree believed, Quincey was the most real of the Harkers. He was the lightning-struck tree smouldering on the lawn while the picnickers tried to make small talk around it. His photograph on the mantelpiece, stern-faced and erect in his lieutenant's uniform, always drew visitors' eyes. Some would gaze wistfully in its direction, keeping a respectful distance. Some would catch Mother's eye and smile sadly. Others would look away, feeling guilty their loved ones had survived.

But no one mentioned Quincey in Father's presence. Father's fragility was too domineering. Outsiders sensed this, treading carefully around the subject of war. And tonight would make things worse. Would Father remember screaming Quincey's name? Would he know that everyone in the house had heard, or would his wife's soothing wash away memories of his nightmare? Abree imagined avoiding her father's eyes over breakfast, blushing whenever Jenny or Mrs. Rogers spoke to them. It seemed worse than anything, this shame of her father.

Mother's voice had lapsed into silence. Perhaps her words were too quiet to be heard, or perhaps Father had gone back to sleep. Abree heard the click of the lamp. The disturbance was over, for now. She settled down on the now-cool pillow, turned off the lamp, and tried to reimagine her pantomime horse. She was too awake to reclaim her dream quickly, but she wanted to feel its flavour once more. Buried in her companion's descriptions of the stars there tingled a promise of something marvellous. Its substance was mystic and enthralling, transcending war and death. The voice of her friend—she still couldn't place it—had seemed to whisper in her ear, even though Abree's head was buried in the thick material that made up the horse's flanks. The dream had designated a name for the friend—Lucy. There was a Lucy once, Abree remembered. She tried to follow the thread of memory back to its source. No, there had been no Lucy at school. It was a name belonging to her parents' story.

Abree thought back to Lucy rhapsodizing about the stars,

trying to remember the words Lucy had used. They had seemed so eloquent, so magical as she described the heavens. But Abree's efforts were useless. Phrases seemed to fizzle on the surface of her memory and then wink out like the effervescence of freshly-poured wine. Perhaps there had never really been words at all. Dreams often worked with essence and symbols. She'd thought she'd heard words, but she'd really experienced something far deeper, an unearthing of the divine.

The little moth was battering against the lampshade and the walls, searching desperately for the light. It came close to Abree's face in the darkness. She felt a little puff of air against her forehead. She thought of Quincey. Quincey with the worms, under the earth in some bleak mass grave in rural France. Quincey with the name of a hero. Quincey fulfilling someone else's dream.

She'd envied poor Quincey when he signed up and left for training. It had felt like an end of childhood for her as well. Shadows had fallen long in the evening as the two of them played out a last game of tennis. They'd lingered over each point, letting the ball bounce from their shoes and run away towards the trees so it would have to be retrieved. Nature hung around them, acorns plump, with the occasional soft thud of an apple or plum hitting the ground. It was almost too relaxed, too complacent, as though every pulse of life for acres around knew what Abree didn't want to know, that everything was on the brink of destruction. The falling plums and apples, the hissing leaves, and the shadows were like merciful executioners, preserving the serenity as long as possible.

Abree had been envious. Quincey was going *somewhere*. She, on the other hand, was staying with her parents. If childhood must end, she thought, it should end in adventure. Hers was ending in a brick wall.

Abree switched the lamp back on and threw off the bed-clothes again. The weight of sleep hadn't left her but she felt too rootless *not* to move, like a limb searching for its body. She slipped out of bed as quietly as she could and padded slowly to the curtains, pulling the lapels of her nightdress close around her neck with one hand, and reaching to tug an opening in the curtains with the other. She gazed into the pre-dawn Belgrave Square with its contours of mysterious foliage and its dark wall of houses some two hundred yards opposite, beyond the gardens. As she watched, a yellow light came on in an attic window. A servant must have awoken in a house just like her own. Dawn couldn't be far away. She looked into the gardens, a sea of undulating leaves, small birds hurling like grenades from one branch to another, preparing for the day. Moonlight touched the iron teeth of the fencing. Someone, a lone watcher, sat on one of the benches. A young man it seemed, from his outline. He appeared to be gazing at the Harkers' own house or at some point very close to it. Abree could just make out the outline of a suit, the paleness of his hands and face. Whoever it was seemed quite motionless, almost as though in a trance.

She moved away quickly and let the curtain drop. Her bedside lamp was on. She could be seen. She listened in the darkness, not yet ready to return to bed. Although the tall beech at the front of the house was not visible from where she was, the sound of the leaves grew like a stream as the breeze picked up strength. She had climbed the tree once to this level, thinking, mistakenly, that she could reach Quincey's room—now her own—and surprise him. But she'd had to shimmy down again and admit failure as the trunk had not come close enough.

Everything came back to Quincey, as much for her as for her parents. Even with eight years between them, they had always been playmates of a kind. They had appeared in the Christmas pageant together. When she was young, he had let her beat him at chess. When she grew older, she, naturally athletic, could beat him at tennis, even when he was trying. It could have been that his reflexes were naturally slow or it could have been the result of a physical anomaly—he had webbed toes—but Quincey was not adept at games. He was always happy to play them with her, however. Losing gracefully was part of his character.

When he left for war, she had been more alone than she could have imagined. The world became frightening, not with the excitement of adventure, but with the sense of things crumbling. It wasn't bullets she feared but those mundane sounds that had taken on an ominous quality: the knock on the door, the squeak of the gate, any hint that the telegram might be coming their way. And the telegram did arrive one Saturday morning. Mother opened the envelope with trembling fingers while Father backed into a corner of the room. Abree knew the world would remain comfortless and grey far into the future. This was growing up. And it was awful.

She moved back to her bed, more restless than ever, and switched off the lamp. The dream had brought something back to her at least. There was a world beyond this, beyond the brick wall that had ended her childhood. She listened for the moth again, but it was silent now. Soon, however, birdsong would rise in Belgrave Square. Dawn would trickle around the curtains. The newspapers talked of the gloom lifting at last, and it was suddenly possible to believe it. Tomorrow she'd have duties. She had said she would go to tea at Lyons with her mother in the morning. In the afternoon, she would meet with her tutor, Professor Reynolds, to talk over her dissertation. He'd winced when she'd mentioned her working title: *From Keats to Whitman: Mystic Premonitions*. She'd wondered then whether it was all really *her*, or whether she'd chosen this approach and this subject to fulfil the ambitions of another. Who could that "other" be but Quincey? Quincey had loved "Ode to a Nightingale" and became emotional when he talked of Whitman. It occurred to her she was trying to carve herself into a living memorial to her brother. How mighty are the dead! She was a moderately successful undergraduate, she knew that. But she perched awkwardly on her subjects, distrusting her right to study and argue.

Through the haze of sleepiness, a kind of conviction was forming. Lucy held the key. If she could find her way back to the dream or to some version of it, she might use Lucy's voice to slip into a more confident version of herself. On the way home from university yesterday, she'd gone to the National Gallery and had found herself gazing for longer than was decent at Edvard Munch's *Madonna* with her exposed breasts, her rivulets of black hair, and her defiant eroticism. This was a secret self. She'd been brought to suddenly by a nearby shuffle of feet. A party of schoolchildren, carefully marshalled away from Munch by a disapproving teacher, tittered and stared. She'd quickly left the gallery.

She knew what people thought of her—friends of her parents, tutors, even some of her fellow students. They thought her serious to the point of grimness. But it was all the wrong way around. She was serious because she was awkward, but the awkwardness had been foisted on her with the loss of her brother and her subsequent attempts at atonement. She had survived. She had never been in danger. How could she justify this?

The first pre-dawn squeaks and chatters came from Belgrave Square gardens. In minutes, light would show around the curtains and the noise would become intense. The final stage between childhood and adulthood is like a new birth. Somehow hers had missed its mark. She'd buckled under when she'd been required to push. But it would have to stop now. Lucy, she imagined, was whispering to her again of the stars and the heavens, not in words but rather in an ambient music that danced behind the rising birdsong. Lucy was hers now. She meant to hold on to this new friend.

2.

A BREE ASKED HER QUESTION out of nervousness, and she was surprised by its effect on her mother.

"Mama," Abree blurted, "did you ever know someone called Lucy?"

There was a moment. Mother looked directly at Abree, her eyes curious. Then her lips formed into a smile. She leaned back, reclining into the past.

The mood changed immediately. The smell of tea, rising steam, and freshly baked bread had permeated Lyons since they'd arrived, but the comfort from the old days had been absent. The gloom of war may have lifted, as the newspapers insisted, but another kind of pall had fallen in its stead. All the young men had been sucked out of England. Although many of them had returned, they had come back altered. They seemed intent on pursuing wilder amusements, and no longer frequented Lyons. And because there were so few escorts to the once-popular tea rooms, there were also fewer women. Those ladies who did go abroad in pairs and in groups lent their destinations a lopsided feel. Though parasols and hats adorned Lyons as in the old days, the few men who were present were white-haired or bald. There was a desperate optimism in the bustle of the waitresses, but Lyons was a ghost from another age.

Abree had been itching to be back at her studies, back to rearranging the arguments she would have to use with Professor Reynolds. An unhappy static had hung between her and her mother since they had sat down. Mother had looked away each time Abree caught her eye. This was so unlike her. She, like Lyons, seemed diminished. If she were a lioness, Abree thought, she'd be in a zoo, not wandering the plains of Africa.

It wasn't just Lyons, of course. The scream was between them too. Father's *Quincey!*—a near-silent, dog-whistle version of it—echoed in the rattle of the trolleys, the clink of china.

But Abree's question first startled, and then warmed, Mother. And Mother, in turn, warmed Lyons. Nostalgia radiated from her.

"What makes you ask, Abree?"

"I had a dream last night. The details are too silly to…"

Mother was still smiling. She raised her cup to her lips.

"But, well, someone called Lucy was in it. It was such a very vivid dream, and I seemed to know her."

"We nearly called you Lucy," said Mother. The static between them was gone. Mother was herself once more, in command, taking her time. Her eyes seemed to twinkle but with a touch of sadness as she laid her cup in her saucer. "I had such a dear friend with that name. If she hadn't died tragically when she was very young, she would have become Lady Godalming."

"She was to marry John Holmwood's father?"

"Yes, she was to marry Arthur. We all had such times together. Your father, Arthur, Lucy, a young doctor named John Seward, and I."

Mother turned. Her back was to the window, but she seemed to crane her neck for a glimpse outside. When she saw her view was blocked by waitresses with trays and an elderly couple, her gaze skittered back to Abree.

"You must have told me about her once," Abree prompted. The simple request, *tell me about her*, was too direct. Mother was best approached from the side.

"She was my best friend," Mother said dreamily. "We spent many happy days here in London and in Whitby. She was so full of joy, so full of fun. We wanted to pay tribute to her when we had a daughter. But then we reconsidered. We thought it might bring you bad luck." She gave a defeated little laugh, then caught Abree's stare. "It was all an adventure, but poor Lucy died." Mother's eyes seemed to gaze through Abree to some faraway place.

Abree had heard some of this before the war, when she was a child. She knew her parents had been involved in some quest and that it had involved John Holmwood's father and some other people. One of them had been a Texan named Quincey. Her brother had been named after him. And she'd also known that her own name, a name that she secretly hated, was from an elderly Dutch doctor called Abraham from the same era. But if she'd known anything about Lucy—and she must have done to dream about her so vividly—she had forgotten it.

Abree took a deep breath; she felt a mini rebellion coming on. "But, Mother, didn't the young man, Quincey, the American, also die?"

"Yes, Quincey Morris, a fine, brave man."

"How?"

Mother's eyes narrowed. "How what, dear?"

"What killed him?"

The sad laugh came again, a gentle, faraway sound, so far away in fact as to suggest something beyond the reach of explanation. "We were in a wild, wild region. There were so many dangers. Roaming Slovaks and gypsies. But he was killed trying to protect us."

She gazed at her daughter with a defiant kind of nostalgia that Abree knew not to challenge. *This is my world*, Mother seemed to say. Abree looked away to an elderly waitress who, with much clattering, was in the process of lowering a tray of cream teas onto a table with two even older ladies. Both of these customers were in the black garb of permanent widowhood.

"How did she die?" Abree asked quietly.

The question took her mother by surprise. Her reverie had been so deep it seemed rather like waking a sleepwalker.

Mother frowned. "She?"

"*Lucy*, Mother. Lord Godalming's first intended."

A wave of something—confusion or pain or perhaps both—swept across her mother's face. She looked suddenly older, lines appearing around her mouth where moments ago there had been none.

"It was consumption," she said, dipping into her purse. "Consumption or something very like it. I can't remember the details."

Mother had taken out some money and now signalled the waitress, who was quick to respond. "I know you are eager to prepare for your meeting with your professor," she said with a quick smile.

Mother was right. Abree had plenty to do, and the idea of coming to Lyons in the first place had been an unwise indulgence. But as she stood awkwardly and strapped her purse over her shoulder, she felt profoundly dissatisfied. The sun from the window skimmed against her eyes as she and her mother negotiated their way towards the door. She was inching towards a mystery but was still a good distance away.

Abree wondered at it now, that she and Quincey had allowed the idea of an elaborate fantasy, like something out of *One Thousand and One Nights*, to be alluded to regularly throughout their childhood but never explained. All that Abree had ever known was that her parents' quest had involved some danger and a journey to little-travelled Balkan areas east of Budapest. There was a villain in the midst of it all—a nobleman, she believed—but she had no knowledge of the precise nature of his crimes nor the reason why they, and not some law enforcement agency, should be responsible for bringing him to justice. Her lack of curiosity sprang, she realized, from her scepticism.

Abree followed her mother onto the Strand and watched the heron feather on Mother's pre-war hat quiver in the breeze. Suddenly her mother seemed like a relic—proud and romantic but out of place. Perhaps Abree had always seen her this way but had never wanted to admit it. The claim of romance and adventure had always been just a little absurd. That was why she'd never probed it too closely. A secret quest for justice or honour was her parents' delusion, and they were welcome to it. In reality, her life, and that of poor Quincey, was more expansive than the lives of her parents. Quincey had gone to war—a real war with a real foe—and Abree was enrolled in university. It had even occurred to her, though she felt rather mean to admit it, that Mother had always known her children would outdo her, that they would venture into areas which had been forbidden to her generation. The foreknowledge had given extra fuel and colour to Mother's vision of a glamorous past, Abree speculated. Anticipation had made Mother jealous of her children.

But beneath all this, beneath all this doubt, part of her wanted it all to be real. Conflict was a muddy thing now. Perhaps it always had been. But the idea of a chivalrous past, where adventure truly inspired, where there was a precise delineation between virtue and vice, was delightful. This secret world of the imagination had existed in fleeting spells during her childhood. Even now she was not quite ready to let it go.

Something niggled inside Abree, something that made her feel valued less than she would like. As Mother's arm slipped through hers, she ran backwards and forwards through their conversation to discover what it was. A tram rattled by and a taxi blew its shrill horn. Suddenly she had it. If her brother had been given a martyr's name, why then had she been denied Lucy?

3.

PROFESSOR REYNOLDS ALWAYS doubled up his tutorials with women. Whether this was because doubling provided a chaperone or because it was simply a more efficient use of time for a man who doubted the value of educating females, Abree wasn't sure. Either way, it meant Abree had to sit through his dissection of Helen Morrison's proposal for *The Rime of the Ancient Mariner* as an allegory of the book of Genesis. Helen's argument made perfect sense to Abree. In fact it made almost too much sense. A paper had to have counter arguments, nuances, and qualifications, but the mariner's act of pointless defiance, his killing of the albatross causing the doom of his shipmates, was so much like Adam and Eve and the forbidden fruit that it was hardly worth stating. Coleridge's father, like Helen's, had even been a clergyman, and the poet's childhood and education had surely been steeped in cautionary tales about the will of God, mankind's inherent sinfulness, and the need for obedience. The bard has merely given his cautionary tale a more flamboyant canvas.

But none of this stopped Professor Reynolds from wincing as though he was in pain whenever poor Helen made her arguments. Nor did it prevent him from twitching in his seat as though he were beset by invisible wasps.

"The danger of pinning a poet too closely to allegory," he said at last, producing the words painfully and tugging at his earlobe, "is that we begin to edit out the variations that *make* his work poetry. The poet's mind, particularly the mind of a romantic poet, is open to a whole universe of thought. We poor academics do him a disservice if we funnel the majesty of his creation into drab modern theology."

There was a nervous smile, there for a second, then gone. The birdsong outside the bright window suddenly got louder. It felt as though nature itself was applauding the professor's judgement.

Helen had been looking at her notebook. From her side, Abree could see the neat row of questions, the odd circled question mark, and a word or two underlined for emphasis. This was how Helen, a careful and meticulous student if ever there was one, prepared for tutorials. The notebook flapped uncertainly in her hand now. Abree sensed she was trying to form a question, but nothing came.

"Now, Miss Harker," said the professor, turning to Abree. Helen's notebook flopped onto her lap. "Last time we spoke you had tangled yourself up in the discredited briars and thorns of *poet as mystic*. I do hope you have re-thought that concept for your paper."

Abree had not re-thought the concept, but she knew now it would be futile to merely restate it. She despised herself in advance. "I'm afraid, professor, I have found myself at a loss for a replacement. I wonder if you might provide any advice as to where I might begin."

Professor Reynolds brightened. He peeled away his spectacles, took out a handkerchief, and breathed hard on both lenses. "Well, you might begin—both of you—with less ambition. Sweeping theories, attempts to understand and define poets within categories of our own creation are altogether too grand for our little sphere." He rubbed one lens, squinted through the glass, and then rubbed the other. "What we should be working on is rather some very specific theme that allows us to perform a close reading through selected texts, or perhaps an analysis of line structure. Meet the poet on his terms, not your own."

The clamour outside the window rose again. The professor gave one of his tight, nervous smiles, and Abree realized this was a dismissal. She found herself rising to leave with her companion.

Abree had always found Helen Morrison likeable but disconcerting. She was more obviously bookish than Abree but, worse, she carried an aura. At first, Abree had thought this was a dedication to work, a seriousness that dwarfed her own. But now she'd placed it more accurately, and it made her shudder. Helen's disconcerting quality was her *goodness*. A year and a half older than Abree, Helen had spent much of 1918 and 1919 as a nurse in a London hospital. While Abree had been busy writing bad poetry, mourning her brother, thinking about the future, and determining which boys might do for marriage provided they returned from the continent in one piece, Helen had been nursing returning soldiers and influenza patients.

A vicar's daughter, her Christianity, unlike Abree's, seemed neither a burden nor an anachronism. To Abree, God was like some cumbersome add-on to be dismantled then reconstructed as mood and situation demanded. Abree attended church with her mother sometimes. Occasionally, very occasionally, Father came too. But it was Abree who felt superfluous. She tagged along like a third wheel while her mother chatted amicably with the vicar about the weather, about the Versailles Treaty, about the new Labour movement—about anything but God.

Helen was not like that. Religion seemed as naturally part of her as the constituent elements of her flesh. Virtue, service, and adherence to the messages of the gospels were encrypted into every cell of her body. She was not pious. Pious people worked hard just to be who they were. Helen did not have to work. She simply *was* good. Beside Helen, Abree felt bedraggled, not quite clean. Abree was the one with a fallen brother. Yet it was Helen who had picked up the stretcher and borne the weight. She wasn't smug or judgmental about it. She gave Abree no excuse to be wary or resentful. Consequently, conversations with Helen were like walking a high wire. Abree had to balance herself delicately to prevent unwanted self-revelation. Helen would never judge her, of course. What Abree feared was judgement from within.

The two of them strolled on the opposite side of the road from Somerset House, gazing at the rolling Thames, green and opaque even in bright sunshine. Helen hugged her notebook to her chest as though mourning her stillborn paper. Abree was more careless; her satchel hung unfastened and swinging from her hand.

"I shall simply have to start again," said Helen, brows furrowed. "It seems such a pity."

Abree felt impatience rising. A cyclist spun by dangerously close, Abree thought. A scrap of paper circled around the gutter then fell like a dead thing near the grate.

"He doesn't want us in college," Abree said. The statement was plain, dull, designed to provoke.

"Who?" Helen's frown had deepened. Both of them had slowed down.

"Professor Reynolds. He doesn't think any of us, any women, any girls, should be at the university." She almost added that they were *wasting his precious time*, but knew that would be far too cynical for poor Helen.

"I'm not sure about that, Abree." Helen tilted her head to one side as though the emotion behind Abree's point, rather than the point itself, might deserve consideration.

I am, Abree nearly said, but didn't. Something had caught her eye further down the Victoria Embankment. By the dark lions, below Cleopatra's Needle, was a familiar figure. A man, young and slim, faintly exotic in profile, gazed at the river. With a high forehead and a backward-tilted Derby hat, his posture spoke of presumption verging on arrogance. A little whirlpool of fire and spittle rose up within Abree—and not for the first time. She recognized this man. He had been sauntering by her in college corridors since spring. He'd appeared in the little squares between the university buildings, hands in pockets, sometimes in conversation with others, sometimes fingering the blossoms with a cool, half-smiling detachment. Each time something about him, some detail of his dress or manner, had both unnerved and angered her. She'd taken him to be a student at first, perhaps a foreigner brought in to fill the university's coffers. With his high forehead and aquiline nose, he didn't look quite English. English or not, she'd imagined his carefree swagger was an affectation; some exaggerated shrugging off of the war and its effects. It was true he seemed old to be an undergraduate, but then so were many others who had fought.

She'd since learned he was a professor, not a student, and it had made her dislike him even more. Professors were serious, formal, and reserved—or should be. This man's languidness seemed calculated. It seemed to imply that he could achieve all that others achieved yet without the appearance of effort. It seemed like an insult.

Today, she particularly fumed at the way he wore his Derby—pushed up as though he had nothing to fear from the world. Worse than this, she saw now as she approached that one of his hands rested on the haunch of a lion. It lay there on the stone with a sense of ownership.

Helen claimed Abree's attention again. "I suspect that Professor Reynolds thinks I am trying to run before I can walk." She was looking at Abree now, quite intently, aware perhaps that Abree's interest was drifting away from Coleridge, Keats, and Whitman.

"But does he *want* us to do well, I wonder?" Abree asked. She knew the comment would not pass muster with Helen, but she wanted to say something irrational—or something *else* that was irrational, something to overshadow her dislike of the man gazing at the river. She was less ashamed of disliking Professor Reynolds than she was of disliking this man. There was at least some evidence to support her distrust of her tutor.

"I'm sure he wants us to get our degrees," Helen said thoughtfully, "although I have to admit his terms can seem infuriatingly narrow."

This was rather generous of Helen, and true to form. Helen was pretending to be more frustrated than she actually was; she believed in solidarity, in not allowing her companion to feel meaner than herself. Abree couldn't help but smile briefly before her eyes were drawn once again to the stranger. He'd taken his hat off now and was fanning himself with it, a languorous, self-confident action; she had seen motion picture actors in the same attitude. But this was London, not America, and he was not Douglas Fairbanks.

What would Helen think, Abree wondered, if she knew how Abree disliked the foreigner, if indeed he was a foreigner? What would she think if she knew Abree had constructed a whole history for the man, building a character of conceit, privilege, and ignobility brick by brick? She felt herself blush as she and Helen drew close enough to feel the breeze from his fanning Derby. He turned slightly to observe them.

Here, again, was an apparent breach of decency. A man may nod at a passing acquaintance. He might even nod at someone he does not know provided there was something collegial about their circumstances. But this man merely *looked*; he didn't nod. He looked, held Abree's stare and, *damn him*, he made her look away first.

Had Helen noticed him too? It seemed she had. She had leaned forward slightly as though to catch some kind of exchange. And now they had passed him Helen could hardly fail to notice Abree's colour. Her face was burning. Abree sensed a puzzled glance from Helen but kept her eyes on the river.

They walked in silence now, the man receding. Abree couldn't speak for the moment. Quincey, she thought. It was all about Quincey. The breeze picked up around their skirts as though in agreement. Why else would she so hate this man who floated so confidently around the squares and pavements of London, who leaned against London's lions and tilted his Derby back as he gazed upon London's river? It was Abree's lion. Quincey's lion. Their river. Not his.

None of these things were crimes. Yet the stranger *had* committed a crime, the worst crime Abree could conceive of. He'd committed the crime of living while Quincey was dead. And not only was the stranger living, he was fearless and happy; he was thriving. He walked like a man who approached the world without the least particle of trepidation, without the least guilt or shame. But her poor brother, her Quincey—with his loping, clumsy run when he played tennis, with his hat rim always respectfully parallel to the ground—was lying beneath the earth in some bleak unremembered field.

Confidence had no place in this city; too much of this quality was an insult to the dead. Abree had seen and heard of a young generation who wanted to leave all the horror behind. She had seen the rather desperate-looking joy on the faces of the young debutantes with their spindly limbs and fringed dresses. Although she had nothing in common with these fantastic creatures, she was of their generation. But Abree did not want to leave the war behind. Abree wanted to crawl back inside the horror she had only known vicariously; she wanted to lie still in the damp earth, to weigh the meaning of Whitman's words about dripping blood and dying breaths, to relive the visions of wounds she'd never seen but had imagined a thousand times. To do otherwise would be a clear betrayal to Quincey. He was alone there, underground, with no one but her and her parents to share his sufferings. The man, the foreigner fanning himself with his hat, was a traitor, unfeeling and vicious; so were the young, silly girls with the big eyes and the fringed dresses. The dream of Lucy no longer seemed like a promise about the future. She seemed like a temptation now, one to which Abree could never succumb. There were no stars, no limitless sky. There was only death, unjust and pointless.

All this Abree considered as she listened to her footfalls, and those of her companion. Helen looked at her and smiled.

"You look like you're a million miles away," she said, not unkindly.

"Yes, I'm sorry."

Helen had taken a backward glance. "The man by the lion. Do you know him?"

Abree was taken aback for a moment. She felt that Helen, good Helen so free from suspicion, had dipped into her soul. My God, what had she seen there? She hardly dared think. "No, I don't know him, but I've seen him around college. Do you?"

"He's a Bulgarian prince, or so I heard. He's teaching history."

A *prince!* Abree might have known. Did this make his arrogance better or worse? With a flood of shame, she found her dislike fading just a little. She thought of her parents, their rather obvious respect for those of higher social standing. Would Mother's eyes have twinkled with such incipient grief had the Lucy from her past not once seemed destined to become Lady Godalming? Would she be claiming there had once been a special intimacy between them and Lord Godalming had he remained plain Arthur Holmwood? Abree was just the same as Mother then. A title had made her think of the stranger differently. The idea of it made her cringe with self-loathing.

"A prince," she said dryly, "working in a university."

"Well, times are changing," said Helen. "I thought..." She trailed off.

Abree turned. Helen was frowning, clutching her notebook tighter to her chest. "I rather wondered..." she said. Abree slowed to remain by her side. "I wondered whether the man reminded you of your brother. He looks similar to the picture on your mantelpiece at home."

"No, he doesn't," snapped Abree. Her heel jolted against the pavement.

Helen seemed startled and bit her lip.

"Well," Abree said more softly, "*I* can't see a similarity,"

"I've only seen a photograph, of course," said Helen, by way of an apology. "Perhaps they wouldn't look alike if standing together."

Abree shook her head. The thought was so jarring. She didn't want there to be any similarity between Quincey and this mysterious aristocrat. It besmirched her brother, even if such a resemblance were merely physical. But she didn't want to make too much of it to Helen.

She did take one brief backwards glance, only because it would seem odd not to. He was gazing at her directly, impudently, leaning back against the lion, haunch on haunch. "No," she said, "they are not alike. Believe me."

They turned right to make for the Westminster underground. They often left college together and went by the same route, alighting at St. James's Park and going their separate ways— Helen to Chelsea, Abree to Belgravia—only when walking together was too obviously impractical. Today, although Helen's comment about the stranger had disturbed her, Abree felt in need of her companionship. After her strange overreaction, she needed that stamp of acceptance that only Helen could give.

There came a whoosh of air from an incoming train as they descended onto the Circle Line. Newspaper scraps and assorted debris whirled around them as they entered and turned the corner to the platform. Abree buried herself in the sea of faces in motion as the carriage screeched to a halt. She was desperate for home, but she knew home didn't exist anymore. London wasn't home. It was a mockery of home. The cocky eastern prince who looked like Quincey—Helen was right, he did a little—rubbed this in.

And in Belgrave Square, the mockery intensified. A father, once strong and reliable, now screamed through the night. A mother, once an anchoring force, seemed suddenly out of her element. Her sweet, good-natured brother was now a photograph on a mantelpiece.

Helen took Abree's arm, squeezing it a little, and they stepped together onto the train.

4.

ABREE NOTICED QUINCEY'S ABSENCE seconds after she walked into the room. She'd had an unwholesome feeling since tea at Lyons with Mother. Professor Reynolds, the prince, and the river had certainly not helped to alleviate this malaise. Time had been wasted. Now, with the energy of the day waning, she was under pressure to make up for all the lost hours. The scent of fresh flowers mingling with the waxy freshness of furniture polish oppressed her, made her sluggish with a sense of unhappy domesticity. This was where she belonged, it told her. She had no business at the university. And something else claimed her too. The sheen from the coffee table, the cushions on the ottoman, and the placing of the Persian rug in the centre of the shining oak floor were the same, but some other detail, connected to these things, was altered.

No framed photograph on the mantelpiece. No Quincey in his uniform.

The house was quiet save for the faint tick of the grandfather clock, but it was a quiet infused with a hard-to-define aura of attentiveness. There was something painstaking about the placement of the vases and the doilies.

There had been a *presence* in this room, it was certain. Whether this was a hint of Mother's scent lingering along with the blossoms and the polish, Abree wasn't sure, but she knew it was more than the residual scent of Jenny and her chores. Jenny merely cleaned and dusted; she didn't leave that unmistakable fragrance of adjustment, that meticulous sense of change.

In place of Quincey—grave and upright in his uniform—was a short vase with forget-me-nots and tulip heads. Abree moved over to the mantelpiece, feeling an ache in her chest. She imagined Jenny dusting too hard, causing the picture to drop and its glass to crack. The maid had not been well this morning. Abree had heard a distant coughing from the servants' quarters—the kind of cough that comes from the stomach rather than the throat. If she'd been sick, it was possible the distraction had made her clumsy. Abree tried to envisage the picture withdrawn temporarily for a refitting of glass and frame. But already she knew more was behind it. Why would Jenny knock over this article in particular? She heard that shriek—*Quincey!* Its ghost echoed through the silence. The photo's disappearance could not be mere coincidence.

Someone had entered behind her, but very quietly. Abree turned just enough to confirm it was Mother.

"What happened to it?" she asked. Her heart picked up an extra beat as she spoke. She couldn't bear the idea of hearing an obvious lie from her mother. But she was even more afraid of the truth.

Her mother hesitated. "You mean the photograph?" There was an attempt at innocence in her tone.

Mother seemed frailer at the shoulder than usual. Tiny red rims showed around her eyes. Abree had rarely seen fear on her mother's face, and never as the result of anything her daughter said. Seeing it now was so troubling Abree wanted to change the subject immediately. But she didn't know how.

"Yes, Mother. Has it been broken?"

A *yes* would have been enough. A *yes* would have ended the conversation and allowed Abree to leave for her bedroom to study.

"No," Mother said. She approached the mantelpiece and drew level with Abree. They both stared at the forget-me-nots and tulip heads. "I just wanted to try a different frame."

"You've taken it to Rowley's?" Abree brightened at this news. This told of care and renewal, of a son and a brother who would be forever preserved by his family.

"Not yet, but I'm thinking about the possibilities."

The grandfather clock ticked. Abree and her mother faced the picture-less mantelpiece. A sliver of Abree slipped away and watched the two of them, gullible daughter and desperate mother, concocting this story together. "We have other nice photos of Quincey too—the day he passed his solicitor's exams, for instance. We could have a double frame perhaps."

Why a *double* frame? thought Abree. The uniform was a disguise. It wasn't Quincey. It was his death mask. Why display it at all? Why not just a photograph of the young solicitor? She knew this was unsayable and felt herself hovering above her own left shoulder, not saying it. A photograph of a man in uniform was sacred; especially when that man perished in war. His curse was to die, and his family's curse was to preserve for all time that vision of death, except that Mother had found a way of escaping that curse, temporarily at least.

"How was your morning at university?" Mother asked. She moved forward like an actress on cue and touched the tulip petals with her fingertips.

"Good," Abree said. "Well," she checked herself, "not good really. I shall have to start again. I have been too ambitious, apparently."

Mother turned to face her.

"And Helen?"

Mother took a lively interest in Helen's studies as well as her daughter's. Despite the fact she had met Abree's parents on perhaps three occasions, Helen had somehow achieved the status of surrogate daughter in the Harker household. Likely it helped Mother to think Abree had a partner in this strange, new, traditionally male world into which she had ventured.

"The same," said Abree. "Too much ambition, not enough close attention."

"My goodness," said Mother, hands still clutched together but restless in some private battle of their own. "How clever you girls are these days! Too much ambition! Who'd have thought you'd come through it all with so much spirit?" She tried to smile, but her eyes became glassy.

She glanced at the clock. "Oh, must get on." Then she was gone. Abree felt the breeze of her sudden departure against her shins. Mother's heels clipped through the hallway, perhaps enroute to the kitchen where she would give instructions for dinner. Abree wanted to fold into herself like a moth returning to its cocoon. Mother was suffering, clearly. The confidence she'd displayed in Lyons, the mastery, had deserted her since. Abree wondered about this, wondered if it was something she'd brought up herself, something about the past. She would be careful not to probe too hard next time. If Mother collapsed, no one but Abree herself would be left to hold up the beams of this crumbling household. And she knew this was beyond her.

Abree went to her room and set herself up for work. She had Quincey's old oak desk, a large clunky affair which sat at the window overlooking the square. She arranged her books, her copies of Whitman, her volume of Keats. But she knew she would have trouble concentrating. She could almost feel the creaks and moving fissures in the house below her, like Poe's House of Usher.

Mother had always been the foundation of the house. She defined them. She had remained erect through the years, the proud "public" face of the family. She had once said, and with a notable sense of pride, that the Harkers were a very English family. This had been only months after they received the news of Quincey's death. Abree knew then and now what it meant. It meant they showed their strength and their love not by embracing each other or by shedding tears but by getting on with things. In their household, when tears threaten to rise, one turns one's back and leaves the room.

This was all fine, of course, and Abree knew the rules well

enough. Her mother would not have wanted Abree's comfort—not comfort that was in any way physical or pointed,
not comfort that would draw attention to grief. She'd been
wise enough not to question this even for a moment. But it
left her feeling rather useless. This was one reason she found
it hard to settle.

Another was that the Belgrave Square in the sunlight of
early afternoon was bursting with life. A shiny band of starlings dropped into the bright pillows of foliage, every one of
the flock, and there were hundreds, disappearing entirely. A
squirrel's tail scooped in and out of the green; a companion of
its owner scurried up an adjacent trunk. A man and woman
walked a terrier by the bed of young roses. The man threw a
stick. The terrier chased after it as though racing for his life. For
the moment, he was lost to Abree; he went under the canopy
of leaves but then he emerged into a pool of yellowy sunlight,
stick in mouth, tail wagging. He was offering his stick not to his
owner but to a familiar-looking man sitting alone on a bench
by the iron fence that marked the perimeter of the square. The
man bent to scratch the dog's ears. The animal raised a front
paw in excitement, dropped the stick at the man's feet and ran
a quick circle on the turf.

It was him again—the "Bulgarian prince." His Derby had
the same nonchalant backward tilt as at the river. On men less
handsome this would have made him look slovenly as well as
arrogant. On him, it looked merely arrogant. A thought occurred to her: The "prince" was on the same bench as the figure
she'd seen before the dawn. She thought of the pale hands and
face, the figure's watchfulness. Could that have been him too?

But there was a more serious worry. Helen was right. He
did look a little like Quincey. His slimness, his height, his age,
his aquiline features. What if Mother were to see him? Worse,
what if Father caught sight of him and noticed the likeness?

Father was at work now but he would return soon—he rarely
worked a full day these days. Her parents often took a turn

around the square before dinner, and what would stop them today? The Square was gorgeous outside, begging its residents for a stroll. And Abree's mother was on a constant quest to bring brightness into her husband's life.

The "prince" scratched the dog's ears again. Then he swiftly took off his Derby as the dog's owners approached, stood up, and made a slight bow at the hips. The three of them stood for a moment, the couple cautious and bunched together, the prince smiling and looking from one to the other as he talked. The little dog looked from owners to stranger and back again, ears pricking and haunches rising and falling in excitement at the social idyll growing around him. His owners were indeed warming to the prince. The man looked more at ease and became more animated. The woman looked at her husband and smiled. Abree was surprised at how friendly the stranger looked now; she had not actually seen him smile before, and his expression and hand gestures, even from this distance, told of humour and humility.

The little dog barked—Abree could hear the sound very faintly through the window—and wriggled its stubby tail. The three of them all laughed together, and then the man stepped forward and proffered his card. The prince accepted it with a broad smile and slid it into a wallet. The men shook hands. The woman nodded, a touch coquettishly, Abree thought. The dog owners left the stranger clearly happier and lighter than they had been before. The little dog ran in a circle around the "prince" before scurrying after its owners.

The foreigner sat down again, this time placing his Derby on his knee. The breeze shifted, bending the overhead boughs and casting dappled shadows over his bench. He looked up suddenly, looked up straight at Abree's window, or so it seemed to her. Instinctively, Abree ducked and pushed herself away from the desk. Fool, she told herself. He couldn't see in. It was far too bright outside. And why, in any case, should he be interested in her?

She thought of the way he'd looked at her by the river. It had seemed presumptuous enough but hardly lascivious, hardly the kind of gaze that suggested yearning of any romantic kind. She realized immediately what this line of thinking implied: that there was a dim possibility that he was here for her, that he had followed her to this square perhaps or had found some other way of discovering where she lived. What irony, she thought, to call him arrogant when the recesses of her imagination were capable of such speculations. He must simply live in one of the houses around the square. His social status, if Helen was right, would put him either here or somewhere far grander.

She moved back into place before her desk, feeling miserable. He was still there, relaxed and apparently content to bide his time. If he was living here, on Belgrave Square, he would haunt the place for weeks or months or years to come. Her parents would encounter him not once, but multiple times. Mother's caution over the photograph, her attempt to remove reminders, would all be for naught.

5.

IT WAS A TERRIBLE RISK, And she'd made up her mind deliberately. Before she could reconsider, she ran down into the drawing room and burst in on Mother who had taken up some needlework. Breathlessly, as though it were urgent, she made her suggestion. "Mother," she said, gulping on the word, "I've been watching the square from my window. It's a lovely day. I think we should take a walk while it's so fine." The request was oddly put, Abree thought. It seemed like a ruse. But Mother was only mildly surprised.

"If you wish, Abree," she said and smiled, then moved her needlework to the side.

A few minutes later, as Abree felt Mother's warm hand around her arm and breathed in the freshness of late spring, she knew she'd made the right decision. Mother had to know what she was up against; she was the one who'd have to build a strategy to help Father in advance of any reminders. Better to confront a hazardous situation straight on. It seemed like such an English approach, and this was comfort of a sort.

"Oh, look," said Mother. They were perhaps fifteen yards from the foreigner. Abree thought Mother had spotted him. But her voice was content, almost joyful. Abree followed her finger. A lone magpie bobbed its tail and glanced at both of them sideways. A silver-green sheen danced on its tail feathers, and it chattered huskily despite the fact that a young oak twig was lodged in its mouth. "One forgets how beautiful it is here!"

Abree smiled but glanced towards the bench. The Bulgarian prince was looking directly at her. Abree re-fixed her gaze towards the iron railing behind him, to the knots and twists of the bushes. But her cheeks burned. She wished her glance had been more natural or that at least that she had not looked away so suddenly. It must have seemed exactly as it was: furtive, deliberate, and cowardly. To make it worse, Mother, skimming the overhead boughs with her eyes, had navigated them to a point closer to the bench. From the prince's perspective it might look as though Abree, not her mother, were determining their direction.

It dawned on her she would have to take this exercise a step further, that circumstances might force her into an introduction. It would be better to seem deliberate and in control than to simply blunder into his space. She looked at the man again, but this time she nodded and let an uncertain smile play upon her lips. As she anticipated, the man stood, leaving his Derby upon the bench. He nodded first at Mother and then at Abree. Abree had no rulebook for such an occurrence, just a vague idea of how extraordinarily awkward an introduction would be when she had no idea of his name.

She felt Mother's hand flutter on her arm. If her mother noticed the man's resemblance to her Quincey, it didn't seem to bother her. Abree sensed merely a slight conflict, as though she was trying to remember where she might have met the gentleman.

"I believe, sir," said Abree, "you are a professor at Kings, where I study."

"I am indeed," he said. The stranger's voice was far softer, far more delicate and sensitive than Abree would have imagined. And there was shyness in his manner, not insolence at all. Not a trace of it. Abree wondered how her assumptions could have been so misplaced. What else did she get catastrophically wrong in the course of an average day? "Allow me to present myself. My name is Ivan Florescu."

His chocolate eyes seemed to smile although his mouth was

tentative. His name was lovely, especially the way he said it—
Flo*rescu*—with the accent on the second syllable. The word
comprised a gorgeous moment of hesitation, followed by an
almost voluptuous opening. Abree thought of the book of
Genesis—or the way Genesis might have been written had its
authors been more concerned with fine detail and beauty and
less concerned with darkness, voids, and the grander elements.
She imagined the pause before the unfurling of Creation's first
petals. She could envision a proud God overseeing the moment.
This, He might say, *is an entirely new object. Some of these I
will call tulips. Some I will call roses. But watch closely. This
timorous moment between stillness and unfolding I will call
a Flo*rescu.

But where was the *prince* in the title? Abree wondered. He
had introduced himself merely with a name. It would have
showed ill-breeding to do otherwise, of course, at least in
England. But it would force her to call him a mere "mister"
or "professor," which might prove an embarrassment later.

"Please," she said, "Professor Florescu"—she gave a nervous
smile and turned to her mother—"this is my mother, Mrs.
Jonathan Harker. I am Abree Harker."

He seemed delighted for a moment, as though the names—
such plain names compared to his own—had sounded like the
most sublime poetry in his ears.

"Mrs. Harker," he said gratefully, it seemed, "and Miss
Harker. I am so delighted to make your acquaintance."

Abree could not think of anything to say. Mother seemed
likewise lost for words, and Professor Florescu looked on them
both, smiling and patient, in no special hurry either to break
off conversation or to offer anything that might serve for small
talk. Abree thought of his title again and of his origins.

"You are, I believe, from Bulgaria, Professor?"

It was a slightly dangerous subject. Bulgaria had been an
enemy three years ago. But the country was far enough away
from the English map, Abree thought, for the detail to be at

least half forgotten, and Mother was never parochial when it came to such things. In 1914, both her parents had been enraged at the looters and vandals who'd ransacked London shops owned by Germans.

"I was born a Hungarian, Miss Harker, from the province of Wallachia. But, unlike those of Great Britain, our borders move often. So it can be confusing to us as well as to those of other countries. Now I am a Romanian."

"What a beautiful country you belong to, Professor Florescu," said Mother breathlessly. Abree guessed her to be in the throes of a powerful emotion, a memory perhaps. A glance to her side revealed that her eyes had misted over.

Professor Florescu's face showed smiling appreciation but also curiosity. Abree thought of a handsome dark animal, an otter perhaps, wanting to burrow through the water after a shining fish but cautious lest some unseen danger lurk beneath the depths.

Mother seemed lost, oblivious to the fact that her statement required some explanation. Abree supplied it for her.

"My mother and father, Professor, travelled in the region long before the war."

"Really?" Now his brown eyes widened in admiration as well as surprise. Yet, there was something else in his expression, something she'd first noticed when he heard their names. Some of the surprise, at least, was feigned. Abree couldn't swear to this, and was not certain where the instinct came from, except that the response was a little too polished, a touch too steady.

"Yes, Professor Florescu," said Mother, her voice still husky. "It was just over thirty years ago, quite the most memorable journey of our lives."

"A honeymoon perhaps?" he asked.

"Oh no," she said rather too quickly, "but an experience nevertheless, one we can never forget."

He looked at her, smiling steadily, waiting for more. But Mother was clearly not going to supply it. "And what brings you to London, Mr. Florescu? You are a professor, I gather?"

"I have the privilege of teaching history here, Mrs. Harker. I find there is so much energy of enquiry in young minds today. We have an extraordinary opportunity."

Abree felt a nudge and wondered whether Mother wanted them to move on. But a glance revealed that she had merely turned to Abree, a sad, sentimental smile upon her face. "You are so right, Mr. Florescu," said Mother. "We have such hope in our children, and there is such a responsibility placed upon their shoulders."

It occurred to Abree that Professor Florecsu must be older than she had thought him. He still did not look more than thirty-five, but the ease with which he and her mother had fallen into the nuance of codes and hidden meanings about young people suggested they recognized each other as generational peers. She searched for lines upon his face. His expression reflected her mother's sense of transience and loss, and there were indeed grooves leading down from the sides of his nose to the corners of his mouth, and spiders' web networks of lines radiating from his eyes, especially when he smiled plaintively as now.

It is often the case with men, Abree thought, that when they remain slim and keep their hair, they seem to retain their youth and vigour for decades. The qualities that delineate women's youth are, by contrast, too narrow to survive the years. This idea, real enough and true enough, made Abree despise herself. These were her parents' generation's judgments, not hers, and yet they were in her, like tumours. The pantomime horse came back into her mind. No one had put her in the back end of the costume. She had done it to herself. She was an imposter belonging to nineteenth-century complacency and inaction. She was *woman* preserved under glass. It was a mistake that she was living in this age. This age was a time of change. Change required courage, not just the kind of courage to make Father's eyebrow arch as she announced she would go to a decidedly non-militant lecture on women's suffrage, but something much more, something that required shattering the glass that surrounded her. Women just like her, daughters of solicitors or doctors, had nursed wounded soldiers and influenza patients. They chained themselves to the railings of public buildings and threw themselves before the King's horse while Abree was, for the most part, meekly waiting until she was thirty, when she might legally cast her vote.

Professor Florescu and Mother continued to talk while Abree drifted into her own thoughts. She felt like blaming all these failures on what had happened to Quincey, but she knew that wasn't it. Others had lost brothers, and husbands, and sons. So what was wrong with her? Mother glanced at her and smiled. She and Professor Florescu thought they were talking about her, but they weren't, not really. They were talking about people, men and women, who took their responsibilities seriously. They were talking about people like Helen.

At last, Mr. Florescu bowed again. Mother, ever resourceful, carried Father's card and often issued invitations on his behalf. She pressed this card into Professor Florescu's hand almost fondly. He bowed to them both again, looking delighted with his new acquaintanceship. Abree managed a smile, but she was worried. Mother seemed blind to any similarity between the Wallachian professor and her dead son. But perhaps Father would see it, and the door had been opened to the possibility, perhaps even a likelihood, of a meeting.

Mother was strangely silent when they returned home. Abree closed the front door as Mother took off her gloves. Only when Abree turned did she notice that Mother's fingers were trembling as she returned the garden gate key to its hook.

Jenny had appeared pale-cheeked and expressionless at the sound of the front door. She took Mother's scarf.

"We'll have tea in the drawing room, please," Mother told her.

Jenny gave a swift curtsey and ghosted off in the direction of the kitchen.

"You'll join me, won't you?" Mother asked Abree. Abree could think of no reason not to. Obviously, Keats and Whitman could wait a little longer. Perhaps they would wait forever.

In a few moments Abree was circling the drawing room, catching sight of the photo-less mantelpiece again, hearing the hollow *tock* of the grandfather clock. Mother sat in the centre of the settee. Abree took the chair opposite.

"A charming young man, didn't you think so?" Mother said. "Thank you for introducing him to me."

"I didn't know him before today," Abree said, "but it seemed silly to walk by without saying hello, considering the circumstances."

Mother smiled complacency. "You girls, you and Helen, you seem so modest, so shy, and yet you take life on your own terms."

Abree frowned.

"It must be so very liberating, not to have to wait for someone else to introduce you."

Abree couldn't think of anything to say. There seemed to be a criticism, as well as a compliment, somewhere in Mother's words.

Mother seemed to read her thoughts. "Or perhaps there was never anything to be liberated from. A change in the times, I suppose."

"We all need liberating, Mother," Abree said and wished she hadn't. It seemed pretentious and angry and she had no idea where it had sprung from. She knew her face must have coloured as she could feel the heat. "Anyway," she added, "I've never been to Wallachia."

This was even worse. She shrank into her chair while mother looked at her calmly. A smile played on Mother's lips.

The door opened and Jenny came in with the tea trolley.

She rubbed her hand down her pinny and seemed ready to serve, but Mother pre-empted her.

"We can see to the tea, thank you, Jenny," Mother said.

Jenny wheeled the trolley closer to Mother, then turned and slipped from the room.

Mother picked up the strainer and started to pour, her hand steady, almost artificially so. "I suppose that there are fewer men now, fewer young men I mean, and this is why your generation of women is thrust into the spotlight." She moved the spout from one cup to the other, the echo of hot tea on china still ringing through the room. She poured again.

"I suppose so," said Abree.

Mother's dark eyes caught Abree's as she finished pouring the second cup. "You take milk, don't you?"

"Yes, thank you." Abree collected her cup and sat down again.

"I went to Wallachia," Mother said in an unusually measured tone, "because your father and his friends had to go there, and I was safest with them. It may be hard for you to see now, but Abree, your father was, and is, a courageous man." Mother tilted her head, listening. "I do believe he's here. Ring for another cup, Abree dear."

There had indeed been a sudden change in the atmosphere of the room, a shift in the air. Abree heard a faint thud from the hallway.

6. ARTHUR HOLMWOOD, LORD GODALMING

WHEN THE DOORBELL RANG, Arthur jolted in his seat. The wreaths of cigar smoke hanging over the dinner table had become a welcome opiate, and he was looking forward to sliding into the oblivion of sleep. Since Alice had left the room, leaving Arthur with John, the mood had changed from awkwardness, to hostility, to a drowsy kind of truce.

There was nothing unusual in any of this, yet Alice would insist on giving that mischievous little smile of hers as she left for the drawing room with a promise to "leave you men to your port and cigars." It was their little familial deception, unless of course Alice seriously thought father and son had anything in common that might make their conversation anything other than strained. This was possible. Women seemed to mystify relationships between men. They saw bonds of affection and respect where there was little but discomfort. Most days, Arthur would have found a reason to leave the table with his wife or even earlier. There was always something he could pretend was urgent: letters he should have written during the day, a phone call. But it was Friday evening, and it had been a trying day, unexpectedly so. He'd been left alone in the house and had, for reasons he could not fathom himself, decided to conjure some ghosts from the past. He'd managed to put all that aside and was at the tail end, thankfully, of one of his unhappy conversations with John.

They'd both made an effort at first. They'd talked briefly of the new combines on the Surrey estate farms, of the challenges of mechanization and maintaining the hedgerows, but then, as the smoke rose towards the ceiling, the conversation had faded. The two of them had started avoiding each other's eyes, and John had taken more and more frequent sips from his port.

John sighed in that habitual way of his. It wasn't the bored, hedonistic sigh some men of Arthur's generation had once employed, but something infinitely grimmer, a signal perhaps that the world was broken and could not be mended. John's manner no longer disturbed Arthur. It angered him, and the anger helped.

"Well, it'll all be up to you, one day, you know," said Arthur sternly.

John looked perplexed. "What will, Father?"

"The countryside, the management of estates, the balancing of books."

John closed his eyes and nodded, blotting it all out perhaps. Then he raised the glass to his lips. Again, the sigh.

Arthur tensed.

John looked at him suddenly. Arthur was surprised at the sobriety in his son's eyes. He should have been on his way to tipsiness—John was rather too fond of his liquor—but what Arthur saw in his eyes was a challenge, steady and clear-headed. Arthur thought his son was going to speak, issue some kind of protest. But he didn't. So Arthur beat him to it.

"You can slide into a funk if you like, John. You can let it all go to rack and ruin."

"Let all what go to rack and ruin, Father?"

"Our way of life, John. Our house here. Our house in the country. Our tenants. Our farms and forests. Or perhaps you hadn't noticed any of those."

"Yes, Father," John said, filling his glass again. "I had noticed them." He shook his head and laughed.

Something in Arthur snapped. "So, what's this?"

"What's what, Father?"

"Is this the war again? The famous battered generation we hear so much about?"

A smile, cheeky, almost triumphant, played on John's lips.

"You think you're the only ones who've ever questioned things?" Arthur said, feeling the heat rise to his face. He knew this was dangerous territory, but he had committed himself. He trusted he could back out of too deep a revelation in time. "It's the disease of the age, isn't it, this guilt of yours, this inertia?"

Arthur placed both hands on the table like a priest in the pulpit, and he knew he was raising his voice. His son's eyes were blinking under the onslaught but the hint of a grin had not quite disappeared.

"It's everywhere, like a contagion, this doubt, and belly aching. Guilt at having survived when others hadn't, guilt over bullets piercing the enemy's flesh. I've had enough of guilt, boy, I can tell you. It's been three years since the last bullet was fired." He took a breath. John was silent. "Man survives at the expense of his enemy, John. It is the law of nature, the eternal law, the universal law, the only law that matters."

John squinted at him. "You really believe *that*, Father?"

"Yes, I believe it. I know it." Arthur's eyes searched the room, the decanter, the mahogany cabinet on the far wall, the deer's head with its shiny glass eyes, the sideboard with the crystal tumblers. "This disgust your generation feels—it's a pose, John. You're like one of the aesthetes from Oscar Wilde's time except your drug is doom and gloom and hopelessness. You don't need the opium."

"Well thank you, Father, for that insight into my true nature."

Arthur realized he was breathing heavily. He could hear the pounding of blood in his ears. He leaned back. "We have talked about this before, John," he said more calmly.

They had indeed talked about it before. In the spring of 1919, Arthur had told him enough was enough. There were lands to manage, tenants to see to, and households to run, heirs to provide. There was, in short, a future. If the country is ever going to recover from the war, he had told his son, it is up to us, to *you*, to show it how.

It had seemed to work. John had buckled down, finished his last term at Cambridge—his academic studies had been interrupted by the war—and had seemed to come back into the world to an extent. Father and son had drawn their half playful battle lines, fencing about the tendency of young people to either take everything too seriously, or not seriously at all. John, of course, was in the former camp. It had never occurred to Arthur that it would go on so long, that his son would be almost twenty-five, a bachelor, and worse, a bachelor without any social life which suggested he might one day be anything else. The battle lines had ceased to be so playful. The fencing had become argument or silence. And occasionally, as tonight, he still saw *that* look in his son's face, the one that seemed to say, *You haven't got a clue, have you, old man?*

Arthur allowed his son's look to settle on him. The judgement was transparent, brazen even. John's eyes narrowed once more, and he filled his glass again. Arthur signed and looked at his watch. It is said that parents little understand their children, but Arthur had added an indecent little twist of his own to that saying. Few among his acquaintance, least of all his son, could possibly guess his own secret. No one could guess at the perverse twinge of pleasure this knowledge gave him, especially now, at this moment when youth claimed wisdom and experience over seniority. No, Arthur thought, it's you that doesn't have a clue, boy. But he merely smiled very slightly. It was a lonely sort of triumph. Tonight it was all rather closer than usual.

Alice had insisted on sitting in the garden before dinner, and it had seemed churlish to oppose her. But he'd known it had made matters worse. The birds had been rising to a chorus as the sun had lowered to embrace the high garden wall. Sparrows and thrushes had darted from bough to bough. And beneath it all Arthur had thought he'd heard the audible hiss of growth, the upward sliding of grass through the soil, the stretching of leaves as they opened and rubbed against their neighbours. The sound should have been a joyous one, but it wasn't. It was unsettling, almost unbearably so, like too-bright scarlet paint on the walls of a dining room, like Tennyson's "Crimson Petal" sung by the white-faced debutante at the Connemara's soirée. The garden, he realized, held reminders. Those blades of grass, leaves, and subtle fronds of nature curled and eased their way through narrow and long-forgotten paths of his memory. They returned him to his life before Alice, before John was even thought of. He saw a slender figure in a pale dress with a parasol and pretty, large-eyed face. He had returned to Lucy, to unstained goodness, the purity before the fall.

Lucy was rarely so vivid in his recollections, and he knew he'd brought it on himself. During the afternoon, when he'd been alone in the house apart from the servants, he'd occupied this time by going through his private documents and papers. At first, he had done this innocently, only half aware of the flutter of the past rippling beneath this impulse. If he'd been in mind to prove his innocence to himself, he might have whistled a jaunty tune. Instead he'd merely spoken a little too breezily, too loudly to Oxborough as the two of them together had unhooked the large oil painting in his bedroom. The view, always one of his favourites, was by a skilled but fairly obscure American transcendentalist. It depicted a waterfall, a mountain, and a ravine at dusk, or perhaps it was dawn. A point of startling light was within the waterfall, as was the fashion in landscapes from that great continent. He'd become sentimental talking about it and only realized too late that Oxborough, embarrassed—or worse, bored by his display of emotion—was staring off toward the window.

The safe behind the painting contained family jewels sometimes worn by Arthur's wife, together with some bonds and banknotes. They were, in theory, destined to be passed on to

John's future spouse were such a creature ever to come into existence.

Oxborough had left while Arthur had been distractedly holding family jewels to the light of the window, returning to Arthur's bell ten minutes later. The restlessness, the sense of an ulterior motive had by now suggested itself to Arthur. He had held it at bay for a while longer by telling Oxborough he wanted access now to a second safe on the ground floor. This alternative stronghold, less obviously placed than the first, but also known to the family's insurers, was in a fairly narrow hallway that led from the main living area to the stairs that, in turn, descended to the servants' working areas, the kitchens, and the butler's private rooms. This safe was not behind a portrait, but a mirror—an undistinguished modern piece that was slightly bronzed and tarnished in the corners. He hadn't needed Oxborough's help to remove the mirror from the wall, but having him there leant a certain legitimacy to his presence in an area of the house where servants would surely jump to see their master.

Again, Oxborough had backed discreetly away but only so far as his own rooms from where he might emerge should he need to inform those under him of Lord Godalming's presence. The safe contained the original deed to the house, which dated back to 1785, now dried and yellowed at the corners with age. Arthur had fingered the deed carefully and sifted purposelessly though his own and his wife's wills, various other legal papers, some bonds, and a curious and valuable collection of stamps and coins which had been passed down through several generations of Holmwoods.

As he closed the safe and enlisted, unnecessarily, the help of Oxborough to re-hang the mirror, his heart had picked up speed. The perverse desire had fluttered again. The existence of the third safe was known only to Arthur, and he had resolved to open it. Unlike the first, this was not hidden in plain sight. Nor was it, like the second, secreted in an innocuous but oft-trodden corner of the house. It was not, in fact, easily accessible to anyone. But by examining, however cursorily, the contents of the other two safes, he'd given himself leave to imagine the opening of the last a logical part of the same routine.

In placing this secret safe, primal fear had sparked a hitherto dormant romantic imagination; he had contrived to make use of an unknown portion of the attic. He had retrieved the necessary keys from the chest of drawers in his room and made his way up a small, disused staircase behind a locked door, accessing a small, deserted room a whole floor above the servants' sleeping quarters. Although the walls were too bare for either a picture or a mirror, some half-finished works of art created by a great aunt with bohemian pretensions were stacked against the wall within which the safe resided.

Arthur had moved some of these aside, uncomfortably aware the sound of shifting and scraping might carry to the servants' quarters below. In a moment, the safe, which possessed both a combination lock and a padlock with a chain moulded into the iron, had been exposed. He had dipped his hand into his waistcoat pocket and fished out the padlock key, alarmed to see as he did so that his white fingers were visibly trembling. But he had quickly succeeded. The chain had fallen loose. His mouth had gone dry as he crouched down and entered the combination.

The safe had opened easily, a welcoming host.

The contents had seemed innocuous at first, even to Arthur. Even so, he had felt lightness in his chest and, for a moment, couldn't move. Inside the safe was a thick sheaf of papers bound together though it was comprised of various sizes of paper—some letter, some legal—of various colours and differing bonds. The red ribbon might put one in mind of a legal brief, but the miscellaneous nature of the papers might remind one of a bundle of exhibits.

He had slipped his hands under the sheaf and drawn it from the safe. Dust had collected in the furrow of the red ribbon.

Again feeling an unhealthy lightness in his chest, he had pulled the ribbon free and laid it inside the safe.

The note was in John Seward's handwriting, slanted and precise, not at all the scrawl physicians were supposed to use. Arthur had glanced through the words:

> *How these papers have been placed in sequence will be made manifest in the reading of them. All needless matters have been eliminated, so that a history almost at variance with the possibilities of latter day belief may stand forth as simple fact. There is throughout no statement of past things wherein memory may err, for all the records chosen are exactly contemporary, given from the standpoints and within the range of knowledge of those who made them.*

This note was a committee effort. Seward authored the first draft. Mina Harker improved it, of course; she always did. Her husband might have chipped in, as had Arthur. It was on its way to being a work of collaborative genius. What better way of giving verity to an unlikely series of events than by drawing attention to its implausibility? And what better way of defending oneself in advance of any charges than by having multiple contemporary accounts all giving witness as one voice?

Arthur's hands had ceased to tremble as he leafed through the contents of the bundle. He had felt suddenly proprietorial about it all, almost proud in fact. He had thought of the many, many hours of work behind the series of diaries, journals, medical memorandums, and letters. Between the first concept and this final collected version was almost eight years of work, planning, and meetings, disparately scattered.

He had looked at the first page after the introductory note: *Jonathan Harker's Journal.*

Poor Harker. Such an unimaginative man, so out of his depth. And yet he'd managed this task well enough with the

"journal." He'd remained true to the sole verifiable details—
his eastward journey to the Balkans to facilitate the sale of
a house to one Count Dracula. And then he'd convincingly
penned details of the mounting terror, his imprisonment in
the castle, the voluptuous women, then his escape and return.
Harker's task, which he accomplished remarkably well, was
to make his pages look like a diary, not a recollection after
the fact. He'd also had to create crimes for the count and
his companions that were so loathsome, so outrageous, that
they would block any thought and therefore any doubt in
the reader. Arthur had been impressed at how such a dull
man had plunged the depths of nightmarish imagination to
achieve this.

Arthur had leafed through Harker's pages. The writing had
faded to a lighter blue but this helped make them seem like
true exhibits. His eyes had settled upon the grieving mother
in the courtyard of Dracula's castle. "Monster, give me my
child!" she'd screamed.

Why she should have screamed in English was a puzzle, but
she was a vivid enough creation as she tore at her hair and
beat her chest, and the reader, by this time, already knew what
had happened to her child. Dracula had given the women—his
daughters from their description—a "wriggling bag." Harker
had outdone himself.

He had continued to sift through. Harker's journal with
its hardened pages, interspersed with letters written at corre-
sponding dates, gave way to John Seward's diary, with letters
and medical memoranda from Van Helsing, saved from 1889
and 1890, the years in which they were written. Finally, Mina
Harker's journal had begun to take up more and more space
in the collection of papers. Harker's wife had neat, slightly
right-sloping handwriting. Everything about it commanded
respect and attention, even the addition, which they had all
opposed at the time, that she should declare the count "the
saddest soul of all." In the end, this had appeared not in Mina

Harker's narrative but as a quote in one of the others. It was more powerful that way.

Harker had added a note at the end about the fact that he had named his own son in honour of Quincey Morris. The detail had given Arthur a twinge of guilt and sympathy for Harker. His hand had trembled slightly as he let the papers run in reverse through his fingers. And there was something worse than Harker's loss. He had caught sight of it in the looped handwriting of some of the letters.

He'd forgotten, or half-forgotten perhaps, that the bundle included letters from Lucy. These had been placed, like Van Helsing's notes, in chronological order, little material ghosts among a series of documents penned by the living. He remembered how they had dealt with the problem of Lucy. They had merely altered the setting. In Seward's version, she had met her end in the crypt rather than her own bedchamber.

Arthur took another puff of his cigar. His son's eyes were on his glass. He'd given up his silent accusations for now. The doorbell, though muffled by distance, had disturbed him. It had come two, then three times. What manner of emergency would justify this at such a late hour?

Even John noticed, and his brow furrowed slightly.

Arthur coughed and waited, unsure how to conceal his growing trepidation. He knew nothing, after all, of the caller. But he'd opened that safe; everything from that decision onwards had been off kilter. Even the midsummer garden had become a place of unpredictable menace. He'd opened his Pandora's box. His superstitious side saw no reason why life would slip back into the same pattern as before.

In a moment, Oxborough entered. "Mr. Jonathan Harker to see you, sir."

7.

OXBOROUGH'S VOICE WAS HUSHED, and he'd left the door slightly open behind him. Normally Arthur would have taken this as an oversight, but he wondered whether Oxborough had his reasons. If Harker was agitated—and the lateness of the hour, the insistence of the bell suggested he might be—the promise of an open door might placate him. There was Alice in the drawing room to consider.

"Better show him in here, Oxborough."

John shifted, backing from the table and placing both hands on the surface.

"Where are you going?" Arthur demanded.

"I just thought…"

Harker entered. Arthur glanced up at him. "Come join us, Harker. You remember my son, John. We are just finishing off our dinner. Fetch another glass, Oxborough."

Arthur was surprised, and rather pleased, with himself. Harker, pink faced and ill at ease in his dinner jacket, was one of the very demons he'd unleashed. But there was no panic in his voice. He sounded fearless and urbane.

Oxborough had waited inside the room, obviously ready for the request. He produced the glass quickly from the sideboard and laid it soundlessly on the table, then he left the room and closed the door after him. Arthur reached across the table and filled it as Harker sat down opposite John.

John placed his hands on the table again. "Perhaps I should…"

"We haven't finished, John."

Harker closed his eyes for a moment. His dinner jacket seemed dishevelled, his tie askew. Had he battled his way through a cluster of thorn bushes on his way to Mayfair?

John stared at his father pleadingly.

"Well," said Arthur, "perhaps you should join your mother. Tell her I won't be long."

He hated to submit, particularly when he guessed at his son's reasons for wanting to leave: guilt yet again. *He* had survived. Harker's son had not. The two boys hadn't known each other well as far as Arthur knew. John was several years younger than Harker's Quincey and had gone to Eaton, of course. Harker's boy had gone to some lesser public school. But John must have taken careful note of every family in his acquaintanceship, both near and distant, that had lost a son. Everyone in the world, it seemed, wanted to crawl under stones in the garden or into cracks in the concrete. Everyone wanted to apologize for their existence. The country had been overtaken by a contagion of guilt. For the moment it defeated even Arthur.

John slunk away and closed the door quietly. Harker's hand shook as he brought the glass to his lips and gulped. He put it down with a clunk, and then wiped his lips with the back of his hand.

"Looks like you need something stronger," murmured Arthur. He rose from the table and went over to the brandy decanter. Overturning a glass, he poured a generous measure. He hesitated, and then did the same for himself. He returned to the table and placed the glass before Harker, again pausing before he moved around the table to his own seat. Delay had become remarkably important all of a sudden. He knew he would not like what he was about to hear.

"It's happened," said Harker, after another gulp, this time of the brandy.

"*What's* happened?" Arthur's tone aimed at nonchalance, and he was quite certain he'd achieved it until he caught Harker's stare, which was feral but steady and determined. Arthur's face twitched.

"A man from the province of Wallachia has made contact with my wife and daughter. He is a professor at King's College, here in London." Harker's voice was unnaturally dull. Arthur wondered if he'd been drinking already, or whether he was keeping all emotion from his words to prevent any suspicion of panic.

Arthur shrugged, but again he knew that his bravado was false and that Harker could see through it. He'd brought it all to life himself this afternoon. It was a fancy, a suspicion, he knew, but a potent one all the same. He thought of the garden again, the hissing grass and the fronds. He felt one with it all, as though his inner world and the garden were fused in some land of the imagination. The tendrils were making their way through his youthful love for Lucy, through her perfect beauty, her sweet face, and trusting eyes. Then they reached deeper into him, curling around visions of her paleness, the way she was when her first illness struck, and then—God help him— through the terrible change that came over her.

"I understand your concern for Mina and your daughter, Harker," Arthur said dryly. He slid his hand along the table ridge, rooting himself into the room. He wished it was day, and that everything in the room—the decanter, the mahogany cabinet on the far wall, the deer's head with its shiny glass eyes, the sideboard with the glasses—were flooded with unromantic light. At the moment everything seemed monstrous, touched with the living hue of candlelight yet shadowed in mystery. Every object conspired with the hiss of the garden beyond the heavy silk curtains. "But those days are long gone. King's College attracts people from all over Europe, from all over the world…"

"His name," Harker interrupted sharply, "is Florescu."

The hiss of summer became stronger. Arthur raised his glass and gulped from its burning contents. His vision blurred a little. The far wall became hazy, Harker's head and shoulders dissolving into the candle flame. Arthur sensed, rather than heard, Harker's breathing. It seemed to be rapid and panting, like an animal hiding from a predator, avoiding detection but ready for flight.

"And the title?" Arthur asked. "Did he use any title, any family name?"

"He did not call himself Dracula or Count. But then he wouldn't, would he? Not if he wanted to get to us."

"But Harker..." Arthur sighed and shook his head. It was too late—almost—to play the rational man talking to the neurotic. His own fear had been too obvious. But he'd been duped by fear—he'd admit that much—just as Harker had been duped. This, he felt, would be the key with Harker; he would simply own up to his own weakness and hope that Harker would do the same. "I agree, totally agree, that this occurrence is upsetting. I even think it's possible this Florescu is related to ... well ... to *him*. But think about it: how many Florescus are from Wallachia? It's a royal name, but does this mean anyone with the name is royal? And let's just say, for the sake of argument, let's just say, he is a relative, a nephew, a third cousin—this doesn't prove ill-will towards us and our families. It doesn't even prove he knows about any connection."

Harker seemed to relax. At least he slumped in his chair. "I dreamed about Quincey last night."

Arthur looked to the door. "Your son?" he coughed.

John's guilt was his all of a sudden. The contagion had spread.

"No," Harker stared across the table at Arthur. "Not my son," he said, "though I have dreamed about him a hundred times."

Was this a reproach? It seemed like it had to be. The deliberate metronomic metre of his words, his pink-rimmed eyes, one twitching, felt like a building accusation of some kind. "No, I dreamed about Quincey Morris. I dreamed about the final battle. The chase, the blood on my knife."

Arthur glanced at the door. "Steady Harker!" he said. But his voice did not command. It quavered. Harker's fear, it seemed, was as infectious as his son's guilt. But there were real dangers here, dangers of memory, and dangers of loose lips. Surely Harker was not so far gone as to forget there were some things that should never be spoken aloud. Harker had more to lose from indiscretion regarding the final battle, as he called it, than Arthur. While Arthur had financed the expedition to Wallachia all those years ago, it was Harker's knife, not his, that had sliced through the count's throat. Poor Quincey, the other executioner, had perished in the act.

From this distance, Quincey's death seemed less terrible than Dracula's. Arthur remembered the arc of the foreigner's blood, a dark rainbow amidst the falling snow. He remembered also that sense of fear, the feeling of being too far from home, even when the mission had been accomplished. Harker's wife had dealt with this part of the story in the manuscript they'd concocted. Although he had glimpsed none of the writing in his sift through that afternoon, he remembered it well enough. Her version of the fight was extraordinarily romantic. She had poor Quincey make the most improbable heroic declarations even when he was in his final death throes. She'd had all the survivors sinking simultaneously to their knees in prayer, and she'd even added a bit about the count's body crumbling into dust before their eyes.

Perhaps she really had seen it all that way. Who knows? It was true, anyway, that the danger had passed. Pride was avenged, and Harker's wife would never succumb to the same vile influence. But the Wallachian rocks and ridges were like inscrutable, eyeless judges. Older than time, they had sat silent in the mounds of grass. The sunset, red beyond the castle, had seemed cold even as it burned. *This is not your land*, nature had seemed to tell Arthur. You have come here solely to commit a crime you could never commit in your own country.

Arthur had known it was hypocrisy, this journey into a lawless land to exact a just revenge, but it had been necessary. They'd all thought it at the time. But it wasn't Dracula's people Arthur feared after it was done. It wasn't his descendants or retainers, or some authority that might take the dead nobleman's side. The peasants, the only witnesses, had fled. They would never tell. Yet he had wanted to take one precaution when instructing the others writing of the tale. He had wanted them to remove any mention of him being present on this final journey. Arthur would be the financer only. He'd had to stay at home to deal with his affairs. There'd been puzzlement rather than protest at the idea. But he'd explained, convincingly he thought, that if the manuscript mentioned Lord Godalming taking part in such an adventure, the whole story, if ever found or leaked, would take on an even more sensational quality. He would become the Lord Byron of his age, a mad adventurer whose every move was a scandal, and this would bring an uncomfortable focus upon all of them. As it was the precaution had never been acted upon. When Seward refused another rewrite, Arthur had stopped asking the others. The count's death was not the worst thing for Arthur anyway, and he realized this soon enough. It was a distraction. Arthur's problem was and always would be Lucy. He could never have married her, of course. Such corruption was complete and irreversible. She would have infected his line. But the solution Van Helsing devised and the fact Arthur had been its instrument would haunt him for eternity.

"Quincey was a brave man," said Arthur simply. He thought to placate Harker by echoing his wife.

Harker nodded. "Indeed. But why would I dream about him now?"

Arthur shifted in his seat, feeling a reflux in his throat. "Because of this man from Wallachia, of course. He stirred you up."

"No," Harker said. "I didn't know about him when I had the dream. Mina and Abree only met him today."

Arthur sighed and took another sip of brandy. "So, what are you suggesting, Harker?"

Harker's brow furrowed. He seemed confused, as though he'd never considered the point. "I can't explain," he said finally, "except that it isn't over. We tried to wipe it out. But it didn't work. It's just come back in a form subtler, more dangerous than before. Think of the war."

"The war?" Arthur repeated. He tried not to sound too like he was humouring Harker, but the more Harker rambled, the less rational he seemed, and the more Arthur felt reassured.

"One man shot in a carriage. Battle lines are drawn. Germany against Serbia. Russia against Germany. Germany against France. War, like a disease, takes over Europe. Millions die." Harker stared at the table as he spoke, and then raised his eyes to Arthur, his expression terrified, bewildered. "Should we have done it?" he asked urgently.

Arthur glanced at the door. "Shh, for God's sake, Harker."

"Should we have followed him to Wallachia?"

Arthur sighed. Then he talked in slow, deliberate tones as if he were a doctor and Harker a patient. "You can't conflate our efforts with the assassination of the archduke. We didn't start the Great War. We had to put an end to a dangerous man. Remember what he did to Lucy. And your own wife, man! We had a duty to them and to others." Harker was silent, listening. But it was too late for Arthur. The hissing had returned with a vengeance. She was before him again, in the very midst of this verdant jungle of memory, the incarnation of Lucy he'd tried to blot out forever, her full red lips, her insinuating gaze, her wantonness when she was with the count. Again, she took Arthur's hand and plunged it into her, and again he pulled it back sharply and thrust her away. That he'd ever needed to do that to Lucy! That she could be so changed he'd recoil from her. Again, he felt an overwhelming sense of loss as he realized her purity and shyness was gone forever. He was angry with Harker for bringing him back to this. His Mina was never changed to the same degree.

It had been Arthur's duty to marry and produce an heir after Lucy was gone, and he had done so. But Lucy, the way she had been before the change, trusting and pure, had always remained with him. She presented the full spectrum of feminine virtue and vice: Lucy "before," the most shining and pure; Lucy "after," the darkest and most wicked.

"Remember, Harker," he said more determinedly, "we were not acting on our judgement alone. Van Helsing was one of the foremost authorities on moral insanity. This was the infection the count spread. Your own daughter is named after the professor, for goodness' sake. How could you doubt him?"

Arthur realized he'd raised himself from the head of the table as he talked and was moving to the side opposite Harker. But he had no clear idea of why or where he was going.

An emotion swept across Harker's face as he looked up at Arthur. Arthur couldn't be sure, but it seemed like disgust. "Van Helsing was recommended by Jack Seward," he said slowly, as though doped. "And Jack took his own life."

"His mind was unbalanced."

"He was in despair, Holmwood. He was in despair because he knew he'd been wrong about so many things."

"You don't know that." Arthur moved a small box, containing Turkish cigarettes, from one part of the table to another. He opened the lid and closed it again. He realized this seemed like a sign of dismissal and felt conflicted about it. He didn't want Harker on London's streets before he could be properly calmed.

But Harker didn't take the hint anyway. "Why else does a man like Seward despair?" he asked. "A man who has seen everything, every kind of suffering, every kind of mental disorder? He was more used to the world and its cruelties than you or I."

"I don't know, Jonathan, and nor do you." Arthur sighed and leaned over towards his guest. "You should go home to your family. You are stirred up, as am I. Neither of us is thinking clearly."

Harker shifted slightly in his seat, gave a slight nod, and rose. "Give me a call tomorrow, when you've ... when everything seems clearer. We'll have lunch at my club." He reached to the wall and pulled the bell cord, then extended his hand. Harker took it and they shook.

"Perhaps," said Harker, as Oxborough returned, "perhaps I need some rest."

"That's it, precisely." Arthur managed a tight smile as Harker shuffled off.

The door closed behind Harker. Arthur stood where he was for a moment and then moved over to the window. He pulled back one of the curtains. Stars pierced the night. Boughs rippled in the breeze like monstrous fingers. A crescent moon, cruel and slivery, hung far above the garden. What happens to a corrupted soul after death? Arthur wondered. Does she belong irreparably to hell or is she reclaimed by Christian goodness as Van Helsing once claimed?

A winged creature flitted from the horse chestnut tree to the copper beech. Arthur had thought he was watching the garden, but now he realized it was the other way around. The garden was in darkness; Arthur knew each feature only by its placing. *He*, on the other hand, was in a lighted space, exposed. His flushed cheeks, his glassy-eyed confusion—these things would be clearly visible from the outside. The night was an ocean of watchfulness. Every supersensitive antenna was directed upon him. Something dropped from a branch, then disappeared entirely into the darkness before it reached the ground. Where had it gone? He closed the curtain, and turned back into the room, disquieted.

8. JENNY O'CONNELL

EVEN FROM HER ROOM on the third storey, Jenny heard the front door open. It was an abrupt sound, a bang followed by a thud, but hardly loud enough to wake anyone. She must have been waiting for him, she realized. The moonlight filtered through the cloth curtain above her head. It had been a night of breezes and lulls. The atmosphere itself had come alive since darkness had fallen.

It seemed an age before there was any other noise from Mr. Harker. Jenny imagined the master standing mutely in the entryway, eyes wide and senseless, door open behind him. Had he been expecting her or Mrs. Rogers to still be up? Then she heard a squeak, followed by the unmistakable sound of the door closing.

She had wanted to be downstairs for his return. She had wanted to speak to him, not in confrontation, but just to let him know, to make sure he had proper warning. Tonight had seemed the perfect opportunity. He'd been out late. Mrs. Harker and Miss Abree had been tired and perhaps worried. As they had prepared to go upstairs, Jenny had resolved to take her time over the evening's final chores, to linger over them as she'd done before. But they had pre-empted her.

"You may go to bed now," Mrs. Harker had said. "Mr. Harker has his latchkey."

Miss Abree had looked from her mother to Jenny. "I'll see to the lights, Jenny."

They both faced her as they spoke. There was no reason to oppose and no excuse for disobeying.

For a moment, as she'd climbed the servants' staircase, the weight of defeat on her shoulders, she'd wondered if they'd guessed. She'd tried not to make a noise when she was sick this morning. And when she'd started work, only slightly late, she'd rushed to catch up. Still, these people were subtle and worldly. People who talked so finely—*erudite* people her aunt Laura would call them—know so much more than they ever reveal. Jenny had lived among them long enough to understand that. Refinement demanded an intricate knowledge of all things unrefined. Only then could conversations dance around their true subjects, ducking and avoiding, teasing all those issues that can't be broached directly.

But they didn't know anything. She was quite certain of this when she'd had a chance to think it through. They were merely afraid of embarrassment. Mr. Harker could come home any moment, and they were worried about what state he might be in when he did. They needed no more reason than this to clear the space urgently.

Something crashed to the floor below. It was likely the tall plant stand guarding the recess between the hallway and the drawing room. She thought she heard skittering earth and stone. Now there was a stirring on the floor immediately below hers, likely in Mrs. Harker's room. The mistress was going downstairs. Footfalls descended softly like heartbeats. Jenny realized her own heart was racing. The idea of the master being drunk and incapable was a kind of torture to her. The lack of pride, the shame. She twisted her sheet in her fingers, trying to guess at the scene below.

Then she sat up suddenly, letting the sheet go. It was Jenny who was in trouble, she realized, no one else. The master would likely be ashamed of himself when he was sober. Mrs. Harker and her daughter would likely be embarrassed the master of the house had come home drunk. But these were minor troubles really. They would disappear soon enough. Jenny's troubles would not disappear. They would grow in the following days, weeks, and months. It was too incongruous to grasp. It never felt as though her problems, the problems of any domestic maid for that matter, could be a tenth as important as those of her employers. But it was true. The man stumbling blindly below, the drunken man who'd lost control of himself, held her fate in his hand. The moonlight peered more brightly around her little curtain. A cloud must have passed.

He'd been tender, she'd remembered. He'd been kind. The first time had been in March when Miss Abree and her mother had been in Brighton. It had seemed quiet and strange with just the three of them—the master, Mrs. Rogers, and herself—in the house. Most men would have migrated to their club while their family was absent. Not Mr. Harker.

Mrs. Rogers had said he haunted the place, but this wasn't quite right. It was his body, not his spirit, that was present. Several times Jenny had come across his mortal form unexpectedly when she was sweeping the floor, dusting the furniture, or laying the fire. Each time there had been an absence of expression, an indifference to his surroundings. He had seemed half alive at best. If he was haunting, then his spirit wandered some other place.

She'd been sweeping out the living room grate when she'd become aware of a shadow cast across the brass. She'd turned to see him there, staring directly at the mantelpiece. He hadn't moved or seemed to notice her when she looked up at him.

She'd seen him again a few hours later. She'd had a chance by then to examine the mantelpiece and guess at what had put him into a trance. So when they'd come across each other on the main stairway that afternoon, she'd smiled at him. He'd looked particularly distracted. His hair was in disarray and his eyes were like those of a hunted animal. There had been no focus in them, but rather a vague fear, an anticipated pain. She'd felt sorry for this man in mourning whose wife and daughter were in Brighton. She hadn't been foolish enough to think them cruel for deserting him. She'd known enough about grief to understand the need for relief and forgetfulness. But Mr. Harker was a man; he had no way to unburden himself, no one from whom he could seek advice. He hadn't responded to her smile, but when she'd climbed to the top of the staircase where she was to start polishing the bannisters, she'd sensed he had stopped, that he had turned to watch her. And then she'd heard his footsteps climbing towards her.

Mrs. Rogers preferred work on the staircase and landing to be done when everyone was out of the house, so it was unusual for Jenny to be here, in the family space. She'd felt a tingle around her shoulders as he approached. She was trespassing, she'd thought, and he was about to reprimand her. But he was silent, and eventually, feeling her ears burn at the strangeness of it, she'd turned and smiled again, this time nervously.

He had been very close indeed, and she had taken a half step backwards. An odour of tobacco and something spicy, perhaps a shaving perfume, had wafted around the small space between them. He was some way taller than her, so she'd had to strain her neck to meet his gaze.

"He was a sensitive boy," Mr. Harker had said.

Jenny had known immediately who he meant, but it seemed impertinent to admit it. She had felt she should ask instead, but the question trembled away on her lips. She had found her eyes welling up.

"You lost someone too," he had said.

She'd smiled at that, the innocence of him, the fact that he'd put them both on equal terms.

"A sweetheart," she had said almost dismissively. She had shaken her head but as she did so, his hand had come down on her shoulder, warm and comforting. She had found herself stepping into a half embrace. It had been so effortless because it was so unexpected.

Soon, his hands had been everywhere. They were not clumsy,

nor were they expert. At first, she had not been entirely sure if he was touching her as an amorous man touches a woman; she guessed it had to be, although the movements of his hands on her body had been more like those of Mrs. Rogers when she kneaded bread. They had been random too; he had neither targeted nor avoided the parts of her that were reserved for sweethearts and husbands. She knew about the tricks and shortcuts. She'd learned the hard way in another household. But Mr. Harker either did not know them or, more likely, he had had no inclination to use them. His hands had been licensed but meandering, unconcerned with results.

There had been a result, of course—the most momentous result possible. As far as Jenny knew it might easily have sprung from that very first occasion. There had been others, four in all, each of them flowing easily from the master's instigation. She'd have been embarrassed at how easily her own body had succumbed to his will were it not for the obvious fact that this was clearly the expectation. He seemed to know so much she did not. Did all maids lie down for their masters? Was this an unwritten requirement of the position?

There was a thump on the stairs below. Mrs. Harker whispered. Her voice carried between floors though it was as soft as butterfly wings. Jenny wished she could ease herself into a dream as quickly as she'd eased herself into Mr. Harker's arms. The breeze had picked up outside again, and something banged against the window pane. It sounded like a clump of earth, but she knew it was likely a loose slate, or just possibly a swaying twig from the beech tree that stretched towards her window. Her stiff little curtain swayed.

If she'd thought of the possible consequences at all, she dimly remembered, the threat of catastrophe had been tempered by the fact that Mr. Harker was a solicitor, a wealthy man by most standards. He would know how to *fix* things. He would not, at least, see her destitute and heavy with child. He'd find some way to atone, although she could not clearly imagine what that would be. She'd had some fleeting vision of a place in the country, a cottage where she would be briefly confined and then begin work as a domestic with an infant about her feet. It hadn't seemed so bad, and there would be a story with it. He'd arrange a respectable past for her, a tragic accident at the gasworks which had taken her loving husband.

The moon disappeared quite suddenly and the room became dark. She'd known for a while that this was no more than a fantasy. There were no such remedies, not for servants. And even if there were, Mr. Harker was hardly the man to find them. She heard the opening and closing of the bedroom door below, sensed rather than heard the faint slumping of a body on a mattress. How could he solve her problems? The poor man couldn't even find his way to bed without help.

Time was running out. She'd be showing soon enough. She imagined slipping out of the door at night with a small bundle of her possessions and a purse with her savings—three pounds, five shillings, and sixpence.

Then what? Leaving seemed like a good idea until she tried to envision what kind of existence would follow. The few times she'd ventured beyond Belgrave Square in the last few weeks, she'd seen the desperate figures huddled in the city's unused doorways, and she'd seen the grimy-faced women with chipped teeth and watery eyes. She could stay and throw herself on the mercy of Mrs. Harker. She was a charitable lady. But she would surely demand to know which young man had caused her predicament. This was how it worked. She knew this from listening to Mrs. Rogers, who had thirty or more years of experience in service. If a maid fell pregnant, her employer spoke to the employer of the young man, usually a footman or a gardener. They would arrange things, make the man live up to his responsibilities.

All the usual routes that might lead to rescue seemed especially closed to her. Her parents were both dead. She had no brother. No sister. Her aunt Laura had only a single room on

Saul Street and had not been at all well. The last time she'd visited her aunt, Jenny had had to give her two pounds. Poor Aunt Laura would scarcely be in a position to return the favour. And what's more, going to her only living relative seemed too shameful a prospect to even consider. Like many East End women who'd skivvied for others all her life, Aunt Laura had an overblown notion of respectability. It was all she had. Jenny could hardly ask her to give it away. The idea of turning up at her aunt's house would make them both die of shame at the same moment.

Jenny had no friends her own age. No one courted her. She was on a small island, and the tide was coming in, lapping at her shoes. She'd lived with this for many weeks now. But something was different tonight. She'd been thwarted earlier when she'd been determined to talk to Mr. Harker. Suddenly it was urgent. She could not let another night pass without action.

9. JONATHAN HARKER

HE'D FORGOTTEN WHO HE WAS. Even as he stared at the milk-white ceiling, he found this curious. He did know the room, after all; he knew the window backed onto a garden that contained tall oaks, several beeches, and generous hedges that quite consumed the perimeter walls and fences. How could these details survive when he could not recall his profession, age, whether he was a married man or a bachelor, whether he had children?

In his dream, he'd been a child playing among daisies. His mother, her auburn hair falling in tresses from her bonnet, had stooped, tilting her basket towards the grass. She'd been picking mushrooms. The sunlight had flooded around him like golden syrup, turning the lush meadow yellow with the intensity of light. The twitter of birdsong had wafted around him like a carpet woven from sound. The overhead clouds had created a pageant: a giant's head blowing a fleet of skimpy sails while monstrous wings flared in opposition, their pale vapour skin drawn tight over ribbed white bones. The whole tableau seemed to depict a Greek god about to plunge into raging conflict with some mythic creature. Nearby hung the creature's disconnected head and flailing tongue. The blue behind the motionless scene had rendered the figures harmless. His child-self had thrilled at the possibility of battle while remaining safe.

Birdsong was the tunnel through which he'd returned from sleep. The carpet of sound was the same, rising and falling in twittering waves. He recognized the bedposts as well as the room. The twisting vine leaves and plump grapes brought him back at last to his marriage and Mina. There had been danger to her, he remembered, but it had passed. It had passed a long time ago. She was no longer young. And since she was no longer young, then it followed that neither was he. Like a beach revealed by a retreating tide, he recalled each detail of his life. It was later, much later. They'd had children. There had been a war. A hole had been torn in their lives: Quincey, his son.

Quincey was gone. Jonathan's bones ached with the recollection. He tried to move, found his body stiff, and his tongue stiffer and very dry.

Quincey. The name had been chosen as a talisman. That small, squirming thing with its pink warm head and the question mark lock of hair on its brow needed something extra, superstitious though it seemed. Quincey would protect him, they had thought. But the talisman had turned into a curse. The child had grown up awkward as a colt, much less proficient at sports than his peers. He'd been decent, honest, and gentle. And he'd always seemed a little raw, a little unfinished. The leather of manliness had not hardened around him. And then he'd gone to war, a war created by others. Not *his* war. Not his war by a million miles.

Jonathan had thought this even at the time. Caught up in a wave of unpatriotic nausea that horrified him, Jonathan had sought to extricate his only son from the situation. Not every young man talked of volunteering, after all. Could there be a medical exemption, perhaps something that would keep the boy away while preserving his self-respect? The doctor had once noted he had syndactyly—the scientific term for webbed feet. Perhaps that would do. It would be easy enough, though socially awkward, to arrange a doctor's letter. And then, as the weeks wore on, other possibilities began to arise. There was talk of reserved occupations, even badges which young men could wear with *On War Service* emblazoned on them.

No one could accuse them of shirking if he wore one of those. The terror of receiving a white feather would be overwhelming for any young man.

But, in the end, Quincey had pre-empted him. While the first autumn winds blew around London, Quincey returned with a brown paper package under his arm. In it was his lieutenant's uniform. He'd volunteered and passed the medical without Jonathan's knowledge.

The house had fallen silent, except for Abree, a gangly fourteen-year-old. She'd squealed, rushed up to her brother, hugging him and begging him to put on his uniform. Jonathan and Mina had become statues, cursed to watch events for which their generation was responsible but which they could not change. The mutual self-reproach was obvious every time Jonathan caught the dark, worried eyes of his wife. Was it his name that had compelled Quincey? When he'd been a small child, Quincey had heard both he and Mina talk about the Texan hero. They'd done so encouragingly, telling Quincey he too would grow to be a strong, brave man, how he too would one day fight for honour and virtue. Later, when their Quincey showed no aptitude in the more muscular pursuits, they had stopped, realizing that it was pressure for the boy. But it had been too late, or this is what they'd concluded at first. The name had burrowed into his flesh.

But Quincey had turned out to be a surprise in several ways. He had been more self-aware than Jonathan could have predicted. Quincey had seemed to understand Jonathan's guilt over the name. He had seemed also to understand his father's sense of regret and responsibility that his son had joined the British Expeditionary Force. After dinner, they had sat on either side of the hearth. He'd looked at his father with mild disparagement and reminded him he was almost twenty-four, that he knew boys of sixteen who'd lied about their age to get into the war. No, he had admitted, he didn't have any stomach for fighting, nor did he understand or respect the reasons for conflict. But that wasn't the point. The fact was this: he couldn't let his peers, his work colleagues, and his old school friends put themselves in the way of danger while he remained safe. If there was an easy way out of it, he wouldn't take it. For Quincey, it had been about loyalty. Not loyalty to the king, not even to Britain as far as his father could tell. His loyalty had been on a simpler and humbler scale. And Jonathan had understood.

All this was long ago now, but he was hungover, and there had to be a reason for this. He didn't think he'd become a habitual drunkard. Something else had happened more recently, something disturbing. He had a fleeting memory of Mina as she'd been over last night's dinner, her pearls catching the lamplight. She'd been speaking in that odd, breathless way of hers about a chance meeting with one of the professors from Kings, a young man from Wallachia. It was all so self-conscious, as though she was determined to believe that nothing but good could possibly come from such an occurrence, as though Wallachia were a golden memory. He understood his wife well enough. Mina was ever determined to transcend the past, to find the promise of ultimate reward behind every tragedy. It was the same sentimental strand that had coloured her journal all those years ago. Mina was a contradiction. One day she was a poet gasping for the stars, the next she was granite—hard, practical, and unforgiving. Last night the poet was ascendant. Her eyes had glistened with sentimentality.

He had tried to nod her words away like a man on a train platform waiting for the carriages to pass. The quicker she spoke, the fewer interruptions she encountered, the sooner this perversity would be over. There would be a pause and he'd be able to change the subject. But she'd clearly decided to dwell on it, asking Abree to confirm her impressions of the stranger's fine manners—which she did quite readily, smiling shyly at the memory. Mina had spoken the name Florescu without an apparent flicker of recognition. At this point it had felt like mockery, as though she was daring Jonathan to object to the acquaintanceship. He'd felt a swirling pressure in his head and stopped nodding. He had tried to stare at her hard. Surely thirty-one years of marriage had given them a hint of that telepathy he'd read so much about. But she'd ignored him; she'd looked unconcerned. Had she forgotten that "Dracula" merely referred to the order to which he belonged, just as Godalming referred to Arthur Holmwood's position, rather than his actual name? Surely she remembered that the man they'd chased down all those years ago was more commonly called Florescu. Perhaps she'd never known it, after all. There were all manner of things she'd not known at the time. Was it possible she was as innocent of any connection as she seemed?

He shifted under the covers again and pushed them off his chest.

Holmwood.

Now he remembered—he'd gone to see Holmwood last night. A wave of sickness came at the memory. He propped his head up against the headboard and swallowed hard. Holmwood had pretended to be unaffected by the news. He'd been patronizing about it, of course. He'd made a show of considering the danger and had then tried to seem certain nothing would ever come of it. But he wasn't certain, Jonathan could tell.

Not long before he'd died, Seward had told Jonathan that Holmwood kept all their diaries and journals from the time in a locked safe somewhere in his attic. It had been Seward's entries, more than anyone's, that had concerned Holmwood, and he had given the poor doctor a hard time about it, demanding rewrite after rewrite and refusing to return any of the rejected copies. The poor doctor's writing, it seemed, had not been quite as convincing as Mina's when it came to assuring any would-be readers of their overall nobility. But then his task had been more difficult. A group of brave men hunting down and killing a villain with supernatural powers was one thing, but hammering a wooden stake through a young woman's heart was quite another. Seward's diary covered this incident, and since Holmwood himself had carried out the task, he wanted to be certain the action seemed justified.

Jonathan, on the other hand, had been rather impressed with the way Seward had maneuvered his way around the difficult subject. Under advice from Dr. Van Helsing, he had done two things. Firstly, he'd described in the most rhapsodic way the evil change in Lucy after she'd come under Dracula's influence. He'd used phrases of such lavish colour: there had been *something diabolically sweet in her tones* as she'd talked to Holmwood; her face had been *distorted, full of rage* as she'd recoiled from the crucifix. Seward had even added—rather cunningly, Jonathan thought—a small child victim of her vampiric lust. Secondly, he'd talked in the most certain, medical terms of her being dead before the worst excesses of her depraved behaviour. If she was dead, of course, then she was no longer really Lucy, just some evil spirit who dwelt in her "undead" body. You cannot kill a dead person. Seward and Van Helsing, licensed medical practitioners, were uniquely placed to date and retroactively register Lucy's death several days before her staking. This and a change of location—from bedroom to Arthur's family crypt—reinforced the sense of the supernatural.

But Van Helsing had disappeared soon after the narratives got underway. Arthur had taken over as editor, and seeing what had been gathered from his companions, he wanted more. Under Holmwood's keen editorial eye, poor Seward had gone back to work on his sections, building up Van Helsing as a man of extraordinary and unimpeachable reputation. The final draft had, apparently, emphasized how fervently they had all believed in Van Helsing, and how faithfully they had followed his lead to the end. In reality Seward had likely started to have doubts about his old mentor.

Even though all the documents in Arthur's possession represented a valiant attempt to paint them all in the best possible light, ultimately this was not enough for him. Arthur must have had a vision that they had not fully realized, a story complete enough in its literal rendering of evil that it would satisfy the friends and acquaintances in the Hellfire Club—powerful people in every sphere of influence with a strong sense of loyalty. Yes, they had done enough to evade the noose. They had turned the evil effects from the count into a physical, transmittable disease. They had even had the count drinking blood, a literal vampire. In Seward's narrative, Lucy had been dead before receiving the stake to her heart.

In any case, Arthur was worried that the papers might fall into the wrong hands and incriminate him. Whatever the reason, he'd become very proprietorial indeed about the documents. It was as though the writings which had been conceived as a shield against future accusations had rather become a bloody murder weapon, something to be concealed and guarded with extreme vigilance.

A movement came from the floorboards just outside the door. Then there was a knock. Jonathan moved again under the sheets, feeling nausea rise again. There was something else he'd forgotten, along with his name, his wife, and his children, and this time it came as an answer of sorts. It wasn't only the Wallachian stranger who'd unsettled him. Something else had occurred before, several days—no, a week or more—before. It lay in his wallet, slipped in between banknotes. He'd been invited to visit a man he'd presumed long dead. This little slip of paper was perhaps his own version of Arthur's manuscript. He could have destroyed it, just as Arthur could have destroyed his bundle of narratives, diaries, and letters. But he hadn't. He swallowed down hard. Luckily, he was too dehydrated to be sick.

"Yes," he replied. His voice was cracked, barely audible. "Come in," he added.

He heard a tray rattle before he caught sight of Jenny. She was such a practical, confident girl, it was odd to see her hesitate before she approached the bed and lay the lap table over him.

"Is anything wrong, Jenny?" Jonathan asked, hauling himself up. He thought of Mina and Abree, caught a vision—vague but terrible—of a sudden illness. He hoped for something more mundane to explain the girl's manner, perhaps some electrical fault or water leak.

Jenny took a backwards step. "Wrong, sir?" Again, an uncharacteristic hesitation, a quiver about the mouth. Her youthful bony hands, pink at the knuckles, remained clasped in front of her as she waited, presumably, to be dismissed.

"Mrs. Harker. Is she downstairs?"

"Yes, sir. In the drawing room."

Jenny often walked around the bed to adjust Mina's pillow in the morning. She would smooth over her quilt when presenting breakfast. It was a comforting, intimate kind of movement, as though she had been born into service, born with the skill to make her employers feel secure in her spirit of reliability. Although he was grateful for her discretion, Jonathan sometimes felt irritated that she should be standoffish with him. This morning, however, was slightly different. She seemed ill at ease but made no move to leave.

"And, my daughter?" he asked picking up the china teapot and pouring the steaming tea into his cup. There were four halves of toast in the stainless-steel rack, and a neat fried egg with two rashers of bacon. Despite the hangover, he felt hungry.

"Gone to the university, sir."

"On Saturday?" he asked, surprised.

Jenny nodded and looked to the floor.

So there was nothing. No illness, no household disaster.

Except perhaps himself.

He'd the vaguest memory of Mina helping him upstairs last night. He remembered the numb tingle around him, the feeling of unreality. The plant stand had seemed to fall very slowly and yet he'd been unable to stop it. He'd first seen Mina at the top of the stairs in her dressing gown. In the dim light, she had looked the same as when they were first married, with her fine smooth jaw, the sense of character upon which Van Helsing had been so fond of commenting. The nightdress beneath the gown had hissed as she quickly made her way to him, and she'd soon led him to bed, her hands under his elbows.

Was his wife angry with him? Was this why Jenny seemed so strange? Jonathan listened carefully to the silence below. No ominous prickle of energy. No footsteps. No closing doors or cupboards, no clue at all as to the mood of the household's inhabitants. Mina was usually too stoic for anger anyway, and if she had been annoyed, she would hardly send this young girl to carry her message of reproach.

Jenny coughed at last. "Mr. Harker," she said.

Suddenly he was aware of how soft and fragile her voice was. It seemed separate from the rest of her, and the delicate tone worried him. Jenny's personality was open and straightforward. She was pretty, yes, but had a certain toughness he'd often seen in the British and Irish working classes. He'd often imagined her in the munitions factory at Silverton where she'd worked before the explosion in 1917, smudges of oil on her face. When she'd come to them at eighteen years old after a year of service at another household, Mrs. Rogers had spoken of her as a no-nonsense, hardworking type, a good girl who just got on with things. And it was this—her low-key working-class indomitability—that made her so utterly reliable.

"I have a problem I have to deal with, somehow." Her foot tilted sideways as Abree's had done when she was younger.

Service kept people childlike in some ways, Jonathan thought, even the tough ones like Jenny. Jenny and Abree were about the same age, yet Abree hadn't seemed in the least childlike at any time since Quincey left for war. And here was this girl, so much more experienced than Abree in so many ways, so worldly and knowing, suddenly reverting to the schoolroom.

"Yes, go on, Jenny."

He prepared for the likelihoods. A sickness in the family, but she had no family. Another job? This was more likely. She was a resourceful girl and the factories were just beginning to hire again. But she would tell Mina if this was her problem. She wouldn't tell him over breakfast.

She coughed and something occurred to him. She was surely not making a claim of intimacy. This would be against the spirit of everything that had passed between them. Jenny had been the very thing he'd once dreamed about when he'd been a boy; she was a half-imagined, half-remembered legend come to life—a being that came from myth. But she'd inverted the ancient story, made it safer and more satisfying. Jenny was a siren who called sweetly not to destroy but to comfort. There had been no conditions and no demands. She'd been that elusive combination of innocence, carefreeness, and rapture. It had all fit so nicely into his needs.

Nowhere in the storybooks of his youth had such a creature or such a circumstance existed. Virtue and sexuality could not take residence on the same page. But recently, just as Jonathan's life seemed to have settled into the rut of disappointed middle age, this girl had proved innocence and the most willing voluptuousness were merely opposing poles of two identical magnets; in Jenny, the two contradictions clamped themselves together as though they made an inseparable whole. St. Paul's Epistles went up in flames and with them every statement that twinned modesty with godliness. Modesty was nothing of the kind. Modesty was mean, concealing, and self-absorbed. Modesty was ungenerous. Real virtue yields to the touch and reaches out towards the need in others. Virtue smiles as it takes a heartsick man into its attic room. Virtue runs its fingers through a man's chest hairs and reaches to caress his ear lobe. It lies down and welcomes a lonely man's foraging hands.

In her abandonment, she had been more than merely virtuous. She had shielded his weakness, even from himself. She had never once caught his eye outside the servants' quarters or given him a knowing or mischievous glance. Even when his interest waned, she had sent him no signs of reproach.

But something had changed. Jenny's feet were restless. Her eyes seemed to claim and then cower from his.

"Yes, Jenny," he said in growing panic, "go on." He stabbed a piece of bacon with his fork and busied himself with the plate as though its contents were a folder of important documents through which he had to sort.

"I..." she stuttered. Her mouth remained open but no sound proceeding from it.

He glanced up, felt the heat rise to his face, folded a piece of yolk onto a ridge of bacon, and raised it to his mouth. Please, he thought, please don't destroy the vision I have of you. Any sign of a demand, any evidence of scheming or strategy would make the rarified paradise crumble into dust.

"I have a problem, Mr. Harker, a personal problem." She looked at him meaningfully. Something approaching a smile played upon her features, then gave way to a rather more desperate emotion. She moved towards his bed, and then circled to the foot, as though to claim maximum attention. Tea slurped over the rim of Jonathan's cup. His fork spun over the tray ledge onto the bedclothes. "Mr. Harker," she whispered, "I'm pregnant."

He tried to blink her away, but her expression—a hopeful smile, inappropriately enough—became more real each passing moment.

He'd known what her problem was a few seconds before she'd spoken the words. His mind had automatically clung to his position as master and employer which, in turn, yielded two most obvious responses. One was a directive: *you must speak to your mistress about it.* The other was a question: *who is the father?* But the special circumstances here meant he could give voice to neither of these.

He had been right about her. She *was* different. Different from the girl he had known earlier in the spring, and different from the other young women he imagined sleeping in London's attics and serving the city's families. She was not the straightforward woman who guards her virtue and keeps order in the world around her. Neither was she the siren-temptress of lore, the malice that brings destruction. Nor, most crucially for him, was she the comfort without penalty he'd once believed her to be.

She was catastrophe. Catastrophe wasn't vengeful or malicious. It didn't beckon from the rocks or triumph at the splintered hull and the drowning sailors. Catastrophe was blind, unknowing. She was supposed to have fought him off. Even at the time he'd been expecting this. He'd been expecting a shriek, a recoiling in horror, a scuttling down the stairs to the servants' quarters.

The shade of a large bird darkened the curtains. Jonathan felt a wisp of self-reproach as the shadow passed over him from toe to head. No, she hadn't fought him off, his friendly girl polishing the banister at the top of the stairs. She hadn't thought of the consequences, but neither had he. Neither of them had thought of anything, and this was the result. For the first time in many years, Jonathan wondered about God. What an extraordinary way to build a universe, to create such outlandish punishments for lapses in concentration.

"You're sure?" he asked quietly.

She bit her lip and nodded.

"Don't worry," he said, and then, as though trying to persuade himself, he said it again. "*Don't* worry." The emphasis suggested certitude. It suggested a plan.

She looked at him calmly now, gratefully, he thought, her eyes clear and trusting.

He heard movement on the stairs and then the landing. So did Jenny. She went quickly to the door and opened it wide. "Will there be anything else, sir?"

"No thanks, Jenny," he said, with a nod. Again he knew his eyes and manner were conveying that message: *I will deal with it.* And again he wanted to believe himself. But as she gave him a small, relieved smile and disappeared, he felt the world sinking beneath him. What on earth could he possibly do?

He heard a quick exchange—Mina's voice followed by Jenny's soft reply. His wife entered. For a Saturday morning in June, her dress—dark with pale embroidery and white pearls—was remarkably sober. He wondered if this was the point, whether her appearance was meant as a comment on his drunkenness.

"So you are up," she said, her dark eyes steady on him. "I was afraid Jenny might have awoken you."

"No, I was already awake."

"Good, and how are you feeling?"

"Very well, thank you." He bit a corner off his second slice of toast and took a sip of tea. Drips from the spillage fell down into the saucer.

Mina seemed to watch this rather too carefully. "Really?" she said. "I wondered whether you would be up to much today."

This was as close as Mina had ever come to alluding to his habits when she thought they had got out of hand. Good taste, like a ring of fire around some unmentionable horror, always kept her on the periphery. But the steadiness of her gaze carried an unmistakable message. She was disappointed in him.

"What did you have in mind?" he asked, picking up the last of his egg with his fork.

"Perhaps we could start with a walk in the square, or we could go to Harrods. We have a Christening present to buy for Rachel's daughter."

Jonathan nodded.

Mina moved to the door again, but stopped suddenly before leaving.

"Jenny seemed to be in here for a long time. Is everything all right with her?"

Jonathan managed a shrug. "I'm sure she'd tell you if it wasn't."

She kept her eyes on his for a second longer, then left. The reaction, a heat rising to his face, was thankfully delayed until Mina was out of sight.

10. ABREE HARKER

ABREE DIDN'T ENTIRELY UNDERSTAND why she'd never mentioned Edward to her parents. The usual reason—they might not approve—didn't quite fit. It was true that he was scruffy and quiet while her mother liked young men to be shiny eyed, witty, and well turned out. It was certainly the case that he was intense and intellectual while her mother appreciated men who were amiable and outgoing. It was even true that, with his thick glasses, unkempt look, and wiry hair, he bore more than a passing resemblance to the cartoon anarchist in *Punch*, a figure depicted with a spherical bomb and lighted taper under the flap of his raincoat. But Abree suspected that despite these deficiencies both her parents would approve of Edward well enough, if only because meeting him would demonstrate she had at least one male friend. It wasn't their disapproval that worried her. It was hers.

Edward existed only on King's College campus. He could only speak to Abree when they were alone or with other students from King's. She could not conceive what would happen if he ever tried to cross over the threshold of her home. She imagined it would be something akin to an anti-magnetic resistance. If this angular, nervy friend of hers were ever to succeed in entering the Harkers' drawing room with the grandfather clock, the Persian rug, the ottoman, and the cushioned chairs, he would be ejected by an irresistible force back into Belgrave Square.

Edward was *different*. He was very decidedly from this age. Abree had heard of the tombs of Egyptian princes, how the archeologists found the dust overpowering. Edward in her home would be an inversion of the same event. *He* would be the unbearable dust and he would infect the pristine pre-war atmosphere within.

Edward had joined Helen and Abree in King's College refectory. As usual, the skin beneath his stubble flushed deep red as he scraped back the chair next to Abree, tea cup in hand. The susurrus of conversation and cutlery was a welcome haze around his shyness. "This could only mean one thing," he said, setting his cup and saucer upon the bench. The tea's murky surface wobbled and over-spilled into the saucer.

Abree looked at him with an expectant half-smile. Edward never joked in such a way as to provoke laughter, but almost everything he said had an element of world-weary cynicism that sometimes passed for humour.

"Professor Reynolds didn't accept your dissertation subjects."

The comment was directed at both Abree and her companion.

"Right first time," said Abree after a glancing smile at Helen. "We decided to pool our collective ignorance and use the library to start afresh. How about you?"

"Oh, he liked it," he said without guile.

"Good for you!" Helen, on Abree's other side, proclaimed.

Abree remembered something from a previous conversation, and envy began to bite her. "So was it a line-by-line examination of war poetry then, Edward?" She knew it wouldn't be anything of the sort.

"No, it's poetry as historical document. The idea is this..." He held his hands a foot apart over his cup as though moulding some invisible form. "We approach war as statistics, as facts and dates and numbers of dead, but our imaginations cannot comprehend these things, and they tell us nothing about the experience. Poetry brings us there, lets us experience the horror. Professor Reynolds thinks I am in the vanguard. Poetry is the new history. Poetry alone incorporates both the scale and the depth of human catastrophe in a way we can understand it. This is how future generations will experience the war."

He shrugged as though aware his intensity had spilled over into earnestness. "Anyway," he said, "that's the idea."

"And Professor Reynolds liked it?" pursued Abree.

"I think it's a wonderful contribution, Edward," Helen said quietly as though to warn Abree away from her jealousy.

Abree thought of Quincey. What would he have thought of Edward's idea? The answer was obvious: he would have liked it. Edward was like her brother in some ways, at least in terms of his sensitivity, and something about his moral core. But he was very different in other ways. Quincey had never been intense, and he hadn't carried indignation around like an invisible sword the way Edward did.

A year and a half ago, when they had first met, Edward had called himself a pacifist. He'd said it openly, almost as a challenge. They had been on a bench in a college square at the time, thin funnels of February snow spiralling around them. Edward had not been dressed for the weather. He'd had a thin, and rather grimy-looking mackintosh. Abree had been with a couple of girls who had moved away quickly when Edward started talking. Abree had stayed, partly because she'd been intrigued, partly because of an indefinable sense that she simply belonged there, talking to this dishevelled young man who was so careless of the dry snowflakes landing on his clothes.

Declaring oneself a pacifist was dangerous. London abounded with bereaved families and wounded men. The empty sleeve, the crutch, the wheelchair were as much a part of city life as the perambulator or umbrella. Abree had assumed Edward's statement, and its vehemence, meant he had been a conscientious objector. His defeated posture, that wounded edge in his personality evident enough in this first exchange, might easily have been the consequence of a punitive prison term.

But this had turned out not to be the case. Edward had tried to join the army, but he'd been rejected because of his flat feet and a tubercular past. He'd winced with self-loathing as he'd told her this. He'd been a coward for trying to enlist, he said. This statement had been thrown out like another challenge, just like the one about his pacifism. The eyes behind those glasses had been half closed with the bitterness of his self-reproach.

Abree had merely nodded and looked away for a moment. A snowflake had hit the paving scattering then into a dozen white ice particles. When she'd turned back to him, his expression was startled. He'd not expected her to understand so easily.

That had been the start of their friendship.

"Yes," Abree echoed her friend belatedly, "it is a wonderful contribution, Edward." She felt Helen's relief.

A figure with a tea cup moved along the opposite table, catching her eye. It was the man's gracefulness that commanded attention. His shadow swooped along the row of chairs as a kingfisher's might glance along the surface of a stream. The quality of physical grace was incongruous here. Graceful was the last word anyone would use to describe Edward, Helen, or Abree. Abree identified him only when he turned and gave a rather stately nod in her direction. It was Ivan Florescu.

As an afterthought, it seemed, he halted, and now waited, saucer balanced between his fingertips, while two, then three, students passed in front of him. Then he approached their table.

Edward looked up at him, and then glanced at Abree, as the stranger drew up. "Excuse me, Miss Harker," he said. He tipped his wrist and glanced at his watch. "May I join you for just a moment?"

"Of course," said Abree, her voice rather strangulated.

Abree introduced Helen and Edward as quickly as her lips would tumble out their names. She wasn't entirely certain what she said but she had gulped slightly over the name *Florescu*. The moment after introducing Helen, she remembered she'd been less than flattering about the foreigner the day before.

Now, to her own ears, she sounded almost obsequious. What did Helen think of her? She didn't even have the conviction of her own spite.

His responses—which were clear, measured, and courteous—made her feel even clumsier, even more *English*. His presence at the table changed the atmosphere entirely. The three of them—Abree, Helen, and Edward—had been like scraps of paper rising and falling in an erratic breeze. Professor Florescu had focused them with his smoothness and his manners, with his faint, exotic scent of spice, like burned paprika. Suddenly they were an audience.

"So you and Miss Harker are studying together, Miss Morrison," he said to Helen. "That is such a good practice, especially when there are parallels in your work. You can dare each other towards greater intellectual perils, deeper insights."

"There won't be too much daring, Professor Florescu," said Abree. She immediately wished she hadn't. It was too cryptic and would require far too much explanation.

Still, Professor Florescu's tea cup remained as poised in his hand as a tightrope walker's pole. The steam curled into a question mark before his face.

"Mr. McFarlane," he said to Edward, who seemed to jolt back in his seat, "Professor Reynolds mentioned your dissertation subject. It is, I believe, to illuminate the history of war through poetry. I find that most fascinating."

A squeak came from Edward's chair leg. His expression was a tug of war between pleasure at the flattery and fear over a sucker punch to come. No wonder, thought Abree. Ivan Florescu was a history professor. For a student of English to venture into the turf of another's discipline was forbidden in the eyes of many professors. But if Professor Florescu intended any reproach, his manner hid his intention masterfully.

"Ah, yes," said Edward. The invisible form had returned between his hands, ready once more to be moulded. But while before, when his audience had been just Abree and Helen, his fingers had moved in a kneading motion, they now remained oddly static, as though he no longer trusted his opinions, as though his invisible form was now in rigor mortis and he couldn't think how to revive it. His words had deserted him too. But Professor Florescu used the pause to expand upon his point: "What you are doing, Mr. McFarlane, is entirely new. If I understand it, you are examining how a collective disaster can be understood best through the lens of personal tragedy. In my opinion, also, it can be understood in no other way."

"No," said Edward, "quite. When we resort to facts and figures, to political arguments"—Edward's invisible form had twitched into life again, it seemed—"it's as though we're searching for permission to excuse what cannot be excused. It lets in ideology." His eyes were suddenly wide with surprise as though his form had not only come back to life but also performed a double somersault before them all. "And the worst kind of ideology is nationalism. That's the modern disease. Ideology forgets everything—the blood it spills, the guns it fires, the widows and orphans it makes. It forgets everything except itself. King and country. Kill or be killed...."

Professor Florescu nodded in approval and took a sip of tea. "You are right, Mr. McFarlane. My own brief experience of war was as a medic in a hospital in France where slogans soon lost their potency. We need a mass rebellion against ideology."

Abree listened, after the fact, for a note of irony, some tell-tale expression that might reveal this educator, an experienced man, saw rawness or naivety in the undergraduate before him. This was what she was used to. Even encouragement, in those rare cases she had encountered it, had been laced with some hint of knowingness. But there was nothing at all in this man's manner to suggest anything but intellectual respect and sincere agreement. There was another reason to relax. He'd been a medic in France. That surely meant he'd been an ally, not a foe.

"I think we *are* having a mass rebellion, aren't we?" asked Helen unexpectedly.

Everyone looked at her. She seemed surprised by the interest, as though she hadn't realized she'd spoken. "Well, that's what the jazz thing is all about, the flappers, the carelessness about everything." Her tone was thoughtful, considered as always. But it was an unlikely connection for her to make, unlikely at least to Abree, as it implied criticism.

"Flappers, Miss Morrison?" asked Professor Florescu, intrigued.

"The flighty creatures we read so much about. Consciously or otherwise, they are the mass rebellion. They are rejecting everything. Most of all they're rejecting the world that sent everyone to war. What could be more peaceful than mindless pleasure?"

Professor Florescu put down his cup and saucer at last and clapped. "Bravo, Miss Morrison!"

Some heads down the table turned. Necks craned to see what the commotion might be about.

"There is your subject for your dissertation."

Abree smiled. "But Professor Reynolds already thinks both of us are too ambitious. And what we were attempting was nothing as wild and dangerous as the idea you're suggesting."

"And you know why he thinks you too ambitious, Miss Harker?" He leaned in towards them and spoke in a low and confidential tone.

"No…" Abree and Helen spoke at the same time.

"Because you are not ambitious *enough*."

"That's an interesting paradox, Professor Florescu," said Helen, "but I wonder if it's true.

"Personally, I think we're not male enough." Abree leaned back and folded her arms over her chest. She'd been thinking this all along, of course, keeping quiet because Helen wouldn't approve. Now she'd at last got the thought out of herself she felt lighter.

"It is the same thing, Miss Harker. You have not used your one weapon ruthlessly enough. Men fear women, especially in this country. You must take that fear and confound him."

"Doesn't seem like an ethical approach," said Helen mildly.

"And how would it work anyway?" asked Abree.

"Don't make your rebellions minor ones. Overleap all his defenses. Overleap all his expectations."

"We'll be sent down in disgrace," said Abree smiling. All of this was play, she thought, delightful, fantasy play, and she was happy enough to go along with it, happy to play the warrior suffragette at last.

"Ah well, wouldn't you rather be hung as a sheep than as a lamb? What do you think, Mr. McFarlane?"

Edward pushed his glasses further up his nose. "If it is a battle, perhaps you should treat it as such."

"Edward!" said Helen. "You're a pacifist."

"When it comes to state-sponsored war, yes. But not in class struggles, not in struggles of justice." He scratched his stubble, deep in thought.

Professor Florescu smiled once more and tipped his wrist to look at his watch.

"It has been a pleasure, my friends." He rose, smiled sweetly, and gave a rather stately nod before leaving with his empty tea cup.

Again, Abree caught his spicy scent in the faint breeze he left behind. She glanced at Edward's face, his eyes, like objects in a test tube, enlarged but obscured through his lenses. She noted his pinkish skin beneath his stubble, redder still where he'd scratched himself. She could picture Helen on her other side without looking: Helen, pale and bloodless, like a harmless sea creature, her limbs soft, white, and boneless. Who'd have thought she'd have the power to theorize about a flapper revolution? Still her two companions seemed rather sad, inferior creatures suddenly. And before she could feel like a traitor for the thought, she realized it wasn't only two of them who were sad and inferior. If she fit so easily with the two of them, she must be the same. They were all of them debris.

Whose fault was it? Why should this city of high walls and monuments play host to a people so terminally drab? Why should a spice-scented stranger with chocolate eyes tease her with this vision of a different way of being?

"Wouldn't it be nice to be free and ambitious as Professor Florescu advises?" asked Helen, giving her tea a belated stir. She had spoken with a sigh, as though the wish was as unattainable as dancing upon the clouds.

Abree felt her old impatience return like an itch. She wanted to throw off something tired, stale, and stifling. She didn't know what that something was or how to rid herself of it, but she had to start somehow. If a person can't bear the way things are, they change them. It seemed an odd feature of her life that she couldn't bear the way things were yet she hadn't changed them. She had a fleeting vision of Emily Davison at the Epsom Derby—that thundering mass of speed and power as the racing horses swept across the screen in the Pathé newsreel. She'd been with Quincey to see Fatty Arbuckle in *Fatty Joins the Force*. The belly laughs had swept away the horror soon enough at the time, but from time to time afterwards, that terrible vision returned of that small, dowdy figure of a lone woman crushed and trampled by a dozen horses.

More terrifying than the death played out in front of her eyes had been the question of why—why on earth would anyone stand in front of the pummeling strength and speed of so much muscle and bone? Had Emily Davison also found herself unable to bear the way things were? The details might have been quite different. It was only 1913. There would have been no brother needlessly killed in a senseless war. There might have been no father screaming through the night. Abree had read that Emily had been poor but determined and single minded. For many years she had fought for a cause she believed in and received only shackles from the police, force feeding to thwart her hunger strikes, and cat calls from a wet-lipped public whenever she emerged from a Black Maria.

Abree had little in common with Miss Davison, yet the vision of the suffragette stepping under the railing and into the path of the horses haunted her then. It haunted her even more now. Queen Boadicea rode a chariot into war. Today's flappers threw off convention and danced in dizzying circles into the night. But drab people like Abree, like Miss Davison, did the only dramatic thing they knew how: they moved off the path of unbearable predictability and let the gods decide the punishment.

"Abree!" Helen claimed her attention, not, it seemed, for the first time.

Abree turned to her friend. The general buzz of conversation, the tinkle of cutlery and the scraping of chairs rose in volume. She realized she'd been blocking it all out.

"You were miles away."

"Sorry." She gave Helen a mild smile. "Yes, I was." Edward had already gone. Abree hadn't noticed.

"Let's get back to it, shall we?" She patted Abree on the shoulder, a Girl-Guide gesture, aimed both at bestowing comfort and relaying the message to *buck up*. Abree picked up her cup and saucer, and her satchel, and got ready to return with Helen to the library.

11.

ABREE USED HER LATCHKEY. It was a rebellion of a kind as Mother preferred her to ring the bell. Jenny or Mrs. Rogers would give her a more dignified entrance, Mother seemed to think, and Abree usually went along with this even though it kept her waiting for longer and interrupted one of the household servants unnecessarily.

So there was a moment of hesitation before she scooped the key from her purse, a conspiratorial smile tugging at her face. But it wasn't easy, as it turned out. She balanced her heavy satchel on her raised knee while she poked at the lock, missing several times. The books within the cloth banged against the polished door, and she realized the kerfuffle would soon bring Jenny or Mrs. Rogers to the door anyway. But before this could happen, the key found its slot. She turned it and fell into the hallway, dropping *Walt Whitman's Diary in Canada* together with a book of highly impenetrable theory about the stresses in romantic verse.

Ivan Florescu's admonition came into her mind: *Don't make your rebellions minor ones.* Using a latchkey rather than ringing the bell was as minor as they came. According to Professor Florescu's reasoning, such token efforts were bound to fail. It seemed as though he'd been proved correct.

Abree looked down at the two books spine-up on the black-and-white checkered tiles of the hallway, a perfect illustration of the whole dilemma. She hadn't made up her mind whose expectations to conform to, Professor Florescu's or Professor Reynold's. The Whitman diaries represented an attempt to widen her themes. The theoretical book on verse was a vice with which she might narrow them.

Jenny—pink faced, startled—stood about twelve feet away before the closed drawing room door. There was a moment—an odd moment—when their eyes met. Abree was puzzled. She clearly wasn't a housebreaker, yet Jenny's expression made her feel like an anathema. Then, like a butterfly, Jenny swooped forward and fluttered down to help Abree with the books.

"Thank you, Jenny," Abree said, lodging the satchel on the tiles to create a base while Jenny slipped Whitman's diary and the other book into the bag. But that same mute electricity still crackled around Jenny. Her cheeks had reddened, and she gave a nervous smile.

Abree wondered about her father. Something must have happened or Jenny would not have been frozen as she was at the door. Was he drunk and insensible? If so this would be a new and dangerous turn. Father had been drinking recently but only in the evenings. She wondered if he'd yelled at Jenny or thrown his glass.

Abree stood, the satchel now secured over her shoulder. "Where is my father, Jenny?"

Jenny smoothed down her white pinny. Again the look returned. She appeared frozen and tongue-tied, as though Abree was talking a foreign language.

"In the drawing room, I think, Miss Abree." The pinkness remained in her cheeks.

Abree thought of her father's scream the night before last, his late and drunken return in the early hours of the morning. How much had Jenny seen and heard? She looked as though she was on the verge of tears.

"Is anything the matter, Jenny?" She reached a hand towards Jenny's shoulder and allowed it to rest there, trying to convey friendliness. Perhaps this was her version of Helen's Girl-Guide gesture. But it was likely warmer, Abree thought, and didn't hold the unspoken directive to *buck up.*

"No, Miss Abree," Jenny said and then hesitated. Something like a smile, nervous and fearful but a smile nonetheless, passed over her features briefly. She had been planning to hold out on something, Abree thought, but had now given up. Jenny looked at the closed drawing room door, and so did Abree.

Suddenly Abree had a moment of insight. Jenny meant to hand in her notice. That was why she was hesitating at the door. She had been about to go in and speak to Abree's parents. She'd just been getting up her courage, and Abree's arrival had interrupted her.

Abree knew what she must do. This was a problem for *her* generation, and it was her chance to contribute, her chance to shine. She hadn't borne stretchers during the war like Helen. She hadn't dressed wounds or held the hands of dying soldiers. But she could embrace the role of an adult at last, a move that would allow her to break out of her natural timidity. Fearful people don't rebel. Of course! One grips onto one's adulthood first, then one strikes off in whichever way one feels drawn.

First, she must take control of the household into which she was born. And this should be easy. She could understand Jenny better than either of her parents. She wouldn't refuse to understand the girl's discomfort like her mother likely would. She wouldn't shake her head in frustration or cut her off. She could explain Father's demons, their source, and the likelihood of them passing. She could even talk about modern cures for mental disturbances.

A film of tears had appeared over Jenny's eyes, and Abree knew she had to be right. "Let's go somewhere we won't be disturbed. Where is Mrs. Rogers?"

"In the kitchen. She's cooking dinner."

"Then we'll go to your room."

There was an extraordinary intimacy, as well as gratitude, in the look Jenny gave Abree. It was as if Jenny had looked right inside Abree, had witnessed the workings of her brain, and had been profoundly relieved by what she had seen. Abree turned towards the main staircase and bade Jenny follow. Turning, she saw the poor girl's hand quivering as it almost touched the bannister post at the top, as though she wasn't comfortable with the relative opulence through which Abree was leading her. They accessed the servants' staircase from the narrow corridor leading off from the wide landing with the green-and-gold carpet. From here, Jenny look the lead, her pinny bustling as she raised it slightly above her shoes. The space was so much narrower here, the floors so much barer.

It was almost fun. Abree felt as though she had a ghost sister, one that lived in the same house but occupied different spaces, perhaps rooms that had once existed on this site in medieval times. Abree could invent a history for this supernatural relationship between Jenny and herself, could imagine how they might have sensed each other's presence many times before, might have even read each other's thoughts. Only on rare occasions, though, perhaps when their paths happened to cross at certain times of the day, did they actually see each other.

Abree followed Jenny into her room. It was a small space with a dressing table upon which stood a jug, a bowl, and a small white towel. Two books stood neatly on a reading table with an electric lamp. The book on top had a worn gold cross in its leather—a bible, obviously. Leaf-dappled light skimmed between the cloth curtains and illuminated the cross. The effect made Abree think of Saint Thérèse of Lisieux, of the piety of quiet servitude. It surprised Abree. She'd thought of Jenny as being more modern, somehow, more liberated, closer to the genuine flapper at least in spirit than either Helen or herself.

Abree turned to face Jenny now. The bare space seemed to enforce even greater intimacy. Jenny's hands fidgeted before her pinny.

"I'm amazed the master told you," she said softly.

The light through the curtains faded. The gold cross dulled.

So she wouldn't get a chance to fix everything, after all, because she clearly didn't understand what was wrong. The wind shifted through the willow just outside the window. Abree had been fooling herself. Not only had Jenny unburdened herself already, but she had done so in front of her brittle and unapproachable father, the very person who Abree had supposed had been the source of the problem. Abree was not only the last to know, but this girl was "amazed" she'd even been told at all. She could not think of an immediate reply.

Jenny took a half step forward. "I've known for weeks. I've been quite alone with it." A tear rolled down her cheek as she spoke. "It's only this morning I had the courage to tell him." Belatedly she raised her arm and dabbed the tear away with her sleeve. She smiled an apology.

The wind stilled now. Abree wanted to make some encouraging gesture, a smile perhaps, or a touch upon Jenny's elbow. But she could do nothing except stand still. Abree knew nothing, nothing at all. She felt overwhelmed by her ignorance. She felt suddenly giddy with helplessness, up in this high room, suspended above layer upon layer of not knowing. The worst of it was that she couldn't bring herself to admit to her confusion. This was not as simple as a maid giving notice. It was something else, clearly, something momentous. A profound sense of wellbeing had accompanied her decision to take charge. She hoped that in a few moments the whole story would unfold to her in a way that would make her feel that *usefulness* she so craved. Jenny need never know she had been bluffing.

"I thought you would hate me, you know," Jenny continued, her words running faster now as though this were part of a great unburdening. "It's such an insult, isn't it, to ... well your mother most of all, I suppose." Jenny stared at the wool nooses fringing the rug. It had been centered somewhat haphazardly, Abree remembered, to cover a very large crack in the exposed floor. A small insect crawled out now from one of the loops. "Such a betrayal," Jenny whispered. She glanced up at Abree again, skin now crimson around her ears and nose.

A picture was forming at last. But it was a grotesque, impossible picture, like a sheep with a man's head, or a snake with horns. Abree's feet moved backwards. Her heart pumped harder. Only with a struggle did she keep her hands by her sides; they wanted more than anything to raise themselves to her ears and block any sound that may come into them.

Jenny hadn't noticed the change in her. She seemed almost happy now, and she circled her little room, moving to the window just for a moment, then moving back again. This was desperate relief, Abree supposed.

Abree still didn't know for sure, and she told herself this. The first explanation for someone's behaviour was not necessarily the only one. But Jenny had known for weeks. What else does a woman know for weeks but is afraid to tell? She'd told Abree's father, but she knew it would be an insult to her mother. What other revelation but the obvious would make an unmarried girl speak to the master rather than the mistress? And what other circumstance could account for the nervousness, the tears, and the apparent shame, followed by this uncorking of guilt and emotion?

"What did Father tell you?" Abree said at last. Her voice was dull, neither friendly nor hostile. It was a voice from the scorched earth of no-man's-land.

"He will deal with it," she said. Her expression was bright now, grateful. Her tears had returned too, but this time they were like the tears of a saint, Botticelli's Mary during the annunciation. There was a certainty about it, though also a touch of pleading when she met Abree's eyes.

"Did he say how?"

A slight frown appeared on Jenny's face, and Abree felt a sadistic impulse that made her mouth twitch upwards at the corner. Abree was rooted now, close to the door; one foot was further forward than the other, and she was mentally, if not literally, tapping the floor with her toe. It pleased her to be guarding the exit like a keeper charged with confining a wild beast. She felt in control once more though she no longer felt *good*. She was no longer the warm-hearted and open-minded daughter of stuffy parents. Her father had outdone her in open-mindedness a thousand times, even if the way he expressed his warm-heartedness was more than a little suspect.

"No," Jenny shrugged, but she began to smile, her belief returning. "But I trust him, of course." Then she held Abree's gaze, seeing something in it that changed her mood. Her pupils shrank, and she held herself more erect. Had she at last sensed a possible enemy? It seemed so. The dappled sunlight, unleashed again, threw yellow spots over Jenny's pinny. Suddenly the maid had a feral look.

Abree became aware how much power this girl held over the household. She slumped away from the doorway as though wishing the wild beast *would* escape. Without meaning to she sat down on the corner of Jenny's bed.

"This is a disaster," she said. "You don't know how bad this is." It was an accusation that she could not readily explain. *Bad for whom?* she wondered. For Jenny, yes. A pregnant, unmarried maid is a pregnant, unmarried maid. There were variations in the details of her projected future, perhaps, but it was bound to be a story of hardship and disgrace. The girl was a fool not to see this. But Abree might have meant herself and her family too. They were in a bad way already. The joists of the household were coming loose. Grief over Quincey, grief and silence, had been working away at the structure for years now, destroying quietly and patiently like woodworm. When Mother finds out about this, she thought, when she confronts her jibbering wreck of her husband, it would be like the wolf's last puff on the home of the little pigs.

Jenny laughed, folded her arms, and looked down at Abree. "I don't?"

"No," Abree said, her lips dry and burning as though some strange fever had overtaken her. "Not if you think my father will help. Not if you think he's even capable of helping."

The bitterness in her voice took Abree by surprise. She thought she understood her father's drunken stupors and his nightmares. But she didn't understand this. She didn't understand how he could put aside his torpor, not for the sake of his wife or daughter, but rather for some grotesque lust for a domestic under his own roof. Something still glimmered within him, obviously, and this was how he'd chosen to spend this precious, dying flame.

Jenny saw all of this—all of Abree's bitterness and hurt. She looked down upon Abree with a combination of pride and disgust.

A fire welled up inside Abree. She wanted her advantage back, and she spoke entirely without thinking. "I'll have to tell my mother," she said. She had whispered the words in an attempt to keep the spite from her voice. But the softness made it sinewy and suggestive, like the curl of a snake through the grass. She sounded evil.

It brought about the desired change though. Jenny's face flushed. She became less rooted on her feet, and the spots of sunlight disappeared from her pinny.

"You can't do that," she said, backing away and shrinking into herself.

"I must," Abree said, still in a whisper. She had to keep a smile from playing upon her face.

It was not so much self-loathing that swirled inside Abree as horror at her own actions. Everything she had said was designed for the sole purpose of wounding this girl as much as possible. What kind of person acts in such a way? It was as vicious as it was shortsighted. The conviction in her voice, pitched to carry the most impact, was entirely false. She did not know whether she should tell her mother at all. She was not even sure that she *could*. The spite inside her was terrifying, like a parasite that burrows suddenly out of the flesh when its host is altogether unaware of its existence.

But it was about to get worse. Abree rose slowly from Jenny's bed. The mattress, she noticed, was so old and sunken that it still held the impression of her weight. She moved silently to the door, an odd tingle about her shoulders. Yes, she was going to dig herself further into a hole—she *knew* she was going to—but it seemed there was nothing she could do about it. Her stung pride, as well as some other less definable hurt, compelled her to make this girl suffer. With one stern, determined look at Jenny, whose hands were now fumbling desperately in front of her stomach, she left.

The implication was clear. She was going to tell her mother of her father's infidelity and her maid's predicament. She had plotted her course with the ruthlessness of a Borgia. Now, if she did not carry out her threat, she would have to admit to the most ignominious of defeats. No one—neither Jenny nor herself—would believe her for a second if she pretended to have second thoughts out of compassion. Only cowardice could explain such a radical and swift change of heart.

She made her way back down more slowly than she had gone up, leaving the narrow corridor which connected the servants' quarters and emerging onto the main landing. She moved even more slowly down the staircase, stopping three stairs before the ground floor.

The drawing room door was, as before, closed.

There was only one way, she thought, to deliver shocking news, and that was quickly.

She heard the faint tick of the grandfather clock even through the door. It seemed the war was around her again. This was the real reason for her vindictiveness. It had all returned—that sense of impending catastrophe, visions of grenades being thrown in some muddy field, shrapnel flying, a telegraph boy's knock on the front door. Disaster was with them again. It was inevitable. What did it matter whether she was vicious or kind? No amount of compassion would make delivering the news easier. She strode down the last three steps and crossed the hallway. Juggling the words on her lips—*Mother, we need to speak urgently in private*—she opened the drawing room door, ready to speak.

12. ARTHUR HOLMWOOD, LORD GODALMING

LUCY APPEARED IN A SWIRL of sunlight. She was as she had once been, her large eyes frank, catching the light, smiling at Arthur. He could taste her sweet fragrance, the very scent of innocence. Neither of them spoke, but the communication flowed easily between them. *I am as I used to be*, she seemed to say. She was Lucy, *his* Lucy. The false Lucy, the Lucy of insinuation and hunger, had been erased as if by magic. Time had run backwards like a blessed stream and washed away the vicious and the squalid.

You killed me, Arthur, Lucy's thoughts whispered. Her expression was a picture of wounded trust. Her eyes held his, demanding an answer.

Arthur sputtered. He felt suffocated. To see her as he did, he realized, he must also be floating like her in this undulating cloud of sunlight, this curious ether. At last he heard himself moan, a childlike, unmanly sound. Then Lucy laughed—a sweet, compassionate laugh with no mockery or unkindness. *It's all right Arthur. I am only teasing.* This was Lucy as he'd always wanted to remember her.

Arthur wanted to believe this was all real. He *almost* did believe it. But something had crept into the scene, an odour at odds with the sheen and sparkle of the sun-cloud that held them. It was an odour not of the spring but of something damp and cloying. It smelled of the earth. There was a noise too, very like the thud of a spade hitting the ground. Lucy's eyes changed. Her gaze was no longer frank and pure. There was a hint of cunning now, a sense she was watching him closely, waiting for something.

A shadow passed over him, and the shadow also smelt of the earth. Then he felt it—the touch of something damp upon his wrist. Lucy laughed, not kindly this time. He was no longer suspended with her, no longer in a sun-cloud. He could feel a clinging dampness on his back. Lucy was standing above him, an earth-soiled spade in her hand. Blood flowed freely from her bosom, and there was blood and saliva over her bared teeth.

He recoiled but could only push himself further into the ground. His lungs filled, but he couldn't speak or move. A clod of earth fell upon his shoulder, then more spilled onto his wrist. She meant to bury him, he was certain. This was her revenge.

He managed a cry at last—an accumulation of animal noises rising in pitch and volume. The earth upon his wrist became alive and suddenly warm. It squeezed him.

He opened his eyes.

It was not the shadow of death. Neither was it Lucy. It was Alice, his wife. It was not wet earth on his wrist but her hand, the lace of her sleeve.

Arthur felt unmanned, naked. His scream still echoed in his eyes. What had it sounded like?

On the library wall facing him was an antelope's head, its horns curling extravagantly, its glass eyes as inscrutable as that of the prey hanging in his dining room.

"Arthur, what on earth is the matter?" Alice's voice came to him muffled as though his ears were plugged with cotton wool. He had deafened himself with his cry. His wife was aghast.

"A dream." His hand had come instinctively down on the stem of a half-full brandy glass. "Just a dream."

Alice glanced at his glass and narrowed her eyes.

Arthur tried to move, tried to look natural, but his shirt was stuck to the leather upholstery. He moved forwards and felt the trickle of sweat down his spine.

"How was your lunch with Jonathan Harker?" she asked with heavy irony.

"Oh, well," he shrugged, "you know Harker."

She looked thoughtful. "It always seems to upset you when you get together."

He felt his face burn.

She stood back from him a little and smoothed down her dress. "I don't know what old adventures you recount to yourselves," she said, "but sometimes I wonder if it's healthy." She looked at his glass again. "Three o clock in the afternoon, Arthur," she said simply. Then she went to the door. "Don't forget you're taking me to see *Salome* this evening."

Nausea washed though him. "Don't worry, I'll be ready."

She slipped through the door, giving him a quick look before she disappeared.

Salome, she'd said.

He'd forgotten about this. Or had he?

Perhaps Salome had prompted his dream. Lucy first innocent, and then transformed; Lucy possessed by demonic lust; Lucy flowing with blood. Perhaps Lucy had always been his Salome, a once-prized woman gorging on depraved desires, driven mad by them.

The opera, by Richard Strauss, was based on Wilde's notorious play. Wilde was back in fashion, it seemed. The opera was far from new, of course, but the production had been heralded in the newspapers as though it were. *Shrugging off the grey years of war*, one of them had said, *London had settled down again and was returning to whence it had come.* The capital was once more becoming its daring, garish self. Critics embracing the works of the playwright who'd they'd pilloried and imprisoned years before the war seemed, oddly, to be a part of this reclamation.

The thought made Arthur shiver. He longed for the grey years again. He could deal with Johann Strauss, with geometric patterns on the dance floor, but not Richard Strauss, with this ferocious passion and a bloody climax he'd read all about. The singer playing Salome was supposed to caress John the Baptist's severed head in her arms. He tried to imagine sitting in his box through such a scene, an ocean of fluttering fans beneath him. It was all too close. If Lucy was Salome, then the holy madman, John the Baptist had to be the murdered count. The rest of them—Arthur, Harker, Mina, Quincey, Seward, and Van Helsing—were all part of his murder. Like composite parts of Herod, they had been forced by Lucy's unbridled depravity to track down and execute the man with mysterious powers. Salome had turned them all into criminals. But, unlike Salome, Lucy had perished too.

Arthur's dreadful lunchtime meeting with Harker, his dream, his wife's sudden appearance as a specter from the past—all these things had brought the events of more than thirty years ago closer than they had been for some time. But then he'd begun it all himself yesterday by opening that damned safe.

Visions of the grave were gone, for the moment at least, but a voice from the past returned: *Go on. Tell me what to do.* It was a raw, callow voice, insistent yet needy. The voice was his, and the words were addressed to Van Helsing. He wasn't really asking advice. He was requesting permission. Arthur had been brought to this precipice willingly enough, but he wanted someone old and wise to nudge him forward. Then he would never have to feel bad about it; he would never have to feel responsible. Van Helsing was old, certainly, and, according to Seward, he was venerated in his profession. He'd given his diagnosis of Lucy: moral insanity. Highly infectious and likely to spread. There was no cure. Van Helsing's white hairs had convinced not only Arthur but the whole group—Harker, Seward, of course, Quincey, and even Mina—of his deep and unfathomable knowledge.

If Arthur had known then what he knew now about passing years and experience, he would never have put so much store in the professor's judgement. Age, he knew now, was merely time. Time can shed wisdom as easily as gather it. Time bestows only the *appearance* of knowledge. But he was glad enough even of this then.

Van Helsing had taken over. They had all listened to his every word.

"Go on," he'd told Van Helsing. "Tell me what to do."

The professor had seemed very old to all of them, but he was likely no more than fifty, several years younger than Arthur was now. Arthur remembered how the professor had stood by Lucy's pillow, his hand on the curved mahogany headboard. There had been something proprietorial about him. He had taken charge of the case. He was like a house master, or more than this, a school principal, and he had them all reverting to the emotions of boyhood. They would compete with each other to be loyal to this leader. They would have followed him to war if he asked them to, and gladly. Mina was gone from the bedside now, and this was important. Lucy had been asleep. She'd been given a draft. Something momentous was about to happen, and they all knew it.

The white silk bed curtains had been drawn back as far as they would go. Arthur hadn't known who was responsible for this, but the very intimacy of the scene—five of them in a semi-circle looking down upon an exposed bed and a sleeping Lucy—had seemed jarring. The folds nearest Arthur had fluttered as a warm breeze wafted from the fireplace. It had been as though the curtains sought escape so they might enwrap and protect their mistress again. It had been hot—Arthur would always remember this—unreasonably so.

Van Helsing had taken something from his grip, the strangest looking collection of odds and ends to emerge from a medical bag—a large mallet and a long thin wooden stake. Arthur had wondered at first if Van Helsing meant them to go about building something. "Take the stake in your left hand," Van Helsing had said.

Arthur had taken the stake and felt the raw wood. A tiny

splinter made its way under his skin.

"Get ready to place the point over the heart. Take the hammer in your right."

Arthur lurched forward, hand over mouth. A swirl of brandy and acid had flowed up from his stomach. He gulped it down quickly. His hand trembled as he lowered it. It was Harker's fault. Lunch time with Harker had brought him back here, to Lucy's bedside. Damn Harker! The wreck of a man had used Arthur for restoration. In doing so, he'd turned Arthur into a wreck instead, while Harker himself walked away quite cheerfully

To an outsider, of course, and to Harker no doubt, Arthur looked indomitable. He'd played the lord as usual. He'd remained firm and sensible while Harker fretted. It was second nature to do so, and for a while it fuelled his pride, his sense of power. He could feel his strength rising as he spoke.

Then when Harker left him, somewhat calmed, somewhat reassured, Arthur had begun to feel off balance. And there was no one to whom Arthur could turn. His ancestors no doubt had sought God after some onerous duty had drained them of spirit and hope. But God had long since turned his back on Arthur, and he was glad of it. The idea of a living deity filled Arthur with unimaginable dread.

Arthur stared once more at the antelope's glassy eyes and remembered lunch with Harker.

At first Arthur had been taken by surprise at lunch. Harker had dreamed up a new catastrophe for himself, not the mysterious Florescu, after all. Arthur had been glad enough of this at first. The idea of talking about some Wallachian who may or may not be connected to the count was oppressive in the extreme. But he needn't have been concerned. When Arthur had obliquely brought it up, Harker swatted the subject away as though it were a fly. Then he had become furtive, twisting, like some curious creature hidden in the undergrowth. He had turned to peer at a table of some elderly men. As soon as he had uncoiled, he craned his neck in the opposite direction and scrutinized a waitress who had emerged from behind the serving doors with a cake stand. It had been a quiet day. Many of the club's regulars had been at Lord's for the test match. Rather than calming Harker, the silence and the space had seemed to make him more vigilant.

As though through some invisible conduit of emotion, a measure of Harker's tension had transferred itself to Arthur. He'd anticipated this. Once more he was forced to be strong as this old comrade in adversity vented his worries and his neuroses. Once again he was left drained and fragile. This was the curse of strength.

Arthur became impatient. He wanted Harker to speak, to lay his problems at Arthur's feet, so that Arthur himself could begin recovering. But silence reigned. The sigh of shoe against the carpet was quite audible as the waitresses crossed the floor. The sun tried to shine through the Georgian windows. It was a typical English June, restrained in its celebration. Sunlight was parceled out primly between clearings in the clouds.

"I'm in trouble, Arthur," Harker said with a twitch of his shoulders.

Arthur gulped, but smiled. He topped up Harker's wine. The slurp of the liquid echoed under the high ceiling.

"It's the maid, Jenny." Harker had that frenzied look in his eye again.

Arthur shook his head, mildly baffled. He held his glass close to his lips and waited.

"*She's* in trouble."

"What kind of trouble?"

Jonathan twisted around again like a snake, again searching. Then he leaned forward. "Oh, come on, Arthur!"

Arthur lowered his glass again. He stared across the table at Harker. *Oh come on, Arthur* could only mean one thing.

Arthur had been indiscreet with a maid just before he became engaged to Lucy. Everyone expected Arthur to be wild, but maids of one's own household are out of bounds. They are like family pets to be looked after and respected. He had muddied his own doorstep, and there was something quite shameful in the feeling. Caught up in guilt and worry over his fiancée, he had confessed the dalliance to Van Helsing, Seward, and Harker. In truth, he'd been afraid they would find out anyway, and at the time he hadn't been sorry that they knew. He'd wanted assurances that his affair with the maid wasn't one of the reasons behind Lucy's sickness. It had been possible in his mind because, in a rapture of sudden honesty just after his proposal, Arthur had told Lucy all about the maid.

Van Helsing had given Arthur the comfort he had needed, and he'd been touched at the time. The old professor had turned his anxiety into the most heart-warming of compliments, one that seemed to speak directly to his soul. Young men, the professor had told Arthur, are all idealists at heart. Arthur had wanted to purge himself of all unworthiness in front of this saintly creature he'd managed to win. The professor had assured him that he must never blame himself for such a thoroughly noble impulse.

This had all seemed so true. And at the time Lucy had taken the news as he'd hoped and expected she would—shock at first, followed by soothing calmness and patience. It was only later, when she fell under the influence of the count, that Arthur had seemed to catch a sense of bitterness, even of anger, from his beautiful intended. He would almost have believed at the time that her dangerous flirtation with the count was either revenge against Arthur or perhaps a kind of rebellion. She'd lost her faith in the purity of love, and she blamed him for it. Arthur had allowed Lucy to see that taint of corruption in the man she was to marry, and, in so doing, he had opened her up to the poisons of the world.

"So," Arthur said, through gritted teeth, "I take it this *trouble* ... the obvious kind, I suppose ... has something to do with you, Harker."

Harker nodded. He gazed at the lace tablecloth, looking like a dog that had just received a blow from its master.

"Who knows?"

"No one," Harker said hoarsely. He picked up his wine and gulped. Then it was Arthur's turn to look around. One of the elderly peers had turned briefly in the direction of their table. Two young men, sons of people Arthur knew, had entered.

"Well, the first thing to do is keep calm."

Arthur didn't stop to consider who benefited from this advice, but it had its desired effect nonetheless. Harker lost some of his furtiveness. He coughed, nodded, and leaned back a little from his table.

"Second, you must be the first to bring it up to Mina."

Harker stared at him, horrified.

"Don't let events dictate anything. And don't give the girl any power. You must control the story from beginning to end." Harker listened attentively, a sheen of red wine on his lower lip. "Tell Mina you have seen Jenny on the street canoodling with some young man. Tell her you are concerned for Abree. You have reason to believe they may have even met together in your garden shed. Whatever sounds convincing."

Harker said nothing, but a pleading look came over his face.

"You asked my advice," Arthur said quietly.

A waitress much younger than the others, pale faced and thin, came toward them with her pencil and notepad.

"I will have the potted shrimp followed by the pigeon," Arthur said.

"The same," Harker said. The waitress scribbled their orders before giving an awkward half-curtsey and rushing away.

"It hardly matters what you say, Harker. The most important thing is that you are the first to say it. Mina will dismiss her, of course, and then you are in the clear. If this girl accuses you of anything after the fact, she will be seen as a disgraced servant spreading scandal about her former employee."

Harker's face had turned white. He mouthed silently, like a small boy who had witnessed a conjurer's trick and didn't know whether to be delighted or disturbed.

"But, what will happen to her?"

Arthur tilted his head and smiled, not unkindly, he thought. "That is not your responsibility."

Harker squinted back at him. "How can it *not* be?"

"What do you think would happen to this girl if she'd never met you, if she'd never been in service in your house? If she"—he threw a disgusted look at the wheels of a passing trolley—"did what she did, and with her employer of all people, a married man, what else might she have done?" He leaned forward. "For all you know," he said quietly, "the story you'll be telling is likely true anyway."

Harker blinked.

"You think you were the first one?" Arthur asked, trying to be gentle even as he mocked. "You think you were the *only* one?"

Harker looked askance.

Arthur realized he had hit his mark. Vaguely, beneath the false certainty, Arthur wondered why he was trying so hard to persuade Harker, to make him feel blameless. He thought of his own misdemeanour all those years ago and how much it may have cost him. Arthur felt almost like a father offering immoral advice to his son because he knew that, in the short term at least, this was the path of least suffering. But Harker and he were the same age. He owed the solicitor nothing, not advice nor comfort. Something bound them together, of course, but it seemed beyond understanding.

"It's just so ... dishonourable," Harker said feebly, but his relief was obvious.

"Nothing is more honourable, Harker, than protecting your own family."

He was still doing it, still trying to convince. He still didn't know why, except that he hadn't protected his own family, his Lucy. He'd let his fiancée hear it all. He remembered Lucy's innocence when he'd confessed.

"But where is the maid now?" she had asked, brow furrowed.

"Gone," he'd said. "Long gone."

It had been intended to reassure, but the furrows had deepened. What had she been thinking about? Arthur wondered. She hadn't asked any more questions though, and he hadn't volunteered anything further. But he'd extricated himself. He'd had the maid dismissed on the grounds of suspected immorality.

Harker nodded vaguely, lost, apparently, in a fog of thoughts. "Yes," he said, defeated but calm. "It's the only way."

Now in his study, the brandy in his hand, a vision skipped through Arthur's mind. The arm of a gramophone was suspended above a record. The record spun, and the same fragment of sound repeated over and over, as a scratch brought the needle back to the same point every time it tried to escape. He did not know the melodies of the opera he would be forced to go to tonight, but the fragment of sound was eastern-seeming, and it featured a wind instrument weaving one way and another in a minor key. It evoked the spires and domes of some Persian city. The record was Arthur. He was cursed to repeat the same actions just as the record repeated the same single loop of music. This unfortunate maid, this Jenny, had shed her virtue for Harker just as Lucy had shed hers for the count. Arthur had nothing against the girl, of course. He may never have seen her, although he'd been to the Harkers' home fairy recently with Alice. The vaguest memory of a girl spilling tea into his wife's saucer came back to him. Perhaps that was her. Why, he wondered, had he not even considered giving more compassionate or fair-minded advice? He felt the splinter easing under his skin once more, felt the weight of the wood in his palm. The impulse was the same, and he was trapped inside it, doomed to relive the moment when he had extinguished Lucy.

13. ABREE HARKER

A BREE HALTED. Her father was just inside the room, block-ing her entry. He was obviously about to leave. Now he stood, blinking at her stupidly. Neither asked the other to move. Neither gave way. Abree had been ready with those words: *Mother, we need to speak urgently in private*—but now she was stumped. She'd been thwarted by nothing more than the awkwardness of stepping past her father. But perhaps there was something else. He used to be much taller than her, Abree thought, almost half a head. Now their eyes were at the same level. Why had she not noticed this before? It seemed incredible, with Father standing no more than two feet from her, that he had managed to get Jenny into trouble. He seemed no more alive than an upturned log.

He muttered something. Abree thought it was *well, well*, or it might have been a cough, Then ditheringly, flapping his jacket pocket, he moved though the doorway as Abree sidestepped away. He closed the door like a corpse re-entering his tomb. Abree could deliver her line now. She had her mother's sole attention. But she said nothing.

She caught her mother's eye and realized something had happened, something important.

"We're going to let Jenny go," Mother said simply.

Abree turned to the door through which her father had just disappeared. She felt panic around her diaphragm, as though several moths were trapped inside her, beating their wings for escape. He couldn't have *told* Mother about it, surely? She didn't want to ask questions about it, didn't want to know. But it would seem too strange *not* to ask, so she did. "What happened?"

"Nothing we need to talk about, Abree." Mother moved to the bell pull. "But it seems she's just not suitable, *morally* suitable, to be a housemaid, at least not here." She pulled the cord. "You needn't stay, dear. It might be quite unpleasant."

She was ashamed at how quickly she left, how swiftly she moved through the hallway, past the dining room. She was ashamed at how frightened she must have looked to any outsider as she disappeared into the conservatory. This was the one place where she might be certain not to come across Jenny, who, at any moment, would be descending to her execution.

When Jenny arrived in the drawing room, she would catch sight of Abree's mother so serious and stern and naturally assume that Abree had revealed everything. The possibility of another explanation would seem absurd to Jenny, as indeed it was. But there was another explanation. Jenny was about to be dismissed but not because of anything Abree had revealed.

The conservatory, a step down from the main floor of the house, was cooler and smelled slightly of earth. Abree gazed at the fronds of ferns—there was quite a collection, with some plants on the window sill and some hanging from the ceiling—and the spears of Mother's dragon fingers, each of these exotic plants packed tight in its own terracotta pot. The trees beyond the windows rolled like proud giants gazing at their growing children within the glass. Above it all, a great oak presided, lighter in hue than all the other trees. Abree heard footsteps faintly descending, and she thought she could make out a distant knock.

So what on earth *had* happened? She thought of her father's dead eyes, her mother's calm determination. Surely he hadn't told her of the girl's condition and his part in bringing it about.

A small group of starlings chased each other in an ascending spiral in the centre of the lawn. She thought of Quincey; she saw him as he had been that final autumn. Quincey and Abree hadn't been playing tennis in this garden. They'd been in a properly marked and netted court in the garden of a friend in Mayfair. But looking at the rippling boughs, she could reimagine their game well enough here. She could see Quincey, with his lolloping run and his air of self-parody, as the ball bounced off his shoes and rolled towards the bushes. She could see herself less distinctly, as an idea rather than a person, but she could remember how she had felt. The young Abree gripped her racket in her athletic, intense way. No one seeing the white-clad figure bent over, measuring the distances between the chalk lines, getting ready to return the serve, would have guessed at the growing fear and longing inside her. She dreaded the future, poor girl, Abree thought. She dreaded the moment when her only sibling would desert their home. When Quincey departed, she would be left in a decaying house in a crumbling city. She knew this, knew it would be the end of all the colour and fun. The gay dress rehearsal of childhood would give way to the dull performance of life.

She remembered the taste of autumn in the air, the sense of longing she had felt as nature sizzled around them, complete with plump acorns and the thuds of apples and plums hitting the ground. What would that hopeful, grieving, fearful girl have thought had she known her father, at fifty-five years old, would get the family maid into trouble, and that she herself, as an adult, would threaten and blame the girl? Could she have known perhaps that Quincey would never return to them? Could she have guessed that without him everything would fall to pieces?

She listened for more noises, for shouting or slamming of doors, but she knew her efforts were in vain. Servants never shout even when they are fired, even when the firing is unjust. They just bow their heads and pack. And Abree's parents, her mother anyway, never needed to shout; she was too much in control for that.

A shiver crept its way up her body, tingling between her clothes and her skin, all the way up to her shoulders, her neck, her ear lobes. It remained, fizzling like the rim of a wave on the sand. There was heat inside the sensation. The phantom wave mingled salt water with lava. She recognized an emotion in all this, something inchoate and raging. It was anger, and it nibbled like tiny-toothed fish upon her ears and the super-sensitive skin of her neck.

But who was she angry with? The question she put to herself was honest, innocently posed. Anger had to have an object, didn't it? She realized the answer straightaway. Worse than blind, she thought, this anger of hers was also unjust. She was angry, not at Jenny, and not at herself. She was angry at her father and mother. She saw Quincey's lolloping form in the tennis court again, the rich foliage waving around him, the bloating sun spilling marmalade hues over the tree tops. Quincey had no place in fields of flying bullets and roaring tanks. He'd been stolen from her, stolen from his home and his destiny. Nature itself should have screamed out in protest and claimed him back for itself. Abree's mother and father weren't responsible, and yet at the same time they were. The war was not started by Quincey's generation. It was started by men of her father's age, and by the women who supported men of her father's age—the women who hung on to their husbands' arms when they went out to the opera or the theatre. She thought of Emily Davison at the derby, the little dowdy figure ducking beneath the barrier and walking into the path of the king's horse, the thundering muscle and sinew, the hat flying off, the doll-like carcass flattened then dragged. The poor woman had long turned her back on the conformity that turns men into either murderers or corpses and women into either murderers' accomplices or widows. Emily Davison wouldn't have let Quincey go to war without a struggle. She would have thrown herself in the way, chained herself to him. She would have stood in the path of the train going from London to the coast.

No, Mother and Father were not to blame directly. They had done nothing to bring about the war and nothing to encourage Quincey to join, but neither had they ever shown their children how to oppose. They had named Quincey after a hero, the Texan of their younger days who was supposed to have sacrificed himself. Modest as Quincey was, surely this image must have worked itself under his skin.

This was the substance and direction of her fury. But, of course, her parents hadn't killed Quincey any more than Abree had killed him. Father had done his best to dissuade Quincey from going to war. Mother would scarcely have been for his joining. Is this how anger and blame always worked? It made a kind of sense. We blame who we can. Those who are really responsible are out of reach.

Still no noise from beyond the conservatory. The leaves and boughs rolled blindly beyond the glass. Quincey and her young self were no longer there, not even as shadows. Abree was trying to conjure Quincey among the leaves again when a thought, a really terrible thought, occurred to her. Her brother had never properly died. She and her parents were still alive to remember him. They could still see his ghost cavorting among the boughs, or hunched over his desk studying. He could still delight or move Abree and her mother. He could still drive his father to night traumas. But one day, when they were all gone, no one would remember him. He would be completely erased from thought and history. If Abree married and had children, another generation would exist to immortalize Abree and likely her parents, but not Quincey. Quincey would fade forever from recorded time.

The air in the conservatory shifted. Somewhere in the house a door had either opened or closed. Abree's chest tightened and her pulse came to life. She thought she should go and investigate.

That was what Emily Davison would do. No, Emily would do more than investigate. Emily would find her mother, hold her by the shoulders, and tell her in no uncertain terms of the gross injustice of firing a servant impregnated by her employer.

A squirrel appeared from a clump of branches, resting for a moment upside down, its head tilted towards Abree in a black-eyed stare.

Yes, thought Abree, I am a coward. All of nature can see it.

There was another movement in the house, this time closer. Abree turned. The bench holding the terracotta pots dug into her back.

The door opened. Her mother appeared, her face a mask of composure.

"There you are, Abree," she said, stepping down upon the conservatory tiles. At first Abree thought there might have been a hint of reproach in her mother's voice, but she soon realized that this was likely her imagination. Her mother had wanted her out of the way, after all. "I'm going to need your help this afternoon." She looked beyond Abree as she spoke, through the glass and into the garden. Instinctively, Abree turned to follow her gaze. But, of course, nothing was there save the rolling branches, so she turned back, feeling foolish. "I've called Mrs. Rogers. We have to find another maid as quickly as possible."

Abree took in a sharp breath. She almost blurted something. It would have been quite out of character for her, but even so the words were at hand, fizzing on her lips though not yet correctly ordered. All they needed was one moment of mental clarity, one moment of focus to find their escape.

Her mother sensed something. She'd been on the point of leaving, but now she stopped and narrowed her eyes at Abree. Abree felt galloping hooves in her chest, a rushing in her ears. Her moment was upon her. But almost without warning, her chance skipped beyond her. She coughed slightly. Her gaze fell away from her mother's curious eyes. The missing words were still jumbling in Abree's head, trying to reorganize themselves after the fact. *You can't do that, Mother. You shouldn't have. The girl is pregnant. We are responsible for her. Casting her out is wrong, morally wrong.* But her lips were dry now, no longer fizzing. Suddenly these things were quite unsayable.

"Come into the drawing room in half an hour," her mother said with an odd smile . "You and Mrs. Rogers can help me plan what to do." Then she disappeared and the door closed slowly behind her.

There was a small buzz in Abree's ears, like the noise of an electric light in the first few seconds after it is turned on. She was both surprised at herself and angry—surprised that she had almost questioned her mother, something she had rarely done in the past, and angry that even this puny and belated rebellion had proved to be too much for her.

Not learning to oppose seemed an unfortunate legacy now. How huge had seemed those unspoken objections when they were on the brink. But they were only words, reasonable words at that. It had been her Emily Davison moment, but, unlike the suffragette, she had faced no danger at all, nothing that could hurt her physically let alone trample her into oblivion. Yet she had not acted. She had stalled.

Abree thought of that odd smile on her mother's face. How much did Mother understand her? They were so very different that it was easy to try and argue that her mother hardly knew her at all. But the smile said otherwise. The smile was more than certainty, more than confidence. The smile seemed to come from an effortless knowledge of another's thoughts. And this brought up another question. If Mother had known Abree had been on the brink of objecting, if she had known at least some of the reasons for these objections, an astonishing confidence must reside in her very core. She'd known her daughter was judging her. But it didn't affect her. And if Mother had known this, then might she also have known her own husband's role in the story? Yet she had smiled.

Abree would have liked to react to all these possibilities with horror. But she couldn't. Morality, that smile seemed to say, was mere self-delusion. Some part of Abree was trapped by the argument. There was nothing remotely moral in anything Abree had done or threatened to do today. She'd said she would expose Jenny merely from panic and discomfort. Ever since Mother had pre-empted this threat, Abree's dominant emotion had been relief.

You'll learn, Mother's smile seemed to tell her now. You'll learn one day not to panic but to act. You'll learn not to be shocked by the world's cruelty, not to recoil like a child when self-interest demands that you strike before you are struck. The thing that terrified her about her mother's smile was its suggestion she knew Abree all too well.

Something banged against the pane behind her. She gasped and turned. Twitching on the turf close to the glass was a fluffy young sparrow. There was a notch in the pane. The small bird, learning to fly, had glided directly into the hard glass and fallen, beak damaged or broken, onto the ground. Its wings twitched again, and then it took off and flew in a straight geometric line before disappearing into the thick foliage on the left border of the garden. Surely it could not survive, thought Abree. Surely the injuries to its beak would be enough to prevent the poor bird from feeding.

Mother had known she would not be able to talk, because she had known that fear would stop her. But fear of what? Mother would not cast her own daughter out as easily as she would her servant, would she?

She wondered if Jenny had left the house. How long would it take her to stuff all her belongings into a bag and leave? Half an hour, Mother had said. That was how soon she wanted Abree in the drawing room. Mother had calculated the time. She'd left nothing to chance. In half an hour, the embarrassment would be gone, tramping east perhaps, seeking some long-lost relatives. What do pregnant unmarried maids do when they are dismissed from their employment? It seemed like a riddle, a question without an answer, a Chinese puzzle designed by a practical joker.

Abree looked at the swaying greenery into which the bird had disappeared. Something tugged inside her, a tangible, physical longing, vivid and fresh. Its name, like Father's scream, was Quincey.

14. JONATHAN HARKER

JONATHAN LAY FULLY CLOTHED and face-up on his bed. He listened to the sounds from upstairs—the muffled, packing sounds. In a few minutes, Jenny would be gone from his home and the danger would have passed. For the moment, though, time could not pass quickly enough. He'd never quite mastered Arthur's trick of doing the *correct* thing as opposed to doing the *right* thing. The *right* thing came from the schoolroom, the pulpit, and the gospels. It was a fairy story, of course, for schoolchildren and priests. But Jonathan didn't have Holmwood's insouciance. He had never been able to lay aside the traditional, middle-class notions of morality. He had discarded them, of course, as Arthur had instructed, but it troubled him. It would continue to trouble him until long after he heard the footsteps descending the servants' staircase and the closing of the basement door.

The *correct* thing was different. Arthur was different, and the longer Jonathan knew him the more different he seemed to become. Arthur had inherited lands and a title, and he represented a line of Lord Godalmings. Jonathan envied him, not for the lands and the title, but for the clearly defined sense of priority. Duty was narrow and sharp, and it came to a point. There was only one perspective that mattered for Arthur, and that was that his tribe should continue and prosper.

Something scuffed across the floor upstairs. Was this Jenny's trunk? Surely, she didn't have enough possessions to fill one, and he'd not noticed anything of the kind when he'd been in Jenny's room. Anyway, she must be getting ready to descend. Soon she would be part of the vortex of things Jonathan should not be concerned about—the trades' union leader, the radical, the pickpocket. None of these people were his concern and neither was Jenny. Arthur had been right about that. Leave Jenny's unfortunate parents or uncles or aunts or whoever survives from her circle of family or friends to make amends for the obvious gaps they had left in her education. What properly brought-up young woman would ever let a man take such liberties? Man's duty is to advance, woman's to repel. Arthur's philosophy, brutal though it seemed, was unsayable but true. You might not find this truth in the official creed of any denomination. But it is woven indelibly into every human cell. The difference between what *is* and what *should be* was the source of all misery and every misunderstanding.

Now at last Jonathan heard it: a steady set of footsteps, quiet and ashamed, making their way down the servants' staircase. He found himself stretching, hands behind his neck. The ordeal was passing. It would be awkward for a while, particularly around Mina. But it would be forgotten.

It had been a while since Jonathan had been to church, perhaps since Easter, but he remembered the priest on that occasion—a young man with a bald patch, reminiscent of the Carthusian tonsure in medieval illustrations. He had talked of empathy and compassion as though they were universal truths. Even at the time Jonathan had wondered whether there was a soul in the congregation who believed him. Gentlemen suppressed coughs, babies cried, and ladies fiddled with their purses and handkerchiefs. How self-deluding and fragile the man seemed. But he had succeeded in uniting the congregation. They all believed he was talking nonsense. Where were empathy and compassion on the battlefields of Northern France? Grenades, rifle fire, and Gatling guns, and then, when all means of de-struction had failed to produce a result, tanks and planes—was all this the language of compassion and empathy? Where was this God hiding during those long years?

Jonathan let these thoughts wash through his mind like water cleaning a flesh wound. Jenny was out of earshot now, but she had likely reached the basement, was perhaps saying her final goodbyes to Mrs. Rogers. What on earth would they say to each other? He shifted on the bedclothes, turning on his side. Did it matter what they said? He tried but could not replicate Arthur's certainty in himself. He reminded himself of the young Dorian Gray trying to persuade himself that Lord Henry's arguments were sound. Morality was a sham. Religion was a sham. He could half-believe these things. But he was no aristocrat, no Arthur, and even Wilde had meant only to satirize such thinking.

For the moment, he dared not dwell on it. He was who he was. He could be no other. It was a shock to gaze from afar at his deterioration: a man lying on his bed in the afternoon, hiding as the servant he'd impregnated left the house, a sack of a man motivated by no more than an impulse for dodging life's discomforts. He wished he cared more, but he cared, *really* cared, about very little. Only one concern festered. Did Mina know? She had watched him, her dark eyes steady, as he had stuttered out his fears for Abree.

He had wanted her to look away, to blush and sit while he told her about Jenny and a young man lost in the shadows of the square. Arthur's idea of a shed did not work—the fictional lovers would have found no access to the garden's outhouse without coming *through* the house, which would have been a near impossibility. If Mina had been embarrassed as he had hoped, his own discomfort would have been less obvious. But she had merely stared, unblinking, until his words had trailed inconclusively into silence.

"Jonathan," she had said, frowning, "I don't understand what you are telling me. Jenny has a young man. Is that it?"

He had turned a half circle, sinking into a chair. "I'm afraid it was the nature of the embrace which worried me. They were concealing themselves."

The contradiction had struck him immediately. If they were concealing themselves, how had he seen them? Unless ... unless he was the kind of man who spies on lovers who don't wish to be seen.

He had snapped up a newspaper, rolled it up, and tapped the sheath upon his knee. "He was a rough-looking fellow. I only saw them because she let him in with our own key. The square is for residents only."

Mina had tutted, and sat down opposite, but her curious—one might almost say suspicious—expression remained.

"I was going to follow them, but then, when they were inside, well...."

"Well?"

"Well, need I say more?"

The clock on the mantel ticked an answer.

Mina had leaned forward and shaken her head. "Well, what do you propose we do about it?"

"I see only one course of action. Regrettable, but necessary. We have Abree to think of." He'd stared at the carpet as he said this. Then, a touch too self-consciously, he had looked up at her. He had become horribly aware that a pleading look had likely come into his eyes. Partly to explain this he'd said, "I could handle it myself of course, but given the delicacy of the situation...."

"Of course, I will handle it, Jonathan," she had said firmly. "I will ring presently." Her eyes had indicated the door, and her hand had come up to move a loose hair from her eyes. She turned to the mantelpiece.

It was her next action that made Jonathan wonder. He'd reached the door and was about to open it when she turned back to him. "Let's hope this young man of Jenny's has honour enough to look after her once she's gone. I can't in all conscience give her a reference after all."

"No," he had said mechanically, but he realized his mouth had become very dry. The word had come out as a mere cough. He had faced his wife, meaning to simply nod. But she had caught his eye again and held it. She'd clearly meant for him to think about her words.

Reproaches weren't often exchanged between Jonathan and Mina these days. They belonged to a much earlier time, an era of playfulness and jealousy. And their quality had been correspondingly hot and volatile yet ready to transform into hasty declarations of sorrow or love. This reproach had been quite different. It had been deathly cold.

Jonathan heard something deep in the bowels of the building, a clunk—yes, the servants' entrance at last!—but the look on his wife's face remained with him. Yes, it was possible, more than possible, that she knew he'd lied to her. The incident would become, like so many others, part of the great mound of debris upon which their lives would continue to perch. He'd not strayed before Jenny, and, if he was honest about it, it was fear that had kept him faithful. Fear not of Mina's anger but of her reciprocation.

He turned on his bed again and shrugged off the memory. But words from a much earlier time entered his mind like a snake: *the saddest soul of all.* She'd said this about the count. Somehow the quote had made it into the document they'd all worked on together, not the "diary" written by Mina herself but in one of the other sections, either Seward's or Van Helsing's, he couldn't remember whose. But it was a reminder. Mina had come under the foreigner's spell more surely than Lucy had ever done. Lucy's infatuation was of the senses. It might have passed in time had they all left well enough alone. But Mina had been reached through her intellect and her empathy. It was more lasting and more dangerous.

All of a sudden it seemed extraordinary. Jonathan had once believed courage and manly virtue would accrue through life like interest in a savings bank. But this, his present self, this shameful creature hiding out in his bedroom, seemed to prove the opposite. But how had Jonathan's life turned out to be so entirely unsatisfactory? He had never planned it this way. This was not the life envisaged by the young rugby scrum half, the boy who had once captained the first fifteen when the regular captain was off sick, the reliable boy who had been clapped on the back by boys and masters alike. This was not the natural destination of the child who had once read Dumas into the night, who had believed in honour, friendship, and chivalry.

One self-revelation stood out as more shameful than all the others: even those moral standards he had sustained for much of his adult life had been held in place not by courage, but by cowardice. He'd managed to conform to some of the commandments because some of them were also laws, and he didn't want to go to prison. Once he had believed in them. A kink, it seemed, had separated him from his true self, had ripped away this part of him—this ignoble, spineless, quivering parasite—leaving that upright man he had once believed himself destined to become as an ideal only, an outline, distant and unrealizable.

He knew where the kink had occurred. It had been long before the war, before Quincey was born. His world, the orderly one he had once known, had been invaded by something dark. It had been invaded by the count. Arthur Holmwood had suffered along with him, but he—"Lord Godalming"—had been insulated by riches and elevated rank. He could better keep the pretense, the starched collar, the lofty stare, but it was surely eating him away from within. They had crossed the most perilous border of all—he, Arthur, Quincey, Mina, and poor dead Seward—the one that divides virtue from vice.

15. MINA HARKER

MIDNIGHT HAG! Mina had just caught sight of herself in the hallway mirror. While the words had not been spoken aloud, they had certainly growled inside her with unexpected vehemence.

Did she really despise herself so much?

She struggled to slip on the first of her silk gloves while balancing her purse strap on her wrist. Her knuckles seemed too enlarged for the fine fabric. This made little sense as they had fitted just fine only yesterday. She wondered if her rate of aging had accelerated at an unnatural pace. Quincey and once or twice even Abree had seemed to grow an inch or two overnight, or take on certain aspects of maturity they had lacked only days before. Did old age take people by surprise in the same way?

Old, old woman. She almost did say it aloud this time. The air hissed through her teeth as she pulled on the second glove, but of course "old woman" is not as damning as "midnight hag," nor is it as vulgar. It was a revision, she realized, made not out of self-punishment, but rather to soften the blow of the earlier, rawer insult.

She hadn't entertained in weeks or perhaps months, but the act of playing hostess defined how she believed herself to look to the outside world. Until a few moments ago she had imagined herself to be slender, graceful—*swanlike*, she'd once been called by Juliet Evans. And this was no mean compliment, as Juliet had been one of the most accomplished and elegant lady acquaintances of her early married life. She'd carried that adjective inside her during all those intervening years, especially in the evenings while she had been preparing for guests, entertaining them at the table, and then leading the ladies away to the drawing room while the gentlemen struck up their matches and lighted their cigars. Candlelight always helped to refine this self-image, as did her pearls, her emerald earrings or any of the several favourite combinations of clothing and jewellery. All these accoutrements made up her armour.

She had not been prepared for the reflection looking back at her in the ruthless light of the afternoon. The woman in the glass was shapeless, dowdy even. All those cozy euphemisms—middle-aged, mature woman—scattered into the corners of the hallway. People were young or people were old, and Mina was old. She was old because her husband was old, and there were no graceful euphemisms that could be applied to him. His progress through married life was like that of a flower withering as summer turns to autumn. He'd once been upright and moral, splendid in his sensitive way. She couldn't trace the stages of change any more than she could map her alteration from swan to midnight hag, but she knew the abject creature still cowering upstairs in their bedroom had little in common with the young man from the Exeter firm who'd courted her more than thirty years before. He still hadn't come down—*damn him*—even though Jenny had been gone from the house for more than half an hour, even though no vestige or trace of her remained.

It was too pathetic, but she refused to share in this part of his disgrace. Mina had not lost her courage, and she found it exasperating that the less Jonathan had to lose—the shorter, sadder, and more dismal the stretch of life left to him—the more he cowered. This change from brave young man to twitching, inebriated old fool made her want to travel in the opposite direction. She wanted to jump through rings of fire and ford tumultuous streams. But who cared about a woman's courage? Bravery is an irrelevance. A woman is judged not by any aspect of character. She is judged by the orderliness of her household, the grace of her demeanour, and most of all, by her beauty. As though some venomous deity were quietly arranging a punishment most apt and most cruel, it was this—Mina's looks—that was coming apart at the seams.

Mina fumbled once more with her purse and unhooked the key to Belgrave Square gardens. She was desperate for air. Her household was also in disarray. Mrs. Rogers had flushed with concern when she'd come to Mina's call. There had already been an exchange between Jenny and the housekeeper. Mrs. Rogers had assumed the girl had misunderstood something, taken to heart some imagined insult, and that her misperception would be challenged and corrected. She had been grave when Mina told her this was not the case. But Mrs. Rogers was less than half the problem. Mina had also caught an accusing look in her daughter's eye.

Abree had defected. She had taken the side of the house-keeper and the maid, and it was infuriating. Mina had felt the heat rise from her chest like an exotic rash, crawling in rivulets up the skin of her neck and onto her cheeks. It annoyed her to be embarrassed in front of her housekeeper and her daughter. Neither of them knew what it was like to bear the frailties of others. Mrs. Rogers had never even married. The title *Mrs* came from rank and seniority among servants; a housekeeper could not be called Miss. And Abree—what could anyone say about her only surviving child? How had such a strange, frightened mouse of a girl scurried from under her skirts to announce herself as her daughter? Abree, it seemed, saw everything from some hidden corner of the room. She was forever hunched against the skirting board, too afraid of the mighty humans to even consider intervening. Was her daughter's generation the one for whom all those fine young men had been sacrificed? It seemed grotesque somehow. But it was no more grotesque than a husband passing damning information about a servant to his wife and then hiding upstairs while his wife arranged for the same servant's removal. She knew, or strongly suspected, of course, there was more to the story than this. But, like flyblown garbage rotting in her flowerbed, it was more than she cared to consider. She had enough coping to do.

Mrs. Rogers and Abree clearly thought there had been an injustice, but neither had possessed the courage to say so directly. Self-doubt and lip biting were the curses of the age. Thinking, the way Abree did it, was corrosive. One chose a side, one's own side—husband, family, children, neighbours—and one defended it. What could be simpler, more straightforward, and, in the end, more morally sound? People win and people lose. This was natural law the world over. The socialists and the intellectuals wanted to rearrange the universe, not realizing that the taint they so feared would merely follow them wherever they went. Abree would question everything. The poor girl would think herself into a maze, not realizing that her thinking would send fissures through the foundations of her own house. There was no such thing as right or wrong. Only children believe in such concepts. There was merely loyalty and disloyalty.

Just as Mina reached for the door, she encountered a sudden vision: Lucy Westenra, large eyed, beautiful, uncomprehending. Lucy staring up at her from her bed, gasping. The sunlight played through the coloured half-circle glass above the door. For a moment, Mina thought she might faint. But she touched the door for a moment longer with her fingertips, bowed her head to let the blood flow, and then gulped the sensation down. Quickly, before she could change her mind, she opened the door, stepped out, and closed it behind her.

The sun was strong, the breeze fresh. An elderly lady Mina knew by sight but not by name crossed the street with a small poodle tiptoeing beside her. The lady nodded at Mina. Mina nodded back and smiled at the dog. She felt revived already.

Once inside the square, she couldn't decide which direction she should take. A lone man she knew to be a resident walked his pug close to a low flowerbed to the right. A young couple, the woman with a twirling parasol, strolled gaily to the left. The two of them seemed irreverent; their steps were too much in unison, and they were swaying together as they walked. Instinctively she resented them.

There was only one other person in the square. Directly opposite, upon the bench and looking at her with a nervous smile, was the professor from Wallachia. Mina could no longer believe in coincidence or in chance meetings, though she had persuaded herself of the possibility when she had come here with Abree.

Foreign words were so much harder to remember. His name, *Florescu*, might sound the same as the count's, yet it might be different. When she and Abree had met the professor in the square yesterday she'd held on to this belief. But she'd known even then that the meeting was unlikely to be chance alone. So she'd reverted then to an old trick she'd known ever since childhood when she'd been persecuted by a neighbourhood dog. Run towards fear, not away from it. Show the master's hand. Shame fear like a cur. It had worked. She'd immediately claimed a common ground with the stranger even though she'd been afraid of him to the point of breathlessness. She'd let sentiment run free, reframing her past and colouring her experience with adventure and longing, as though her whole life had been like one of those Dumas novels her husband used to love. She had even pressed one of her husband's business cards into his hand, and then, at home, she'd talked glowingly of the encounter over dinner.

She hadn't been sure how much Jonathan had taken in, but she'd wanted to dare him to have courage too, to run towards fear just as she had. She'd wanted him to know this was the way the Harkers should behave. Perhaps some of the message had found its way through after all as he'd sat there, listening patiently. He'd even nodded and smiled once or twice. Of course, the night had been different, as she'd feared it would be. He'd run away somewhere, his club no doubt, and then shamed them all on his return.

Mina was more frightened of this man today. This time she was alone. She considered for a moment whether valour might wait, whether a simple nod might be enough. But he was smiling at her very directly. He'd removed his hat and was about to rise. Abree, thought Mina. Abree had made the difference yesterday. Reluctant though Mina was to praise her daughter Abree had helped her find the courage she needed. Young people can be so very useful. Quite automatically, they become the medium of all conversation, and this is what had freed Mina to be brave and sentimental. At the very least, it had helped. Now Mina was alone, and something else worried her. In the shade, with the boughs swaying gently above him, the professor looked rather like Quincey, an older version. Vague notions merged with the foliage rippling around him. She imagined how the greenery might spread around them both, closing in, how it might swallow them whole.

But she made her way in his direction as she knew she must. To compensate for her daughter's absence, she focused on her surroundings, her smile taking in the whole square—a rustling creature high in the boughs, a bed of young roses, their red, bright mouths beginning to open. She let her gloved fingertips touch these. "Ah, do you not love this time of the year, Professor Florescu?" she asked as she reached him. The voice didn't sound like hers, and neither did the words. If he were well acquainted with her he would know this, but, of course, he was not. For the moment, she was safe from the suspicion of artifice.

"Yes, Mrs. Harker, I do." He held his Derby respectfully at his waist. "In my country, summer is swift and sudden. Here it approaches by stealth—daisy here, a chaffinch there, the lawns slowly becoming greener. One doesn't notice the season rise to its peak until it is all around you. It is a seduction."

His eyes, frank and not at all insinuating, were on hers. She found herself blinking, reminding herself that he was, after all, a foreigner. He could not know how far such a sentence had curved beyond the bounds of English propriety.

Suddenly, he smiled and looked to his shoes. "Pardon my poetic effort, Mrs. Harker. I should perhaps stick to my own subject. I am a mere historian."

She smiled also, but the sense of disquiet remained. A ring of shadow danced behind him. There was something too frank about this man, too sincere. It was as though he was playing with the *idea* of sincerity, as though frankness and openness were props, as though even his blunders were calculated.

"I am influenced by my father, even though I was very young when he died."

"I am sorry to hear that, Professor Florescu." It was a standard response, Mina supposed, but the way it was received—with that same smile, steady and open—threatened to confirm something quite disturbing. Mina wasn't sorry his father died when he was only a child. How could she be? The boyhood of this man of thirty-five or so meant nothing to her. More importantly, he *knew* she wasn't sorry. Such obviously feigned emotion would usually elicit an embarrassed half-smile, or perhaps a shrug. The moment would be filled with mutual discomfort. But Professor Florescu still gazed at her, as though welcoming more such dissembling.

Mina's eyes were drawn once more to the rustling creature high in the boughs, and this time she saw it was a thrush, young tufts of feathers marking out its youth. By the trunk, green eyes intent, a black-and-white cat was watching its prey intently. She felt like calling to the thrush, warning the young bird of the eyes on its every movement.

"My father, Mrs. Harker, loved England."

Mina felt the heat rise to her face. Those brown eyes of his, timid yet watchful, would not allow her to look away. She knew the declaration called for a platitude, but her lips would not budge. Seeing that she had no answer, he continued. "He came here to live for a while, and I was to follow, but unfortunately he had to return home to Wallachia." Again, he stopped, awaiting the obvious question. Mina stuttered over it:

"What"—a sharp intake of breath broke her question in two—"interrupted his visit?"

His smile became broader. "I have never been able to find out for sure. In any case, he was overtaken before he reached his home." Again, the pause, the expectant silence. Her heart wasn't pounding, but there was a noticeable change, a picking up of speed, a readiness.

"Overtaken, you say?"

"Oh, Wallachia was a land of brigands then, you can be sure. Not at all like the ordered, peaceful society he had enjoyed briefly in England." His gaze left her for a second. She felt a slight relief as he seemed to take in the square and the houses beyond. "There were, I believe, some English tourists in the vicinity too. I almost wonder, I mean I like to think, they would have helped rescue my father had they been close enough to intervene."

"Indeed, we were in the area ourselves *once*, Professor."

Her voice had held steady enough, but her breath felt thin, and she had put a rather artificial emphasis on the word "once," as though to imply their visit and the misfortune of this man's father could not have happened at the same time. He titled his head as though there had to be more, which, of course, was logical. The most obvious question had been skirted.

"We were there…. My husband would remember the exact year," she said, stuttering. A breeze had helped with the distraction. It had loosened a lock of hair and stirred up some specks of grit, making her blinking seem more natural. "When did this unfortunate event take place?"

"It was in the year 1890, Mrs. Harker. I think you said you too were there a little more than thirty years ago."

A sudden movement claimed them both. High in the boughs, the black-and-white cat lowered itself onto a level branch. The young thrush was in its mouth, outstretched wing twitching.

When Mina scrambled into her hallway again it was as though the breeze had tumbled her back home. Leaning back against the front door, jamming it closed, she listened for sounds of others in the house. Abree was likely studying. Mrs. Rogers would be in the kitchen, and Jonathan—well should she care about him? Maybe she had to.

Mina could not delude herself into thinking her sudden departure from the square had done anything besides confirm the professor's suspicions. But she didn't like to panic, so she measured the distance between normal, civilized, and sensible reactions and how she had, in fact, behaved. "Oh," she had said, when she had seen the bird in the cat's mouth, "how awful." Then, muttering something about not being able to stay, she had merely wafted away, finding her way in a matter of seconds, she supposed, back to the house. Part of her had meant what she'd said. She'd hated the cat's action. Most of all she'd hated the inevitability of it. Why should nature always follow that same predestined course? It seemed every children's book, and many verses in the Bible, promised something different. The lion will lay down with the lamb. Sometimes it seemed as though the only unexpected thing about life was its dreadful predictability.

The sunlight played through the glass above her head and danced queasily upon the black-and-white tiles of the hallway floor. She thought again of Lucy Westenra, beautiful, uncomprehending Lucy, staring up at Mina from her bed. This time she could not keep the memory from returning in detail. Lucy's voice came into her mind, soft and surprisingly rich.

"Please," Lucy said. "They're going to come back." She gripped Mina by the sleeve. "Stay with me, Mina, please!"

Mina steadied herself against the wall and then stood and

began to peel off her gloves with difficulty. But the thoughts of Lucy persisted. She would have been about Abree's age then, a delicate, pretty young woman. But Abree had never been like her old friend. Lucy, before her sickness, had been so utterly fearless. This was what made Lucy's fear so memorable and so startling.

Lucy had had good reason to be afraid. The professor had announced that she had an infection and that they had to cut it out. Mina had heard this announcement herself. The men had gathered on the landing outside Lucy's bedroom door. Then, at Jonathan's nod, she had slipped into the room to comfort her friend. As she had looked down at Lucy's white hands gripping her sleeve, even as she smelled the breath of her sick friend, she wondered at the professor, that he should have spoken loudly enough for his patient to overhear. But dear Dr. Seward had been there too. Although the young doctor had been anxious and troubled, he hadn't questioned the plans of his mentor. No matter their individual eccentricities, collectively there had to be competence, surely. Surgeons did cut out infections. She knew that. But, with Lucy, the physical reality of the act had been a conundrum. The men outside had been murmuring about "moral insanity," not about a specific tumour on her arm or her leg. How does one surgically remove moral insanity? Like a baffled child who wants to accept what her parents tell her, Mina had believed there had to be a way, and that some simple explanation must lie just beyond her knowledge.

"Please," Lucy had said. "They're going to come back." She had gripped Mina by the sleeve. She remembered Lucy's breath, how it had been made stale by too many hours of lying in bed. "Stay with me, Mina, please!"

Mina shivered and nearly dropped the key, which she now replaced on its hook. She had not stayed, despite Lucy's pleading. In her memory, she had even twisted her arm away to rid herself of Lucy's grip. Had she really done this? Perhaps she had merely wanted to. It pained her more than anything that her friend might have felt betrayed by Mina so close to the end. She *had* tried to smile reassuringly—she remembered this—while she had backed towards the bedroom door. "The doctors will make you well," she had said feebly. She remembered how this had felt wrong. Hearing those words on her lips—the dullness of her voice, the dismissive hollowness—had made her realize that she did not believe her own sentiments. And worse, Lucy knew this. Her eyes, tired and defeated, had followed Mina all the way through the door.

Mina peeled off her coat and hung it up, suddenly aware of Jenny's absence. The maid had usually arrived to help even on those rare occasions when Mina didn't ring the bell. The house seemed emptier now. It seemed a sad house. The glass behind Mina threw undulating colours on the tiles, conjuring some half-forgotten lines from Omar Khayyam:

The Moving Finger writes; and, having writ,
Moves on: nor all thy Piety nor Wit
Shall lure it back to cancel half a Line.

Jonathan had brought the Persian poet into their marriage quite soon after Wallachia. He had pored over verses night after night. Soon Mina had joined in with enthusiasm. Mysticism seemed an all-encompassing balm; it yielded the comfort of infinite context. No tragedies or mistakes seem as vast when viewed as part of a limitless universe.

The particular lines about the moving finger had always seemed rather mournful, but at this moment Mina found even these ancient words comforting. Mistakes move into the past. Each passing day diminishes their importance. And mistakes are expected. Omar Khayyam anticipated this. There was no way of avoiding them. Had she betrayed Lucy? If so, it was only a moment of betrayal amidst days, weeks, months, and years of faithful friendship. The thing that made this betrayal seem so dreadful was the fact it had taken place the last time they had spoken. She had thought they all knew what they were about—Professor Van Helsing, Arthur, Dr. Seward, Jonathan, and Quincey.

She heard a stirring on the stairs and looked up to see a middle-aged man with stooping shoulders and a pale, frightened face. How little he resembled the man she'd married.

"Where have you been?" he asked.

Curiosity was not part of Jonathan's personality, especially these days, so this was an odd question. But it was a good one too. Mina's first instinct was to give a literal answer: she had been in the square, but only for a minute. But quickly she realized two things. Firstly, that this was only a fraction of the truth, and secondly, that it was not the part of the answer her husband wanted. She had indeed been to many very uncomfortable places in the last few minutes. She had been opened up in the most subtly violent manner by a clever man whose father she had helped track down and kill. Or perhaps her own guilt had opened her up. Perhaps he really did not suspect her, as she feared. But it hardly mattered. Speaking with him, she had remembered the pounding of horses' hooves in the desolate Wallachian wilderness. For a second she'd seen the arc of blood as her husband's Kukri knife pierced the count's throat. But most unpleasant of all, she'd stood above Lucy's bed, reliving the uncertainty and shame as she'd twisted her wrist from her friend's grasp and then backed out of her room with those defeated eyes upon her.

But none of this could be said in the hallway with her husband looking down from the stairs, so she merely said, "Jonathan, it's time we talked."

While she might have expected fear in her husband's eyes, instead she saw a kind of acceptance.

He nodded.

Mina made her way to the drawing room. After only a brief hesitation, her husband came down the remaining stairs, following, and entered after her. He turned and closed the door after them.

16. JENNY O'CONNELL

JENNY COULD TELL SOMETHING was amiss the moment she turned the corner onto Saul Street. A circle of people stood around the ground-floor entrance of Aunt Laura's home. She saw men in cloth caps, their fists digging into their hips, and women standing with their arms folded over their chests.

If Jenny had been a keen observer she would have noticed that one of the younger women, who was dressed in a flowered-print dress rather than in one of the plain smocks worn by her elders, was watching the loose stones at her feet; she did not have her arms folded. But trauma homogenizes everything, and Jenny was doubly traumatized. She'd been ejected from her employer's home, and now, noticing her aunt's absence from the crowd outside her home, she knew with cast-iron certainty that Aunt Laura was no more.

If she had nurtured any hope that she was mistaken, this too would soon be dashed. Mrs. Bradley raised her head at Jenny's approach and said something to one of her neighbours, a thin woman Jenny didn't recognize. This neighbour also looked at Jenny. One of the men scratched the back of his head and moved away from the circle. Two others broke away.

Mrs. Bradley and some of the other women turned from the circle to face her.

"She's gone, dear girl. Your aunt. She died this morning."

An emotion trembled through Jenny's body, and she was ashamed of it. She was not sad. There was no soft and longing sentiment rising within her, no urge to cry. And there was no vision of her aunt at all. She was merely frightened, not for aunt Laura but for herself. She'd come because she'd had to. Her employer had offered both wages and an unspecified financial compensation. Bizarrely, she had refused both.

Pride is a strange thing. It can vanquish all common sense in one swoop. It can trump such urgent and essential matters as the need to survive. She'd said she didn't need the money, and for a moment, in her head, she'd really felt this way. She'd really thought there was a treasure trove hidden in her bag, perhaps a tiny gold strongbox, and that a turn of the key would spill riches into her lap any time she needed them. This was all very strange. She'd considered her rashness quietly as she'd left Belgrave Square for the last time, listening to her oddly hollow footsteps on the pavement. She had little in the way of savings, only three pounds, five shillings, and sixpence. Why had she chosen this, of all issues, as her greatest point of rebellion, when there was so much more she could have said?

Mrs. Harker's words had circled around the reason for her dismissal, and this indirect approach had been part of the problem.

"Jenny," she'd said, "I find that we will no longer be able to keep you on. It appears there is an issue of conduct. I will not go into details, of course, but this issue makes your presence in the home inappropriate."

There had been almost no movement at all in Mrs. Harker's face while she had spoken, only a slight glassiness in her eyes, which had been focused directly on Jenny as she spoke. Only at the end, on the word *inappropriate*, had Jenny seen a slight twitch in the corner of her employer's mouth.

She'd been too in awe to reply at first. Her husband's infidelity, and Jenny's role in it, was worth only this, a slight twitch of the mouth. This fact made Mrs. Harker seem so lofty, so much above the reach of ordinary human understanding. She was like a Greek goddess, able to regard insult, war, tragedy, slaughter, the whole sweep of human turmoil, with the same dispassionate eye. Waves of terror had swept through Jenny. She had wondered if she might faint. She had wondered if she could control her bladder. But Mrs. Harker had merely twitched—a movement so slight Jenny had barely noticed it. Jenny was an ant before a lioness.

Mrs. Harker had continued after a pause, hands coming together in an attitude of dignified prayer. She had no longer looked directly at Jenny. Her eyes had gazed towards the bottom of the door behind Jenny, as though she found the subject indecorous. "Of course, I will compensate you for the inconvenience. I will pay you until the end of the month. The bank will reopen on Monday, and we will leave the money with Mrs. Rogers or, if you prefer, have it sent to you. Further, as I will not be able to furnish a reference, we will add a sum to tide you...."

"There is no need," Jenny had said suddenly. "I would rather you didn't. You do not need to forward my salary. I have saved quite enough. I will leave straightaway."

The trouble was, of course, she'd been lying. Three pounds, five shillings, and sixpence—the sum was tattooed on her brain. Unlike a tattoo, it would change; it would get smaller. What kind of a room could she get in London for such an amount? And for how long? She'd left a sovereign with her aunt Laura on her last visit. Her only living relative had been too sick to work of late. It hadn't seemed important at the time. Now every pound, shilling, and penny had a heightened significance.

None of this information could be passed on to Mrs. Harker. Their conversation existed in a world devoid of such details, devoid, indeed, of any details at all. And this was the real issue. Everything had been in the abstract. Everything had been in code. This was why she'd had to refuse the money. It was all she *could* have done. She couldn't have yelled. She couldn't have complained. She'd been too afraid, yes, but also the words had not existed. The words *it was your husband's fault too* were not within the boundaries of any available exchange. The accusation could exist only in a fantasy, as inaccessible from the calm, frosty presence of Mrs. Harker as the imaginings in Dante's *Inferno*. Daylight, the careful *tick* of the grandfather clock, the ottoman, and the Persian rug prevented any such sentiments from ever finding voice. The words would merely scatter into the air like fragments of a nightmare. The only rebellion she had was to refuse the mattress Mrs. Harker had proposed for her landing. Only this would prove her point and assert her relative innocence. She would not let her employer be reasonable. She would not let her be kind.

She'd realized all this on her walk eastward.

Even before she'd turned the corner and seen the gathering, Jenny had regretted her decision. She'd been defiant with Mrs. Harker, but now she would have to humble herself to Aunt Laura. Aunt Laura had lived a life of hard work, frugality, a nun-like spinsterhood, or so it was believed. Either way, she'd always had a formidable kind of goodness about her, and it was this quality, this unsmiling virtue, that had kept Jenny from visiting since the last time, when she'd compensated for her lack of duty by leaving a pound from her meagre savings. So, she would have to apologize first. And then she would have to explain the reason for her visit. She had never before claimed or asked for any kind of intimacy with Aunt Laura, but now she would have to tell her of her utter disgrace. And then she would have to ask for a space on her floor to sleep.

And now, even this was not possible.

"Can I see her?" Jenny asked Mrs. Bradley.

One of the men, cap obscuring his eyes, sniffed in reply. "She's gone, girl. She's at the parish at Spitalfields. We all chipped in. The landlord's already come and changed the locks. Taking no chances."

Jenny felt the weight of the bag over her shoulder. It was perhaps twenty pounds and held all her clothes—minus her uniform, which she had left—a few books, an apple, and a pie Mrs. Rogers had insisted she take with her. It might pass for something a niece might carry to her sick aunt, but she wondered if the man with the cap had guessed at her intention of staying with her aunt. She wondered if this was why he mentioned the changing of the locks.

"Poor lady couldn't pay last week's rent," he concluded. "Too sick to work."

Jenny knew what was required. She scooped her purse from her bag, angling it so as to prevent a view of the clothes within, and opened it, spilling a sovereign into Mrs. Bradley's palm.

"Service will be tomorrow, ten o'clock," she said.

The silence was oppressive. Jenny knew she should ask some questions. How was it at the end? Did she say anything? Did she suffer? But she couldn't bring herself to begin, and these people didn't really expect her to. It was as though they knew all about Jenny's circumstances, as though the girl had turned into glass and they could see clean through her exterior and gaze upon her quivering, homeless soul.

She turned slowly and began to tramp back the way she had come. So, not three pounds, five shillings, and sixpence. Only two pounds, five shillings, and sixpence now. Aunt Laura was dead, she told herself. Surely this was more important than the amount of coin in her purse. But she felt a tingle of cold around her shoulders despite the warmth of the late afternoon. Where would she sleep tonight?

The landlord had already come and changed the locks. Why? Aunt Laura had no relatives but Jenny, and Jenny had never once stayed the night. As far as anyone knew, until a few moments ago anyway, she was gainfully employed. Had the landlord smelled her fear from halfway across London? Had these people sensed it too, in the larger-than-usual bag, perhaps? Or in the quiet way she'd received the news of Laura's death?

Jenny was moving westwards now, out of the East End, into the heart of the city, but she had no idea why. London seemed malignant suddenly, all of it, east and west, north and south.

The very brick dust seemed to swirl around her, spreading news of her homelessness far and wide. She caught the eyes of a workman, flat-capped like the man who'd told her the way was barred. His eyes, dark and unfeeling, seemed to enter her thoughts. Two idling boys in shirtsleeves and shorts stopped their game to watch her pass by. One nudged the other, who giggled, and then they continued to play football with a stone. Who but an East End child would play football with a stone? Not an old apple, because it would have to be eaten; not a fir cone, as there were no trees; not a piece of bark or branch for the same reason; but a stone, a lifeless thing with no memory of warmth or growth or life. This was London. But unfeeling though the boys were, they seemed to know about her. How could they? It made no sense, but like the brick dust, they knew the look of destitution. They knew the fear that preceded it.

Jenny still didn't think about where she was going, but she continued in the same direction, getting closer to Liverpool Street Station. It occurred to her to leave the city. She had enough for a ticket somewhere. But a city, even an evil brooding one like this, held places to hide, alleys to sleep in. Her employer, or rather her former employer, was in the west. It seemed she was drawn back there as a severed digit might be drawn to a bleeding stump. It was too ridiculous. One short meeting and she was homeless and jobless. Had Mrs. Harker really meant what she had said about the money? And if so, was it really too late? Jenny had sounded so utterly decided about it when she'd answered Mrs. Harker. It had been one of those odd moments in life where she'd been impressed with herself—or at least impressed with the person she might have seemed to be from the outside. If only she really had been that confident young woman with enough money to refuse Mrs. Harker without regret.

She'd transferred her purse from her bag to her skirts as she'd become concerned about some of the looks she'd received from the roughest people. She could feel its lightness in her skirts.

The indignation struck her like lightning. It was Mr. Harker's fault. He was a gentleman of social standing, and she was a servant. She was not responsible for his fragility. And in any case, even if it were her fault, an employer should not fire someone unless they could afford to pay their notice, if they had the money at hand.

There was something extraordinarily luxurious in the breezy way Mrs. Harker had talked about the bank opening on Monday, and about giving Mrs. Rogers what she was owed, or having it—and the additional, unspecified sum—forwarded to her. Again, the details were missing. Mrs. Harker wouldn't have had any idea what address to send this money to. Somehow Jenny couldn't even imagine her asking for this information. There was no paper or pen in the room that Jenny could see, and the extraordinary poise of Mrs. Harker seemed ill-suited to a sudden search for these items. If Mrs. Harker had neglected to make provisions for noting down Jenny's particulars, how could she be trusted to go to the bank and withdraw Jenny's wages?

There was something oddly prescient about all this. Mrs. Harker could afford to ignore details for the simple reason that they were not important to her. Jenny saw her again, indomitable and unbowed. Her husband's infidelity, his fathering of a servant's child, had caused neither fury nor sobbing, nor the collapse into an apothecary's care, but only a very slight twitch. And even this had been difficult to detect. If huge events mattered so little, how would a tiny task like delivering a sum of money to a former servant possibly lodge in her mind until the end of the weekend?

There had probably been a fleeting intention to go to the bank. But by Monday Mrs. Harker would likely have forgotten. The more a person has, the more the world pays attention to their wants. The less a person has, the more invisible their needs. The Harkers had taken everything from her, and Mrs. Harker had not so much as asked where she would spend the night.

Her predicament necessitated her removal from the house; otherwise it was of no interest.

A shiny car purred past her slowly. Jenny didn't know the makes of cars, but it was mauve and black with elegant curves. At the wheel was a chauffeur, in the back a middle-aged couple. The woman in flowing silks looked into a compact mirror with that same dreamy nonchalance Mrs. Harker often had when she sprayed the fronds in her conservatory. The man fiddled with a silver cigarette case.

Every hair and fibre smarted with anger now. This fury was better than the dullness she'd felt outside her aunt's home and better especially than the self-recrimination. A rising fire means action not defeat. She had no idea what that action might be, or why she had just been swallowed by Liverpool Street Station with its high arching glass and its frame of iron. Jenny gazed around her just as Jonah must have gazed around the inner walls of the whale's stomach, following the curved outlines of its monstrous ribs. It was past five o'clock now but it was still warm. Pigeons scattered before her and circled in giddying heights under the glass and iron. A hiss came from three platforms away, and then a great cloud of steam rose up to the cathedral-like ceiling.

Soon enough it would be night, and she'd be in need of a bed. She knew this, but it seemed far away at the moment. The station was like the munitions factory. It was perpetual movement, constant change. She could almost feel that night would never come here, just as it never came in the factory. She found a bench that overlooked the platforms, opened up her bag, and pulled out the pork pie Mrs. Rogers had insisted that she take. She was glad of it now as she was hungry.

She felt self-conscious, hunched over, digging her teeth into the pastry, especially when pale crumbs began to scatter down onto her skirts like snowflakes. A uniformed boy sucking on a lolly stared at her as an older woman tugged on his arm. His ill-fitting red jacket—boarders were never "off," even on

Saturday—meant he had to be from the Catholic boarding school hidden amidst the jungle of stone somewhere around Westminster Cathedral. The woman with him was in the dowdy garb of a governess. When she caught him watching Jenny, she tugged his arm again, but he continued to stare anyway, looking backwards and craning his neck. They moved off the platform and disappeared into a swirl of people as they approached the human drain of the Underground.

But it wasn't them who might sink into the sewer. It was Jenny. She was in real danger, and she knew it well enough. But a new determination had started to warm her from within. She would not submit. There had to be a reason she was travelling west, and the answer was simple. She was on her way to Belgravia. The Harkers had not seen the last of her yet. People continued to swirl into the Underground. Pigeons spiralled above, and the trains hissed and billowed. The night seemed closer suddenly. She could feel it in the shadows cast by the high girders holding up the glass. But it was no longer menacing. She was no longer worried about finding a bed. The night and Jenny seemed to beckon to each other like old friends. She would lose herself in its ripples and folds. The night would be her comfort and her bed. It would hide her until she decided to strike.

17. JONATHAN HARKER

THEY HAD BEEN TALKING in circles for almost an hour. Still Mina wouldn't let up. First she'd asked him about his nightmares. This had been a relief, initially. His first fear when he had followed her into the drawing room had been that she'd meant to confront him about Jenny. He'd half expected it even before she'd returned to the house looking so pale and strange, so unlike herself. Everyone had delayed reactions. It would be like Mina, so businesslike, so organized, to get the practical side of the problem—Jenny under her roof—sorted and then deal with the pain of likely infidelity.

But, no. She'd wanted to dredge up something far more obscure. She'd wanted to pick some scabs, and she'd started—nonsensically, it seemed to him—with the nightmare he'd had the other night. What did he dream exactly? What was the image that had awoken him? Soon the repetition of the question became unbearable.

"You must remember, Jonathan," she said for at least the fourth time. They were seated now, in armchairs at right angles to each other. Even with the coffee table wedged into the space between them, she had seemed much too close for comfort.

"I was asleep. How could I remember?"

"You screamed, *Quincey*, at the top of your lungs."

Mention of the word *lungs* made his chest burn. It was as though she'd lit a taper under his ribs and the soft tissues had begun to smolder. "You don't have to remind me," he said.

He could feel the inner arm of the chair against his hip. It was as though he was trying to escape through the fabric, stuffing, and wood. In a way, of course, he was.

"I don't have to remind you? So, you *do* remember?" The words, whispered, came out in a hiss. "Did you dream about our son or Quincey Morris?"

"I told you. I don't recall the details."

"Really?" She stared at him, incredulous, almost giving up.

"Maybe it was both," he said grudgingly.

The light from the garden had deepened into gold. If there was anything indecent about having this conversation, it was having it when it was light outside. And it was still some while before evening. Quite soon they would be called to dinner. Mina's hunger for knowledge and answers would still be directed at him, but would be muted at least for the duration of the meal. What a mournful event it would be. There would be no Jenny to serve, so Mrs. Rodgers would come and do it all herself. What would Abree make of that?

His watchful daughter. She was bound to ask what had happened to the girl, and in her own sullen, quiet way she could be as dogged as her mother. Jonathan didn't think he could stand any more questions, not after this.

"I'm going to tell you something, Jonathan, something that will upset you." She rose from her seat and began to pace. "I met someone on my walk, someone who seems to know all about us." She paused with her back to him, holding her hands in front of her, one on top of the other, like she was about to dive into a swimming pool. At first he thought she might be praying, but then he saw she was scraping one palm against the other, like Lady MacBeth trying to rid herself of Duncan's blood. And then she told him, quietly and calmly. She had spoken to *him* again, the man she'd rhapsodized about just a day before, Professor Florescu.

So she did remember the count's name, after all. He'd assumed she had forgotten all the most pertinent details that might link this stranger to their past. But part of him had suspected. She'd simply decided to outface the past by first embracing the young foreigner and then by talking about him casually in front of her husband and daughter.

She wasn't casual now, however. She trembled while she spoke, something he'd hardly ever witnessed in his wife, and her eyes looked moist. He was the son of the count, she told Jonathan, it was certain, and worse the young man knew, *somehow* he seemed to know, they were responsible for his father's death.

Jonathan listened, pretending to be calm, but all the while dull hammer blows pounded in his chest. He furrowed his brow, took his eyes from her, and fixed his gaze at the green lines on the wallpaper, at the Persian rug, at the clock, everywhere but at Mina. In the corner of his eye, he saw her theatrically raised hands and her Lady MacBeth scrubbing motion. Finally, when she finished, she let her hands slide down her dress as though drying them. Jonathan took on his most serious lawyer's tone and looked at her with the same determination he'd used with clients who'd been in danger of spoiling their cases through their own indiscretion.

"I can see how upsetting this may be. But there is not the slightest evidence to suggest any crime. There were no witnesses, no authorities within many miles." He paused. She was looking at the rug now too. "Do not speak to him again. Say nothing. Do nothing. No one can harm us."

She looked up at him. "And what of Abree?"

Something clutched at him. "She must leave the university immediately," he said with some vehemence.

Mina moved back to her chair, her hands in motion once more. "She will want to know why. And … and I don't think we can do it. It wouldn't be reasonable."

"No one from this family should contact this man," Jonathan said evenly.

"But, if there is nothing to fear, if there is no evidence, why should we suddenly change our plans? If we do change our plans for no reason, it will be taken as evidence that we have something to hide."

A slow fire was burning inside Jonathan again. He had given her his opinion, but now she was merely using it to fashion her own contrary view. He felt his lips tremble with incipient rage. "Why did you ask my advice if you were going to ignore it?"

"Jonathan!" she said, as though shocked. But it was a certain kind of shock, the shock of someone who sees a pattern repeated for the thousandth time. It was the numbed shock of exasperation. "We are having a conversation. I did not ask you for the answer. We are discussing this situation. *Together*."

He looked at her, aware of the cynicism that must have been in his eyes. Her own expression was open, questioning. It felt like a trick, as though his wife could manoeuvre him into any position she wished and then back away, hold up her hands, and claim she had never intended to do so.

"It isn't just you, Jonathan," she said quietly. "You are not the only one who's afraid."

Jonathan felt suddenly ashamed of his transparency. Not only could his wife see through him, but she had to be especially careful not to do or say anything that might harm his pride. Referring to his fear had been a last resort, clearly.

"You think about the count and what we all did to him," she said, "but I think about Lucy. About that night."

"Stop!" Jonathan's hand flew to his mouth. It would have made more sense to plug his ears. He was aware of this immediately, and he found his actions curious even as he performed them.

Mina sighed. She had *that* look, the one he had become used to seeing during the night when he woke, the one he had seen when he had come home drunk last night—conciliatory, patient. She sank into her chair. "What is to be gained by avoiding the subject now? We both know what happened wasn't right."

"We don't know," he said. Now it was his turn to stand up. He did so awkwardly and walked over to the mantelpiece. Something was different about the display there. The photograph of Quincey was gone. When had this happened? A vase with forget-me-nots and tulips was in its place. He turned and looked back at Mina. "We don't know it wasn't right. Professor Van Helsing was directing us. He was the foremost authority anywhere in the world ... in his field."

"Which field, Jonathan?" she asked as though in pity. It was infuriating. "A professor of *metaphysics*? What does that really mean? Nobody would take him seriously now."

Jonathan leaned against the mantelpiece, felt the ridge hard against his back. "It was the best advice we had at the time. You have to remember what Lucy was like, that dreadful change that had come over her." He shook his head, feeling his skin burn. There were other reasons, more deeply threatening reasons, why the subject embarrassed him.

"Yes," Mina said quietly, "I remember."

Jonathan wondered what exactly she remembered. He felt like he was back at the Holmwood residence witnessing Lucy so hungry, so brazen. Jonathan himself had been sitting on the other side of the count, and even from a distance he had felt Lucy's breath, hot and suggestive, wafting over. What must it have felt like to the count, with her hungry eyes on his, her hot breath so close? This was the beginning of her illness, and the contrast was so grotesque. Just a few weeks before she'd been that sweet, pretty-featured young woman. She had perfectly balanced the spirit of a new woman with the decorum of her own long line of gentlefolk. The worst thing about the evening had been witnessing Arthur's own distress as he'd looked down at his beloved from above. Red in the face, with a blue vein running down his neck, Arthur had intervened, demanding she go to her room to await the arrival of a doctor. This had turned out to be Dr. Seward, and he, in turn, had sent for a specialist: Professor Van Helsing.

"If you remember how Lucy was transformed into such a"—he said the next word quietly—"*depraved* creature, you will admit that something had to be done."

"*Something* had to be done, Jonathan, yes. Lucy had become infatuated. She was engaged, and she had lost all sense of reason, all decorum, yes. But what Arthur Holmwood did, under Professor Van Helsing's instructions…"

Jonathan turned once more to the mantelpiece, staring into the space where Quincey's photograph ought to have been. Mina wouldn't end the sentence, and he was glad of that. Although Seward had written an account of the incident, he couldn't imagine the words spoken out loud. There was another horror churning like a malignant river under this story, and it was just as detestable to him as the one to which his wife had drawn his attention.

Lucy infatuated, yes. But she had not been the only one, had she? He could almost imagine saying it to Mina. Perhaps Mina was right, after all. Perhaps Van Helsing had been wrong about the count's magic powers, his ability to change people and infect women from within with lust. Perhaps it was merely coming from the women themselves. Seeing Lucy as a victim had been a type of flattery. And if this was so, then seeing Mina's near escape was flattery too.

"Moral insanity," Jonathan said, turning. He spat the words like they were weapons. "That's what Van Helsing called it, and that's what it was."

Mina sighed deeply and looked to the floor. "Jonathan, the insane are kept in asylums. They are treated with water baths, and given padding to wear when they are violent. Dr. Seward knew that. They are not impaled with wooden stakes." She had said the unsayable, and Jonathan was numbed for the moment. His heartbeat came to him as if through layers of cotton wool, loud but indistinct. He had to piece the scene before him together; it was as though it had come apart into small fragments, which had to be rejoined into a picture. Mina had leaned forward. She had whispered her last sentence very quietly. The very hush had given the words a deadly emphasis.

"It was not our decision," Jonathan said, his voice no more than a rasp. As though aware of the weakness of the statement, his knees had started to ache. "We relied on the specialist."

"Professor Van Helsing."

"Yes."

"Who disappeared soon afterwards and could not be found."

Jonathan felt an itch in his pocket. He felt the weight of his wallet, remembered the letter slipped between banknotes. It was foolish indeed to argue with his wife on these points, foolish and futile. The insane, Mina had said, are kept in asylums, treated with water baths. Mina was not an imaginative woman, and it was imagination that excused the inexcusable. He moved over to Mina's ground, the simple facts, stated plainly.

"Dr. Seward trusted him."

"Jonathan, Dr. Seward committed suicide! The poor man couldn't cope with what happened. He'd been duped and he knew it."

It was on the tip of Jonathan's tongue to say *we'll just have to agree to disagree.* But the statement was even weaker than the previous one. In fact, it was grotesquely, comically weak, especially when laid beside the image of Holmwood with the stake, the dint of white flesh on Lucy's breast as its point was lowered, finding its mark.

When Mina continued, her voice was tired, as though she was giving up. "Jonathan, you remember all those diaries Arthur Holmwood made us write, all the trouble you went to writing about your journey to Transylvania, the way Bucharest wasn't wild enough for Arthur, the count's strange habits, crawling down the castle's walls, keeping you prisoner, casting no reflection for goodness's sake, bringing a baby so his daughters could suck its blood?" She shook her head as though suddenly realizing after all these years how distasteful, as well as ridiculous, this last idea really was.

Jonathan remembered it all very well. His own "journal" came back to him like a very long and arduous dream, entirely vivid in every way and, like a dream, churning fragments of reality into streams of invention so the whole was a whirlpool of impossible fantasy grounded, however distantly, in fact. Mina watched his expression carefully. Then she continued. "It's as though we were all lost in a madness, as though we'd all been caught up with it. With each event, each time we acted, we forced ourselves deeper. We forced ourselves into even more acts of insanity, each trying to justify the last."

"Well," he said, and then shrugged. He didn't disagree. There was simply nothing else to say. Her use of "we" was rather kind, as Mina had not hammered a stake into her friend's heart. Nor had she physically helped to assassinate a foreign nobleman. There was an ulterior motive for her generosity. If you mean to challenge an act with maximum force, you must first claim you are partly responsible for it. Jonathan braced himself.

"Well, the fantasy is over. Seward is dead, so is Quincey Morris. Van Helsing, well, he must be dead by now. We can surely be honest about it all to each other."

Jonathan felt his face twitch. "To what purpose?" he asked.

She looked at him, startled. "*To what purpose?*" she repeated.

Part of Jonathan understood her shock, but this was one of those times he wished she knew just a little more about the law. The more sensitive an issue, the more careful one had to be. Words, written or spoken, had power. In their situation, each word hid a noose, coiled and invisible to the eye, but ready to show itself should either of them be thoughtless about what they decided to air in public. If there was no practical or urgent reason to speak, one kept silent. He didn't say any of this, because he could predict the disparaging look he would encounter if he did. He merely let the question hang.

"Jonathan," she said, throwing up her hands and rising once more. "What am I to do with a question like that? We've been living with untruth for more than thirty years. We've been busily creating a legacy of untruth." She ran her palms down her skirts again. "We liked Quincey Morris well enough, but did we really want to name our son after him?"

There it was again. They were back to the same question. And this time, because Mina wasn't looking at him—she had turned her back for the moment—he allowed himself a moment to think about it. Why *had* he called out the Texan's name in his dream? He'd thought, or rather assumed, that he had seen a vision of his friend in danger. Quincey Morris really had hacked through Dracula's "gypsy" train and had received a wound in doing so. But Jonathan had screamed not out of fear for Quincey's life, but rather out of fear for what Quincey was about to do. The gypsies had scattered—although Jonathan could see now that they were not actually gypsies but rather plainly clad cart men of the region. Some were behind the rocks, watching with horror. Another was holding his arm where Quincey had slashed him. This was the carriage driver. This driver did not back away but rather stood, incredulous and stunned, watching as his assailant, Quincey, followed closely by Jonathan himself, clambered into the carriage.

The count was not, as Mina's diary asserted, within a clearly labelled coffin mounted on a cart. He was sitting upright, the sole passenger inside the carriage. Far from the red eyes and vindictive look Mina's story had described, the count looked curiously fragile and, for the first time, rather middle-aged. The face that gazed back at Jonathan was a little bewildered, perhaps, but worse than this, it was weary. It was as though this were the last in a long line of inexplicable horrors. He merely wanted to be home, his expression said, but he knew these English people who had ambushed him were going to stop him from getting there.

"Are you going to kill me too?" the count said. There was a touch of humour within his tone of resignation. The question would haunt Jonathan in the years to come, partly because the word "too" confirmed the count knew about Lucy. Who might he have told? And worse even than this practical consideration was the impression of a sane man addressing a group of maniacs.

The special curse of Jonathan's dream was not that it had warped reality and made it grotesque. The curse was that it presented his memory with remarkable fidelity save for one detail. In the dream, he had screamed *Quincey*, but in reality he had not spoken at all that he could remember. As far as Jonathan could now tell, he had screamed out in his dream for two reasons. The scream had been to wake himself up, but it had also prevented the Texan from assaulting an unarmed middle-aged man, hauling him head first into the snow, and then plunging a bowie knife into his stomach.

If Quincey had gone through with this during Jonathan's dream, Jonathan would also have been forced to repeat the actions of the past. He would have had to take his kukri knife and slash with eyes half closed. Again, he would have seen the foreigner's blood arc and fall with a burble into the snow. His scream had nothing to do with saving the Texan. He had merely wanted it all to stop.

If there were a simple way of telling Mina this without getting back into the details, he would. But he wanted Mina to stop too, and she seemed very reluctant to do so.

Jonathan was back to that same question: *To what purpose?* It had been the right thing to ask, no matter what Mina thought. Count Dracula was dead. Lucy Westenra was dead. "We are all responsible for what happened, Mina," he said in his most practiced, confidential tone, "but it is too late. There is no reason to talk about it. Ever."

Mina shook her head. "But the fury of it," she whispered. "The *fury*! There must be something else, some other reason for it."

When Jonathan said nothing, Mina lowered herself onto the arm of her chair. She spoke evenly, pausing between phrases.

"When you returned to England, you introduced the count to Arthur Holmwood. Then the two of you inducted him into the Hellfire Club. This was above and beyond your commission. Were you returning a favour?"

He thought of getting up and ending the conversation straight-away, but to do so would be tantamount to an admission. So he merely waited out the silence. Like the slowest sprouting seed, this thought of Mina's had waited more than thirty years. Although Jonathan could feel pools of heat swimming around his face, there was also an easing somewhere in his stomach. He couldn't imagine childbirth, but he sensed this was what it must feel like to give birth to a monster. Even as one recoils in horror at the thing that has come into the world, one must also feel relief it is no longer inside.

In May of 1889, Count Dracula had been dwelling not in a castle in the middle of the Carpathian Mountains but in a large, modern town home in Bucharest. He'd seemed a modest man, despite his wealth, and Jonathan had not even known about the title until he had seen the count in the company of others. In their correspondence, he'd merely been Mr. Florescu. Jonathan had been sent, just as his journal stated, as an agent of Mr. Hawkins, where he was introduced to two women who were visiting the count's home. This was where Jonathan had got the idea for the female vampires. There all similarity between journal and reality ended. The two women were not Florescu's daughters, as Jonathan's journal had claimed. Instead, Florescu's family, which comprised a wife and small son, remained in the count's country home while he attended to business in town.

The women, Jazmin and Zsofia, were beautiful. Their job was to be beautiful. The scent of them came back to Jonathan. It was something spicy and sweet, not flowery like the French perfumes English women wore, and the dresses Jonathan first saw them in—delicate black lace over flesh-coloured silk—made him stutter and blush. An English woman would have ignored his embarrassment, as it would have meant acknowledging her own allure, but Jazmin and Zsofia did not. Jazmin's chocolate brown eyes held his gaze, and she smiled. Zsofia moved behind him and, hands like warm trickling water, slipped off his coat.

Mina was no fool, and Jonathan had no flair for fantasy. Jonathan had brought these women into his narrative, and Mina had known that there had to be some basis in reality. The business with Jenny had no doubt brought it back to her. Suddenly, for the first time in more than thirty years, Jonathan was the object of jealousy and suspicion, not about Jenny, curiously enough, but about encounters from 1889. Jealousy was such a strange emotion to have lain dormant for so long. Should he feel glad about it? Should pleasure at the rekindling of a decades-old emotion send the blood of desire pumping through his arteries? It almost did for a moment. But then he realized the passion he was feeling was not for Mina but for the memory of Jazmin and Zsofia, and, worse than this, he realized that Mina's jealousy was not for Jonathan, the middle-aged solicitor with a grown daughter and a dead son, but rather for the ambitious young man he had once been. For the Jonathan of today, she could muster nothing better than mild resentment when she suspected misbehaviour.

"I know about Arthur Holmwood," she continued. "I know what he confessed to Lucy about his maid..."

"Mina!" interrupted Jonathan.

Mina stopped. She gasped slightly, as though she couldn't believe what she had just said. Her lips came together with a just-audible *pat*. Jonathan's head started to ache. The clicking of the clock was invasive, getting louder each moment. Despite this, Jonathan felt a rare moment of power. He held his wife's gaze until she looked down at the rug. No words were necessary. Decorum had been breached. He might not have meant to cause her shame with his interruption, but it was a serendipitous effect. Wives do not mention the infidelity of friends, particularly when the friend in question was a peer of the realm. Jonathan had cowed Mina for the first time in many, many years. Despite his pounding head, despite the ticks from the grandfather clock cutting like scissors into his brain, it was an unexpected triumph.

"I meant to speak only about ourselves, Jonathan," she said, still quiet, eyes still cast down. Then she looked up at him, troubled. "What did happen in the count's home?"

He kept his eyes on her, saying nothing. He could feel the embers burning beneath him as though the chair's stuffing was made of live coals, but still he resisted. Jonathan knew what his expression must look like—smug, defiant, angry, and afraid all at the same time. It was a lawyer's expression, an expression that knew no matter how likely something seemed, it could never be proven.

For the moment, he thought his wife would react angrily, but, quite unexpectedly, her eyes went dull. She had given up. Whatever sparks of anger or jealousy had been behind the question, they were gone now.

The door opened. It was Mrs. Rogers, red-faced and flustered, in her apron.

"Dinner will be ready in a moment, sir, madam." Her formality seemed awkward, as though she were an actress uncertain of her lines. Jenny usually announced dinner, and Mrs. Rogers was not happy about her new dual role.

Mina nodded and stood up. Now Jonathan felt frustrated. A moment ago, silence had given him the upper hand. But his refusal to answer his wife was now the great matter between them while his own questions about Mina's conduct remained unsaid. The count had been understandably disappointed with the Hellfire Club, and for the first time Jonathan had seen this most privileged of inner sanctums through a foreigner's eyes. The Hellfire Club was nothing but a group of drunken, bored English men who from time to time spiced up their predictable appetites for drink and overindulgence with equally bored and overworked prostitutes. The Hellfire Club didn't celebrate the glamour of evil. It was merely pathetic, and, to the count, it was inexpressibly vulgar. Lucy Westenra, however, was not. Neither was Mina. These well-brought-up English women were something else; they were a challenge. Even Jonathan could see that, in different ways, Mina and Lucy possessed a sophistication that their chosen male partners lacked. There was a part of Jonathan that regretted his own dullness. He might have read more, perhaps, shown some interest in philosophy, fiction, and poetry rather than just law and the public issues of the time. There had been a flutter of intellectual curiosity after the traumatic events of 1899 and 1900, an interest in Omar Khayyam, for instance. But it was too little, too late. He caught it in Mina's eye now as she turned to leave the drawing room, that sense of *disappointment.*

She was gone now, and the door remained open behind her. For a moment, Jonathan wondered whether he could follow. The long rectangular hallway, with its oak panelling and white-painted plaster seemed a forbidden land, part of a family home he'd once dreamed of but which had now slipped away from him with a finality that came like a thud from a mallet.

The moving finger had not continued to write. Instead, it was tracing its way back into the past, etching mistakes deeper into the fabric of time. He was a murderer. So was Arthur, and all of them—Van Helsing, Mina, even poor Seward—were accessories.

He moved quickly into that forbidden space, aware of his daughter making her way down the stairs in that awkward sulky motion of hers. He ignored Abree and looked straight at Mrs. Rogers, who was standing before the dining room door like a maître d'.

"I find it is imperative I go out, Mrs. Rogers. There is an urgent work matter I must deal with. Tell Mrs. Harker I will return later."

Then, avoiding his daughter's startled eyes—Abree had stopped where she was on the staircase when he'd started talking—Jonathan went to the front door and quickly left the house, closing the door after him.

18. JENNY O'CONNELL

JENNY ARRIVED AT COVENT GARDEN as the quality of sunlight was changing in readiness for the evening. A hint of gold flooded the sandstone walls of the market together with the higher red-and-white brick surrounds, unifying everything with a sense of possibility. A bank of clouds gathered ominously to the east, but even this seemed to add to a sense of happy pageant. Every ancient myth had its war, after all. Every triumph had its dangers. She was on the precipice of exhilaration, at the pinpoint centre of a crossroads. At this place, at this time, she could believe in anything. There was a Saturday-evening bustle. The market was getting ready for the morning. Two Sundays in June allowed for the opening of the stalls and shops, and the tradesmen and merchants were making the most of them.

Barrows rattled past. Lorry engines roared, and men in cloth caps yelled unloading instructions to the drivers. Jenny smelled the dust from potato sacks and the diesel from the engines. The opera crowd was arriving also, the men like starlings in their shining black jackets and top hats, the women like more exotic birds, some with high feathers, and many with stoles or fur linings despite the warmth of the evening.

If she was being practical, she knew that the only open pathways led to desperation or crime. But there was nothing practical about this place. Despite everything, despite the rain that might come from the east, Covent Garden held a breathless promise. She felt she was seeing the world afresh.

The sleek operagoers either emerged from taxis close to the porticoes or wove easily through the market. They passed the carts and trucks loaded with fruit. For the moment, Jenny wasn't hungry. She could tell herself the magic of the evening was a diversion from ordinary life, rather than its terminus. She could forget that the apples that passed her at eye level would be an irresistible temptation once the last of her savings was gone in a few days. What would she turn into then?

She had passed huddled figures in the doorway on her walk from Liverpool Street, and she'd dared not look down. On previous outings, she had often cast a coin in the direction of one of these homeless figures, but this time it was all too close and she didn't dare accept their existence. She'd wound her way through Threadneedle Street and up Fleet Street, with scraps of old newspaper circling around her ankles and dragon's talons, griffon's craws, and lion's tails bearing down at her from the buildings. She'd been on a mission, not expecting to stop until she entered Belgrave Square, where she'd intended to embrace the leafy recesses of the square itself until nightfall. She knew she'd look and feel like a fugitive, but then this was what she was. Patience and planning were no good to her now. She'd either have to slink her way through the gate while another resident entered or left, or she'd have to mount the railings on one of the more hidden sides of the gardens, where high laurel or low-branched oak boughs would conceal her from the houses over the road.

But here, more than halfway through her journey, she no longer felt the urgency of getting to Belgrave Square. The golden light, the bustle, and most of all the unselfconscious mingling of the market lads with the finely clad opera goers, the unexpected sense of oneness in it all, held her suspended. Nothing terribly bad could happen here. This was her feeling. Providence was all around. It didn't just exist for the rich or even for the lucky, and Jenny, despite everything, was a child of providence.

She had often heard the story of a young woman being turned down by inn after inn until finally gaining admittance into a stable. Everyone must go through a tunnel of fire before arriving at fulfillment. The golden light around her was a reminder of this. She did not know whether she would have to beg or find a way to sell flowers, or whether she would successfully challenge the Harkers and shame them into providing for her. But a child was growing inside her. God would not allow it to starve.

She stood in front of one of the low pillars by the market, feet cushioned by a cabbage leaf as her eyes caught the sheen of a top hat in the sun. She found herself smiling. How could anything be impossible here? One of the operagoers caught her eye, a tall man with a thick moustache like an upturned horseshoe, a leftover style from aristocrats from the end of the last century. It was a mark of distinction and made him look proud, as though he was solemnly frowning at all he surveyed. He seemed to be judging her too, even though she was surely far beneath his notice. She recognized him, or thought she did. The wife had a similar air to her husband, haughty, unsmiling, and Jenny felt another prick of recognition. If Jenny had been compelled to describe their manner, she would have said both of them were there as an obligation. They had to be at the opera, and they had to be seen. Any idea of enjoyment seemed the furthest thing from their minds.

She realized who these people were just as they disappeared behind one of the entrance pillars. The realization depressed her, brought her back to the day's events—her confrontation with Miss Abree, her brief interview with Mrs. Harker. Worst of all, it brought back to her the fruitless eastward tramp and Aunt Laura's death. She fingered the remaining coins in her skirt pocket. This was all she was now, all she was worth. She was far more alone than any of these people. Barrow boys, girls selling flowers, taxi drivers, porters; they all had something, an occupation.

The gentleman had once been a guest in the Harker home. He was lord of somewhere or other, an unlikely kind of place like Bognor Regis or Golders Green. Mrs. Rogers had been flustered at his visit. Her nerves had affected Jenny too and made her tense. The lord's wife had wanted a slice of lemon rather than milk in her tea, a request that had caused confusion and delay with the serving. In the end Jenny's hand had trembled as she'd handed the lord's wife her cup. Some of the tea had spilled onto the saucer, flooding the lemon slice. They hadn't made a fuss about it, but neither had they said anything conciliatory, which would have been easy enough for them to do. Seriousness seemed to hang over this man—Lord *Godalming*, she remembered now—like a cloud. Seeing him now broke the spell of Covent Garden, made her more aware of the clouds gathering like an approaching army over the roofs and turrets to the east. London was not as large as she would have liked to believe. The tendrils of her disgrace could easily connect the city's disparate parts—Belgrave Square and Covent Garden, solicitor and lord, and every class, location, and person in between. She had been fired from her position. She was pregnant. It would likely rain tonight. There was no refuge.

She decided to head west after all.

19. JONATHAN HARKER

JONATHAN HAD NOT DECIDED he was going to go to Hanwell until he stooped under the bonnet of the cab, closed the door, and smelled the leather. He had to say something. The driver's porcine head was half-turned, neck rippling under his cap. It was as though he sensed trouble. Had he hailed the man before? Jonathan wondered. Perhaps in his cups? The name just came out: "County Mental Hospital, Hanwell." He couldn't visit Holmwood again. He couldn't face his own club; the members were bound to ask questions about Mina and Abree. Even at the best of times he felt out of place, and he had no son to whom he could pass his membership.

Going to Hanwell coincided happily with what he'd told Mrs. Rogers. As the cab driver sighed, turned the wheel, and moved off, Jonathan noticed the cloud bank high over the chimneys, still miles away but approaching quickly, like ink on blotting paper. The driver clearly wasn't happy with his commission. Was it too long a journey perhaps? Or would it be too hard to get a return ride? Jonathan checked his wallet. He had more than enough money—two fives. More importantly, he still had that letter nestled between the banknotes, the letter from Hanwell's governor. He hadn't lied to Mrs. Rogers. This fact became dreadfully important as the taxi bumped westwards towards the Kensington suburbs. It allowed him to retain a small seed of self-respect, even after so much had been stripped away. He hadn't lied. This journey *was* to do with work. He had received the note from the Hanwell governor while he was in his office, after all. He could pretend that it had come to him because he was a solicitor.

His journey, however, was about much more than work. It was about everything. The note had presaged his recent nightmares. It was the thing that had built up to his scream, to his coming home drunk last night, to Jenny telling him her news. Without the note, none of these things would have happened, or so it seemed to Jonathan. It was almost like his forbidden fruit, except that he'd opened the envelope innocently, not as a response to a dare. The return address on the top left-hand corner had merely been that of the hospital. It had held no prior warnings.

Van Helsing was still alive. This was the astounding news that had opened up to him as he unfolded the paper. The old professor was residing at the County Mental Hospital at Hanwell. The governor wished Jonathan to visit, felt it might alleviate his patient's mental torment and affliction. He'd even said that Mr. Harker could be accommodated after hours or on the weekends if he was too busy with his practice during the work day. Jonathan had hidden the note in his wallet because he didn't want it on his desk where his secretary might notice it. And then he had tried to forget about it. But the note had remained there in his wallet. Hidden among the bills, it had worked away at him slowly, quietly. It had burned right through into his dreams and nightmares.

It had even spilled over onto Mina. *Van Helsing*, she had said. *Well he must be dead by now.* It was as though she knew, as though something had already hinted to her of a possibility to the contrary. The air had become electric with intuitions and super-sensitivities.

It wasn't long before they were through the suburbs and into open country, private estates, and farmland. The sun grew more bloated as it lowered, scattering crimson and gold on the midsummer foliage, the brick walls, and buildings. The light seemed unusually rich and intense, as though it recognized the narrowing opportunity to dance with the night as the rainstorm approached behind them. Like an impressionist, Jonathan saw leaves and grass as every colour but green. The gold outside the window battered his eyes, and he had to look away briefly.

"You visiting someone, guv'nor?" asked the driver. It was the first time he had spoken.

"Yes, you can wait for me."

The answer seemed to relax the man. His shoulders dropped and he started whistling through his teeth.

Soon Hanwell appeared like a city state, its pale walls subdividing sections of the grounds, long buildings with endless windows, a spire, and some curiously-shaped towers—some octagons, some ovals. Jonathan had never been here but he knew about it, and something quivered inside him as they turned towards the long entranceway. Seward had committed suicide. Van Helsing was in an asylum, not as a doctor, not to diagnose or deliberate on moral insanity. He was here as a patient. The world was closing in.

The tires crunched over the gravel and came to a halt in the centre of a horseshoe loop under an imposing ash tree. Omar Khayyam said the moving finger moved on, but for the second time tonight, Jonathan rebelled against the poet; his moving finger retraced every mistake over and over in perpetuity, just as a mouse runs upon a wheel but never advances.

The driver was quick to move around the car and open the door for Jonathan. He looked both fascinated and afraid as he surveyed the grand main building and then turned to look at the patches of surrounding parklands. Perhaps he was concerned about violent lunatics crouching in the bushes, waiting for an opportunity to make away with his car.

Jonathan thanked him. "I'll be less than an hour," he said. In reality, he had no idea how long he'd be, but it felt better to sound certain. It calmed the turbulence in his stomach. He was a lawyer. He must act like one. This was always a kind of shield. A guardian of the law must be firm, and he must say and do nothing until he was certain of his course.

Knocking on the front door of such a vast organization seemed absurd, so when he reached the top step he merely turned the brass handle and found, as he had expected, that the door was unlocked. He stepped into a rather pleasant, grand lobby, with black-and-white tiles much in the style of his own home's entrance and a square spiral staircase ahead of him, its oak bannister disappearing into bright artificial light. It seemed to Jonathan that upstairs was where business was likely done. He imagined a wide-open ward with a lofty ceiling from which electrical lights hung down, their inverted cone shades dismissing all shadow and accentuating the starkness of the simple iron-framed beds and white sheets. White-clad nurses and orderlies would cluster in groups and wheel around trolleys with mysterious electrical gadgets, rubber tubes, pincers, kidney-shaped bedpans.

But Jonathan could hear no faint rattling of wheels, nor was there any other indication of movement. It was possible, he supposed, the main building was for administration only. He walked towards the grille, his footsteps echoing in the silence. Pulling out his wallet, he opened it, and slid out the note from the governor.

"This came to me last week," he said. "I was away." His hand trembled slightly as he slid it through the inch-high gap at the bottom. The man put his hand to his glasses and read. He said nothing, and Jonathan's feet became restless. He was suddenly eleven years old again, awaiting the cane from his headmaster. "I am a solicitor," he blurted.

Jonathan immediately regretted this. He'd suggested he was the patient's solicitor, and he now might have to explain that he was not, so the information was not only irrelevant but misleading. The man looked up at him, his eyes magnified by his lenses.

Jonathan got ready to take back the statement, but the man spoke first. "The governor is not here at present, Mr. Harker." Jonathan was surprised, and a little disappointed, by the man's accent, which was not the precise Teutonic one he'd been expecting, but rather the flattened vowels of the London-raised lower middle classes. He might as well be a bus conductor. "But since the note comes from the governor himself," he continued, "and you have come all the way here, I will call up to the appropriate wing to see if someone can take you to the patient."

He'd already picked up the phone receiver and was starting to dial. Jonathan felt a flood of panic. This was all too easy. The imposing place, the grille, the man's accent had promised obstacle after obstacle. Visits such as this one usually promised forms and bureaucracy and the near certainty of being turned away. But the man was already talking to someone in low mumbling tones. And then he nodded and put down the receiver.

"If you'll just wait here for a few moments, Mr. Harker, someone will come and escort you to the patient."

Jonathan felt dazed as he followed the young orderly down the corridor. As it turned out, Van Helsing was on the same floor of the same building. There were no wards, apparently, just a series of long corridors with white, numbered doors. The light source—evenly spaced reverse-coned shades—was the only detail he'd guessed correctly.

He'd given up control, and it worried him how easily it had happened. The further he moved through this narrow corridor, the deeper he burrowed into the asylum building, the more he was trapping himself in its honeycomb maze. He felt breathless and shivery, but he couldn't stop. He couldn't tell the young man, who had a quick smile and an eager-to-please manner, he'd changed his mind.

The key ring was jangling on the orderly's belt at present,

but in a moment, any moment, he would pause, raise the keys, and unlock one of the doors. The closeness of Van Helsing, thirty years on, made the fact of him no more real to Jonathan. This was how he imagined death must be to the terminally ill: Knowing it was coming, knowing it was inescapable, but not knowing the exact time.

"Here it is," the orderly said, lifting the keys from the ring without removing them just as Jonathan had imagined he would. His voice was quiet, calm. He knocked briskly twice, waited a second, then slipped in his key, turned, and entered. He motioned for Jonathan to follow.

Seated at a desk on the far wall was a man in a white shirt with black braces and slacks. Books were piled haphazardly on his desk. At first Jonathan thought it was a mistake. The man looked like Van Helsing in a vague kind of way, the same stocky, compact frame, the same height, but it was a too literal incarnation. For a start, he was too young. Jonathan had been expecting a heap of crinkled, leathery skin and bone, something barely recognizable as human; the older people were the less they were expected to resemble who they had once been. The man before him was old, certainly, but not entirely decrepit. He might be Van Helsing's son, perhaps, if he possessed one, but surely not the man himself.

The inmate had twisted his frame to see his visitors. His hair was longer, straighter than Van Helsing's. Van Helsing's hair had stood like a brush going back from his forehead, and it had been white but thick. Patches of pink scalp shone through this man's hair. His eyes though, swollen under thick-lensed glasses, were on Jonathan. They seemed to recognize him.

Jonathan realized this had to be Van Helsing. It had been only a short leap for Van Helsing from middle to old age. He must have been very much younger than Jonathan had supposed in 1890.

"I'll leave you two for twenty minutes, Mr. Harker, and then I'll check back."

The door closed. Jonathan heard the key turn in the lock. He became aware of Van Helsing's breathing.

"You've come," Van Helsing said. He did not smile. His mouth seemed crooked. Was he embarrassed? Afraid?

Everything was quite different from how Jonathan had imagined it would be. This was a room, not a cell. The bedframe was wood, not iron. The walls were papered, not bare brick. Practices had changed since Dr. Seward's time.

"You were expecting me then?" said Jonathan.

"My young friend," said Van Helsing, "we all expect the angel of death sometime."

The statement jolted Jonathan. Van Helsing saw this. His mouth formed a smile. Then he removed his thick glasses with a flourish, as though they were a hat being doffed for the sake of deference. He laid them on his desk. Van Helsing's eyes seemed raw and exposed without the lenses, surrounded as they were by little pink wrinkles. It was the face of a creature just born, skin until recently swimming in amniotic fluid, eyes too delicate for the light.

"Will you take a seat, my old friend?" He gestured to a chair in the corner of the room, close by his own.

Jonathan hesitated. Taking the chair would bring him further into the room. He wondered if this old man was really safe. But Van Helsing's eyes were on him, expectant. He succumbed to the pressure, moving silently to the chair, turning it to face the old professor, and lowering himself into it.

"Seeing an old comrade-in-arms is a pleasure I hardly dare anticipate these days. And this is a pleasure indeed." Jonathan had quite forgotten about Van Helsing's old world courtliness, the sense of certainty and conviction, as well as the charm. His manners seemed to represent the wisdom of generations.

"Why?" Jonathan said, but then paused. The hesitation turned into a silence. He didn't know how to continue.

"You wish to know why I would see you as the angel of death"—Van Helsing's eyes were full of humour—"but you are too delicate to ask." He clapped his hands together and gave a little soundless laugh. "Oh, how I miss my old English friends, my Jonathan Harker, my poor John Seward, Arthur Holmwood, excuse me, Lord Godalming!"

"Yes," said Jonathan. He flicked some imaginary dust from his trousers.

"But it is so, is it not, my dear Jonathan? You have thought about the old days, about mistakes and uncertainties. They have, as you English say, snowballed through the years. You wonder about that professor from Utrecht who came to advise you with all his odd notions, his garlic, and his talk of moral insanity."

At the last phrase, Jonathan's eyes wandered the room. It wasn't deliberate, but he realized his message was clear. Van Helsing smiled. "And here is this old professor we trusted so much with his talk of sane and insane, evil and good. Here he is in one of your English asylums."

"Yes," said Jonathan, "here you are."

"You wish it was him, the strange old professor, who was dead and not dear Lucy, so beloved of Arthur."

Jonathan was silent.

"Your dreams are troubled. The old days have returned. I know you, my friend. You believe that you can wipe away sin and crime with more sin and crime."

A jet of anger flashed within Jonathan. "I have committed no sin, perpetrated no crime, and have no intention of harming you."

Van Helsing smiled again.

"I had forgotten, my dear friend, Jonathan, that you have been a lawyer for many years now."

"I'm sorry?"

"Silence and denial, my dear friend—these are your tools. Words, too many of them, are your enemies, are they not?"

"I can't imagine what you mean by that, Professor Van Helsing. I am not sure what I would have to deny, or what my silence means beyond not having anything to say."

"Yet, my friend, it worries you when I say something and do not explain it."

"For instance?"

"For instance, how are you my angel of death?"

Jonathan shifted in his seat and felt a heat rise up beyond his collar. "You must feel free to explain it, if you wish."

"My friend, I am coming to the end of my journey. I am about to rejoin the great ocean from which we are drawn." He put one hand to his ear. "I already catch the echoes of eternity. It is large and hollow indeed. But these echoes, my friend, allow me to glimpse just a little beyond my five senses."

He leaned forward and reached out towards Jonathan, his pink, swollen hand—the same one he had used to cup his ear—lowering onto Jonathan's knee. Jonathan didn't want Van Helsing's hand on him, but he knew it would be churlish to object.

"My friend, I know you. You would like to believe it was me, and not your friend Arthur, who gripped the hammer that pounded the stake that ended dear Lucy's life. You would like to believe it was me who killed the count."

Jonathan felt a faint battering in his chest, like the wings of some flying insect trapped within his ribcage. "You did provide the instruments, Professor," he said. "You urged us towards these tasks."

"Yet the decisions were not mine, nor were the crimes. You were so like children, charming, frightened children!" He smiled and lifted his hand from Jonathan's knee. "Your young ladies, dear Miss Lucy and Madame Mina, were like beloved toys that were broken. You needed some adult to fix them for you or throw them out of sight and replace them. Is this not so?"

The battering in Jonathan's chest became more intense. It was no longer an insect, more like a hummingbird. "Our so brave Arthur," Van Helsing continued, "pardon me, Lord Godalming, could never had been happy with Miss Lucy after she'd been known by the foreign count. I know you English boys so well! He needed someone to tell him it was right for him to act as he did. I did him this service. I knew you could not be happy with so dear Madame Mina if you suspected the same fate had befallen her. But you were already married. A man may kill his fiancée more easily than his wife." He smiled rather sadly at Jonathan. For a moment, it seemed like real pity. "So, how could I help my friend, Jonathan?"

Jonathan wanted to stop him, felt an urge to leap from his chair and cover the old man's mouth. But he merely coughed and stiffened.

"An evil influence, to those of a superstitious bent, is a supernatural influence. And you boys, you sweet boys, were superstitious indeed, despite all your so rational talk."

"You were rather superstitious too, I remember," Jonathan said. He had begun to tremble deep inside.

"I was as you needed me to be, my friend. A supernatural villain would excuse your so dear wife, so this is what Count Dracula became. I persuaded you it was in your power to root out this extraordinary evil and punish this foreign demon for besmirching your love. But it was you, not me. It was Lord Godalming who struck Lucy with the stake. It was you who ripped the count's throat with you Kukri knife."

Jonathan's throat tightened, almost as if someone were strangling him. He knew he should issue a simple denial, especially about Mina. Van Helsing really had deviated from history here. Mina had been charmed by the count; it was true. She had been flattered. He knew this. But she'd always been a long way, a very long way indeed, from degrading herself as Lucy had done. There was no need to excuse her for anything. Why did the old man not see the difference? It was possible the old man was senile, and if Jonathan could convince him he was wrong about Mina he might even be persuaded it was all a delusion. Perhaps this was what the governor meant by calling for his help. He had perhaps heard Van Helsing's mad ramblings and sought out a rational person who had been involved in Van Helsing's past to put him right.

He leaned back. The battering sensation faded, along with the deep trembling. Only one thorn remained. Mina. Why had Van Helsing implied there had been something more than flirtation?

"How much of this have you told the governor here?" Jonathan asked calmly.

"None of it, my friend," said Van Helsing. "None, as yet."

"Really?" Jonathan wanted to disbelieve him. "So why did he send for me?"

"*I* sent for you. I asked the governor if he would send the request in his own hand. He was happy to oblige me."

Jonathan paused for a moment, saw the crinkles around the old man's eyes, and weighed his courteous, formal phrasings. Of course, this old man would have been able to persuade the governor to do anything.

"But impending death is a strange thing, my dear Jonathan. It makes one selfish. You would think, would you not, one would be thinking only of the wellbeing of those one leaves behind? But I am dying, my dear Jonathan, and I worry for my soul. I can't afford to be generous." He smiled. "In the last few months I have become a Christian, a Jew, a Hindu, and a Muslim. I wish to cover every base. Is this not how you say it? Suicide is a mortal sin, so this is not an option. Protecting others by keeping my secrets is also a sin. I must unburden myself as I prepare my soul for the hereafter. I must plague others with my selfishness. I must threaten harm to my dear friend Jonathan Harker, his so sweet wife, Mina, and my old friend Arthur with his fine, strong arms."

A vision flashed through Jonathan's mind—Arthur with the mallet and the stake. Van Helsing's eyes held his, and then he shrugged.

"What harm?" Jonathan asked carefully.

"I am planning a full and open confession of everything. I have been working on it for weeks."

Jonathan's gaze scanned the surface of Van Helsing's desk. There were books, but there was also a fountain pen and what seemed to be an open journal. "You can't," he said after too long a silence. "No one would believe you." His throat constricted again.

Van Helsing's eyes seemed to wrinkle in pity. "And yet *you* all believed me, did you not, when I showed you a way out of your grief thirty years ago? The trick of getting people to believe you, Jonathan, is simply to tell them something they want to hear. There are radicals enough in your modern police force who would like to name a lord and a solicitor among their prey."

Jonathan's hand trembled, and he laid it down flat on his chair so Van Helsing wouldn't notice. He wished the old man would stop. He should not have come. Was it laziness or curiosity that had brought him? He could almost believe Van Helsing had summoned him through some supernatural means, but blindness and stupidity needed no special help. Jonathan was merely a fool.

"I am sorry, my dear old friend," said Van Helsing. "There is only one way you can stop me. This is why I referred to you in my quaint way as my deliverer."

A tap came. A key turned and the door swung open.

"Give us five more minutes, my friend," Van Helsing said to the orderly.

The orderly looked at him for confirmation. Jonathan nodded unevenly. The orderly smiled, closed the door, and again came the sound of the key turning.

"If you die from another's hand," said Jonathan hoarsely, "the sin, if you call it that, will remain."

"Oh, but no, my friend!" Van Helsing reached out once more, touching Jonathan's hand lightly with his own. The old man's fingers were warm. "My *intention* would have been to confess. It makes all the difference in the world. Death is the best of all excuses, is it not?" As he spoke he let his hand fall from Jonathan's. He turned to the desk, pushed aside some papers, picked up a letter knife, and then turned back to Jonathan. "My fingerprints are on it—you need not worry. Your own are easily explained. Once you have stabbed me, remove it with this handle and claim I killed myself before you could stop me."

Jonathan began to shiver wildly.

"Courage, my friend! Do this for your dear Madame Mina just as Arthur struck for Lucy."

Although he was scarcely aware of it, Jonathan must have glanced at the papers on Van Helsing's desk as the professor said, "Don't worry about those. The governor has been told that in the event of my death, all my personal papers are to be burned unless there are instructions to the contrary. He will carry out my request to the letter. Have no fear."

Van Helsing turned the blade in his hands so that the wooden handle faced Jonathan. It was light, but the blade was very thin and sharp. The metal caught the hanging light.

"Do it for Mina! You know, don't you, that the count defiled her just as he defiled Lucy?"

Jonathan began to shake his head. "No. No, he did not." But the handle now rested in his palm. His fingers curled around it and gripped it so he might keep from shaking.

"That fine son of yours. The one who so bravely died in the war—I kept up with all the news of my friends, do not fear—you know he was really the count's."

"No."

But Van Helsing was looking at him in pity, not cunning. The movement came like a spasm through Jonathan.

Van Helsing gasped. His hand trembled and came down on Jonathan's. "My boys," he whispered. "Good boys!" There was a moment, a smile. Then blood spouted from his lips. The eyes remained open but the life was gone. His head bowed slowly. Blood continued to fall like a stream onto the carpet. The pink of his scalp shone in the overhead light.

20. ARTHUR HOLMWOOD, LORD GODALMING

ARTHUR WAS GROWING MORE and more uncomfortable as the evening progressed. The heat of so many bodies, the fluttering fans and coughs were a familiar enough background to any performance. As he and Alice were in their box far above the press of flesh, he was spared these most obvious evils. But there were other sources of unease: the lurid stage lights; the eastern, oriental sets with arches and shimmering silk; and the shining cloth, its peacock-themed pattern dotted with dozens of turquoise eyes, that hung across one wall of Herod's palace. Each of these eyes seemed to stare through him. Worse than this, the piercing light of the artificial moon, achieved through some effect Arthur couldn't guess, seemed to freeze him in its spotlight. Arthur wished his wife, who had been absorbed in the opera but detached from him, would move closer. If it would not have seemed so entirely out of character, Arthur would have budged his own seat closer and taken her hand.

No wonder the Lord Chamberlain had banned the opera in Britain when it first emerged from the sewer of Oscar Wilde's imagination. It was hideous and disturbing, full of lust and immorality. Only a country suffering from some dreadful moral malaise would even consider allowing its performance. Narraboth, one of Herod's officers, is sick with desire for Salome. But Salome is full of perverse love for the half-naked prisoner, John the Baptist, and repeatedly begs to touch the holy man. Narraboth kills himself when he sees her love for the Baptist, and Herod, bizarrely, slips in his blood. Herod himself takes on Narraboth's foul passion for the beautiful but grotesque Salome, his stepdaughter. Arthur understood these details from the program only, as the company was presenting Salome in the German translation, a perverse self-flagellation given the number of sons and brothers of audience members who had been felled by German bullets. According to the program, Wilde's original had been written in English and French.

All this was all bad enough, but Arthur knew, from what he had read about the opera, that worse was to follow. As the grumbling mass of humanity took their seats after intermission, he braced himself for the onslaught of bad taste that was to come. Intermission had provided a respite of a kind, but it had given also a hint of the unexpected. He'd as soon have stayed where he was, but when Alice had risen, seemingly ready to move out into the foyer for refreshments, Arthur had stood and passed over her stole, which she had wrapped serenely about her shoulders. They had passed through the door, which had been opened for them by the attendants.

The first thing he had seen though the rising cigar smoke in the heavy carpeted area was a clergyman's daughter he'd once pinned a medal on for her nursing service in the war. He hadn't remembered the name straightaway, but he knew from something he'd been told once by Mina Harker that she was a friend of Abree, her daughter. Such was the stranglehold of London. No one of note is ever invisible. Everyone is always on display.

Arthur might have considered ignoring her and indeed could have done quite successfully; an attendant had come to them with a tray of hock and he'd had to turn away from her slightly to take his glass. But then, as he'd glanced over, she had caught his eye and had smiled in recognition. Given the nature of their connection, her service to those stricken in battle, he had been unable to justify turning away again, and so bowed first at her and then at the finely dressed dark-haired man at her side. It was he who moved towards Arthur and introduced himself. And when he did so, a dual reaction occurred in Arthur's chest, both a tightening and a relief. Such a sensation ought to be impossible, like seeing water run simultaneously east and west in the same river, but it was not. This dark-haired stranger was the very Professor Florescu whose presence in London had sent Harker into a panic. Talking to him might have been a concern but for the man's impeccable manners and for the fact he was with a sweet-natured clergyman's daughter. The danger had passed before it had begun.

"I am afraid, Lord Godalming," Professor Florescu had said, "that the subject matter and style of tonight's opera has taken us somewhat by surprise."

"How so, Professor?" Alice had asked, somewhat argumentatively. Arthur's wife concealed her natural reserve by appearing to disapprove of people who were new to her.

"I am used to Puccini, Lady Godalming, to romantic love expressed *as* romantic love. This seems a barbarous tale."

Arthur had laughed. "I couldn't agree with you more, Professor. A simple love story is what this country needs, especially these days."

The professor had smiled and held Arthur's gaze.

Arthur had looked down at his wine. A wavering stream of bubbles had danced to the surface and then disappeared with a barely audible hiss. Alice had begun talking to Helen Morrison, asking her a little too pointedly about her studies and the uses to which she might put them. The professor's gaze had remained on Arthur in a way that had seemed far too steady and intimate, a slight smile playing on his lips.

The bell had rung, thankfully calling them all back to their box. Arthur had nodded at the young professor, who appeared not to respond, except to continue looking directly at him. With a tight smile at Helen Morrison, Arthur had taken Alice's arm and placed their glasses on the proffered tray. Even while he turned, the professor's eyes had remained fixed on him. Arthur had wondered if perhaps he had unknowingly interrupted the professor, and if this was the reason for the prolonged stare. The foreigner was confused, possibly. It was likely he didn't realize how out of touch with etiquette his manner was.

Now Salome cavorted under the piercing moon. The holy man's metal cage beneath her feet, she peeled one of her veils from her body and held it aloft. The scarlet fabric rippled as she circled to the spiralling melody. The thought struck Arthur: the professor had only been polite and charming while the ladies had been part of the conversation. When they had distracted each other, when the professor had held Arthur's attention alone, this had been when his stare had become insolent. This was not a man unfamiliar with etiquette. This was hostility, deliberate and calculated.

Was it possible Harker had been right? Did Professor Florescu know exactly who they all were? As Lord Godalming, no doubt his name and position made him more memorable to the foreigner than the others. No doubt he'd be held more responsible too.

Arthur felt a weight dropping like a stone onto his chest. The music, loud and exotic, the dancing woman, the men in a semi-circle around her, the too-vibrant colours, was all too much. He tried to take a breath, but the air would not come.

He was thinking of another circle of men, another scarlet woman.

"This is no longer Lucy," Van Helsing had said quietly. His hand had rested on Lucy's carved mahogany headboard. As though demonstrating Van Helsing's point, the white silk bed curtains had been drawn as far as they would go, exposing Lucy entirely to the collective gaze. It had been the truth. This woman, drugged and sleeping, had been Lucy no longer. Lucy would never have laughed and flirted the way this woman had flirted. Lucy would never have licked her fingertips and stared across the dinner table at a foreigner the way this woman had done. Lucy would never have taken Arthur's hand and plunged it where she did, and then laughed when he had pulled it away, horrified.

Salome spun, unwrapping another veil. Herod held its corner. The music lulled. Paused in profile, hand on her thigh, Salome resembled Lucy. Her hair was dark, while Lucy's had been fair, but the nose, slightly upturned, and the brow were like his former fiancée's. Arthur was there again, prickling with anger, incredulous that she should be smiling at him after her performance on the settee with the count. He'd brought her into his study, escaping for the moment the intense embarrassment of the scene she'd made in front of their friends.

"What do you think you are doing?" he'd fumed. He had felt the steam of anger rising. But still she'd smiled even as she'd moved behind a leather chair and placed her hands protectively around its shoulders.

"Arthur!" she'd said half coaxing, half afraid. "It's nothing, really."

Her cheeks had been flushed, her eyes rather darker than usual as though her pupils were dilated. She'd started laughing, suddenly and desperately, like a mad woman, Arthur had thought. He had turned to the door behind him, hoping the sound had not carried. When he had turned back, he found she'd emerged from behind the chair. She'd stopped laughing now and something else had come across her face—a pained emotion, distorting her features. "I just want," she had said, struggling, "your maid."

She had said no more. He had known to whom she referred, but she'd trapped him into asking for clarification.

"Which maid?"

"You know the one, Arthur."

She'd been coming closer to him with each exchange. "I tried to make it not matter. I tried to not care. You were my prince!"

Her eyes had shone as she said the last part. Had this been an explanation for her behaviour—her finger licking at the dinner table, gushing provocatively to the count afterwards on the settee? Suddenly, she had seemed more like the Lucy he knew; her voice had been infused with such hope, such belief in him. He had allowed himself to move closer, readied himself to comfort her. No real harm was done, after all. He'd merely been embarrassed in front of his friends. If she'd meant to use her allure seriously with the count, she'd hardly have done it so openly.

"What happened to her?" she had said.

He had stalled, becoming rigid again.

"Who?"

"The maid, the one who..." She looked down. Her lip trembled.

"She left," he had said. "I don't know after that."

Lucy had looked to the side as though receiving a blow. "I understand," she had said, but it had sounded odd, as though she had been forcing herself to say it. "I understand that it's different for men." She'd closed in on Arthur again. She'd reached for and taken his hand, and had stroked his fingers feverishly in her own. He'd been expecting her to curl his fingers and press his loose fist, locked in her own, close to her chest, as she had done once before on the day of his proposal. It had been a sweet, chaste moment, all the more tantalizing as it had also promised a world of licence to come after the wedding, and he had treasured the memory. The gesture had been many times diminished after all her brazen flirting with the count, but it had been something to hold on to.

But she had not repeated the action. Instead, she had plunged his opened hand into the space between her legs. And when he had pulled back, startled—had he pushed her away too, by the shoulders? He couldn't remember—her hand had flown to her mouth. At first, he'd assumed this was because she had been shocked by her own actions, but then she'd started laughing for the second time, laughing so hard that tears began to spring from her eyes.

Arthur had backed away hardly knowing what else to do. But her eyes had remained on him even as her laughter had coughed to a halt. Was she laughing at *him*? "Arthur!" she had said, her voice rasping as she tried to clear her throat. "Why are you afraid of me?" There had been an odd pleading in her eyes, and Arthur had felt stifled by the weight of the perversity. "What about the maid? You didn't fear her." "She was a servant," he had said harshly. "You are supposed to be my fiancée."

She had taken this in, her expression suspended but questioning. Then her face had crumpled. The tears had been from grief this time. "Oh Arthur, I'm sorry. I don't understand myself." She had come closer but kept her arms to her sides as though she were a ship's figurehead. She had known that she had revolted him, her attitude had seemed to say; she had known he did not want her touch at this moment. "Help me, Arthur! Can we go back to how it was?"

"Lucy," he had said. The tenderness in his voice had taken him by surprise. Some up-swell of emotion had come over him, an emotion that was for who she had been rather than who she had become. "I promise you, I promise I will make sure you are always the woman I fell in love with."

Salome still danced. Another veil, this one green and translucent, was held aloft for a moment. Then it fluttered down into the outstretched hand of King Herod. Salome turned. Herod fell to his knees. The contours of Salome's body had become quite clear through the remaining veils. Some flesh-coloured stocking material no doubt covered the performer's skin, but he could sense the discomfort from the stalls below, the coughs, the embarrassed fluttering of fans.

It affected Arthur too. He tried to take another breath, and it seemed difficult, like there was a weight upon his chest. His eyes watered, blurring the veils. What had he meant by the promise all those years ago? Had he already guessed what he might be forced to do?

He remembered the feeling of a small splinter entering his palm. "This is no longer Lucy," Van Helsing had said. The phrase played and replayed in his head like a phonograph disk catching a needle at the same point. The splinter had come from the rough-hewn stake in Arthur's left hand. It was the splinter that had done it, Arthur remembered. The effortless piercing of his hand had been a premonition. It had purged him of any doubts. Skin was to be breached. This was its purpose throughout history: Jesus on the cross; Lucy before him. He'd been hesitating. But he had known it was inevitable. It had been the only way out. Van Helsing had said the count knew her already; he had breached those most intimate seals not only of the mind, but of the body. The delicacy of Van Helsing's phrases had contrived to make the reality even more obscene than if he'd used the language of the gutter. But the result was the same. Arthur couldn't marry her, nor could he break his engagement without loss of honour. *Take this cup from my lips*, he'd wanted to say to Van Helsing. But there had been no going back. The moment had been upon him. Thunder had filled the air. It had taken a moment to recognize that the thunder had been coming from within, not without, that his own heart, his own pulse had been the cause. Something terrible and momentous had been upon them all. He had been the instrument of this change. He had been expected to bring about a purging. Van Helsing, the wise old professor, had expected it. His friend, John Seward, sensible, serious John had expected it too. So had Harker, who'd known the count before any of them.

"Go on," he had asked Van Helsing. "Tell me what to do."

Arthur had received the stake and the mallet.

He couldn't see Salome anymore. She was a blur. He felt dizzy, and the stage was receding. Lucy, however, was clear. He could see her pink lips parted in sleep, her white brow furrowed, and he could feel the expectant energy of those around him—Seward, Harker, Quincey Morris, and Van Helsing. It was true, everything the professor had said. The foreigner had soiled her. How could he marry the brazen lustful creature she'd become? How could he lie with her in his marital bed knowing that Dracula been there already, perverting and tantalizing her senses so much that she had become as depraved as any whore in a London brothel? What monsters would Arthur and Lucy produce if their union ever bore children? He could picture them—white-faced, red-lipped imps, deformed of body and mind.

It had been his mistake initially. Arthur knew that. If he hadn't confessed about his affair with the little domestic, if he hadn't tried to wipe the slate clean, she might not have come under the influence of the suave foreigner. She had been too fragile, the framework of her morality too delicate. She had been unable to cope with this secret her fiancé had tried to foist upon her. For the life of him, Arthur could not understand the noble, misguided influence that had caused him to tell her all this. His role as future husband had been to protect, not confide. Once she had plunged into what Van Helsing had called moral insanity, there had been no escape. His confession had opened the box and it could not be closed. Sweet Lucy had become a carnal monster. She had been broken, irrevocably, and he had been unable to be in the same room with her, let alone marry her. But a gentleman does not go back on a promise. As long as she lived he *must* marry her. He'd been over and over the point. There had been only one way out, and Van Helsing had held out a promise to him. He was a doctor of metaphysics, half scientist and half priest. He'd insisted her soul would be preserved in all its sweet innocence if only she were brought through this ring of fire, this cleansing.

He had placed the point over her heart, heard Seward gasp, and turned. He'd half hoped for an interruption, for someone to find a reason why this could not be done. But the young doctor's eyes had been fixed upon the stake. There had been agony in Seward's face, but it was the pain of anticipation, not of warning. John had trusted Van Helsing.

"Be like Thor, young Arthur, my friend," Van Helsing had whispered. "You are the only one on earth with the right to perform this deed because she has given herself to you in betrothal. Be fearless and swift!"

Arthur had raised the mallet, ready to strike.

The music continued, eastern, disorganized, rising to cacophony. He'd given up trying to breathe now. John Seward was before him in Arthur's study, serious, white-faced John, still young several years on, but haunted by troubles. Arthur had asked his friend to sit, but John had not done so. He'd tried to pour him a drink but he'd refused. "I've done everything you've asked of me, Arthur. Everything," he'd said. Arthur had known, from his stance, from his tone, this was a parting of the ways. "I've moved the action from her bedroom to her crypt. I've made it as clear as I possibly can that she was a vampire and that she was already dead."

Arthur had had his arguments ready. "Yes," he had said, "but she is too much like a living person in this scene. She is too much like herself. And worse, she actually calls to me by name. This is not a complete possession. What demon leaves a vestige of its host's personality?"

"I don't know about demons, Arthur," John had said stiffly, "and neither do you."

"It was Van Helsing's idea," Arthur had said. He had thought he meant the diaries, but when he heard his voice and saw John wince, he had realized it applied to everything: how they had dealt with Lucy, the stalking of the count. It sounded pathetic. He'd tried to recover. "The point, John, is to have something that would convince the Hellfire Club should we ever need it, should we ever run into legal difficulties. I think your training in psychiatry has prevented you from depicting a full, supernatural event. It might be a little more honest this way, but also more dangerous."

They'd been through all this before, but Arthur had found it more comfortable to patronize than to plead. The Hellfire Club boasted several London judges, a number of barristers and lords, and many MPs. Unimaginative and dull as they were individually, their web had provided a safe landing for many who'd been in trouble. Arthur had known many more members than John. It had been easy to sound more worldly than his friend.

"We're writing our history, John, like any conquering army. It's our duty, for our children, their children, for everything that follows to make it an ennobling story." Arthur had almost smiled. This was true, he'd thought, and it was universal. Life was a scrawl, scruffy and distorted. We make sense of events only long after they have occurred.

But the physician still hadn't looked impressed. "Arthur," he'd said. "I've lied too much already. You have the final draft I will write. I don't need the Hellfire Club or anyone else."

John had turned and left soundlessly. The final words *I don't need the Hellfire Club or anyone else* had resounded oddly in the silence. At first Arthur hadn't known why, but he soon would. Seward would end his life before the next morning.

Everything had gone dark. He felt it again—that splinter, scooping into his flesh, saw the dint of white around the point. Cymbals crashed, and drums rolled. Arthur saw the hammer pound onto the stake-head. Lucy. John Seward. The count. So much death. So much madness. But whose madness?

He was aware of a hand on his shoulder. A woman's voice, not Lucy's, was calling to him. A minute ago, it seemed, he'd been watching Salome peel off her final veils as she danced, but he'd also been standing over Lucy with the stake, then looking up at John Seward in his study. He could still hear the music, Eastern and cacophonous, rising to a crescendo. But the hard floor had risen against his back. He had fallen, swirling in the darkness. The woman who had called him was Alice, his wife. He knew this now. He knew also that he was dying.

21. ABREE HARKER

DINNER WAS BRUTAL. Abree wished that she and her mother had skipped it, that for once they had foregone the duty to go through the rituals of eating and talking as though nothing was wrong.

Where on earth had Father escaped to now? This was the question that hid behind every clink of metal on china, every blink of the eye, and every suppressed cough. Did he have a secret assignation with Jenny? Or perhaps he had decided her firing was too great a punishment, and he had decided to go and rescue her.

But Mother seemed up to the task despite all this. She talked rather more than usual, skipping lightly over the subject of the flowerbeds. They had let things slide too much this year, she had declared with apparent sincerity as she cut through her meat. She had seen tulips in the most delightful colours in Green Park, and she was determined not to miss the boat when it came to planting bulbs.

Abree chased a pea around her plate with her fork, listening, nodding. The lamb chop was rather dry. Mrs. Rogers was distracted and out of sorts. Abree made no attempt to eat more than a mouthful or two, although she noticed that Mother had finished all that was on her plate. She had also drunk two full glasses of wine, which was unusual for her.

Of course, Mrs. Rogers was likely the sole reason they were eating dinner at all. They must keep up appearances for the servants. What a curious paradox this was. The servants were there for the convenience of their masters, and yet the masters behaved in the way they did because of the servants. She thought about Edward, and her mood became darker instantly. Sometimes it seemed as though Edward's cynicism, a more dynamic version of her own, flooded her spirit. It was only at these times that was she a fully motivated person in her own right. Except of course, it wasn't *her own* right. Her sentiments at these times were borrowed.

What would Edward say about Abree and Mother eating together, talking about tulips and flowerbeds? He would be disgusted at the hypocrisy. He would see it as a metaphor for a vile and depraved system, for the alliance between injustice and mendacity. He'd say that deep inside this behaviour was a profound self-loathing and that the only reason people kept servants was to impose upon themselves a form of social control. They were policed by their "inferiors," by a constant desire to show themselves worthier, wiser, and better behaved than those they employed.

Dessert, a rather watery trifle, had come and gone, and still Mother was chatting, this time about trying out some more exotic plants outdoors as well as in the conservatory. Mrs. Rogers had refilled Mother's glass, which, if she finished it, would make a third. Abree had never seen her mother drink three glasses of wine.

The gold of the evening deepened to dusk, and a breeze began to stir beyond the window, scattering dust and pebbles. Mother sighed and squinted at the glass, the only sign so far that she was worried about Father.

"I should ring for Mrs. Rogers to pull the curtains," she said, taking another sip.

"It's all right, Mother," Abree said. "I'll do it."

Abree was glad to get away from the table for a moment. Dinner had been much longer than it might have been if Father were with them. It was as though by elongating the event, they might delay the inevitable moment when they would have to admit he was not returning until they both went to bed. They both knew this would mean another drunken homecoming, another hushed rescue by Mother.

Night had fallen so quickly that when she reached the window the onyx-like pane threw back her reflection with alarming clarity. She was glad to make it disappear quickly behind the sweeping velvet curtain. She'd seen a thin, anemic-looking young woman with sunken eyes and well-developed furrows on her forehead. Had she encountered such a face on the street or at the university she would have used a phrase like *moth-eaten* or *spiritless*.

She gave herself a moment before turning back to the table. Mother was no longer outfacing her worry. She too was frowning, fussing unnecessarily with a napkin that no longer had any purpose. As she sat down again, Abree braced herself to ask a question.

"Mother, where do you think Father went tonight?"

Mother stared directly across at Abree, her eyes suddenly intense. Abree wished she hadn't spoken. Something was off kilter about Mother tonight, first all the talking as though nothing was wrong, then the third glass of wine, and now this forbidding look. Mother took another sip of wine before answering. "You know your father. His club, I imagine." She leaned back in her chair and gave Abree a bitter smile. "And how about you, Abree? Whose heart are you intending to capture at that university of yours?"

The question, the timing of it, gestured toward an implicit competition between Abree and her mother. Had Abree suggested her father was somehow inadequate as a husband, and that his weaknesses reflected badly on Mother?

Abree fiddled with the stem of her glass. "I went to university with a view to a career, or at least to the improvement of my mind, Mother, not to find a husband."

"But there must be someone, all the same?" Mother seemed

friendlier now, almost playful, but Abree sensed she might still turn. "And that little friend of yours, Helen. She seems a sweet girl, honest and straightforward. Surely she must have many would-be suitors?"

"Mother!" Abree said with a half-laugh. "Nobody talks about 'suitors' these days." Her tone was an attempt at playfulness, but, again, she'd miscalculated. Mother was offended.

"I see," she said, throwing her head back. "I am old-fashioned."

"It's just the word, that's all," Abree said, but the damage was done.

"What word would you use?"

Abree felt the heat rising to her face, and she gripped the base of her glass. "I don't know, Mother. I don't use any words because I don't have any ... suitors, or admirers, or beaus."

Mother blinked at her, three or four times, and then sighed. "Well, clearly I have outlived my usefulness in this strange new world of yours." She folded her serviette neatly beside her plate and rose to her feet.

Abree heard the swoosh of Mother's skirts as she moved through the room to the door. When the sound ceased unexpectedly, she turned to see her mother looking back at her, a curious expression on her face. It wasn't hostile now so much as frightened. "It is natural enough, Abree, for children to criticize their parents..."

"I wasn't criticizing..."

"Hear me out, Abree."

Abree, neck still craning to see her mother, held her breath.

"I said it is natural to criticize. But remember this. We have one chance to get it right. One chance to be a wife, a mother, or a friend. One chance to be a useful person. Once a mistake is made, a serious mistake, you move on. You have no choice. Remember Omar Khayyam's moving finger?"

"Yes, Mother, I know," said Abree, trying to keep the impatience out of her voice. Omar Khayyam's poetry was one of the few passions Abree's parents shared. The esoteric verses, which had been written many centuries ago but had flowered in the Victorian imagination, were rather like a drawbridge securing her parents from the modern word, separating them from Abree. Omar Khayyam was a secret code. His verses drew together everything her parents' generation valued—mysticism, medievalism, and most of all esotericism. The Persian poet confirmed to them that, however much the younger generation thought they knew, they knew less than their elders.

Her mother opened the door but turned back again.

Abree pre-empted her. "I don't know of any mistakes that you have made," she said conclusively, willing her mother to leave and shut the door after her.

But her mother was not about to leave. She laughed, and her eyes became pink with tears. She came back into the room, leaving the door open behind her. She raised her hand and put her half-closed fist in front of her mouth like a perverse version of a giggling school girl. A tear rolled down her cheek and pooled around her knuckles. She was standing only a yard away from Abree now. Abree wished she would back off. "Well," Mother gulped, still smiling, "there were mistakes. Large ones. Life and death mistakes."

"You mean Quincey?" asked Abree.

"No, not Quincey. We couldn't stop him from going to war, though he may have been part of it all."

"Part of it all?"

Her mother made a noise—half groan, half yell—and picked up the nearest serviette as she straightened herself up and dabbed her eyes.

"Mother," Abree said with some urgency, "what are you talking about?" She didn't want to know the answer. She just wanted to shock her mother into sobriety. Any kind of assertion from Abree would be a shock.

"Lucy." The word came out in a sigh. "Lucy." Her tears stopped, but still Abree's mother put both open hands in front of her face before sliding them down to her sides. "I let them murder her."

The phrase *let them murder her* whirred around the room like a bedraggled moth. Abree remembered something about foreign gypsies and ruffians in the stories of her parents' younger days. The details had disappeared into the general haze of childhood memory, but Abree supposed her mother must be referring to these events. An image flashed through her mind of a desperate band of Eastern-European ruffians emerging from a covered wagon—they had pistols in their belts, and long moustaches and cowboy hats—and a delicate young Victorian woman tied to a tree with rope. But it made no sense. Mother had told her that Lucy had died of some disease.

"Who, Mother?" she asked after a pause. "Who murdered her?"

Her mother took a breath. "Your father. Your father and his friends. Lord Godalming, Professor Van Helsing, Dr. Seward, and the young Texan, Quincey Morris." She'd listed these people dryly like items on a shopping list, nodding after each one. With each name, something coiled tighter within Abree. She wished her mother sounded more hysterical, more like she'd sounded just a minute before. The calmness of her tone gave too much veracity to the words. Her mother did not exaggerate as a rule. She hadn't talked about negligence, medical or otherwise. She had talked about murder. Murder is deliberate. It is a mortal sin. It is a crime that involves courts, prisons, and the hangman's noose. And disgrace. Instantly, Abree was ashamed of this last thought—it was a selfish one. Everyone connected with murder, including daughters of murderers, moves instantly from anonymous respectability to public shame and infamy.

"Mother," Abree said as sternly as she could manage, "you don't know what you're saying."

Her mother looked down at her with a glassy-eyed serenity. "I wish I didn't, but I'm afraid I do."

The coil within Abree tightened even more. She shivered. The danger felt urgent, imminent. There was a noise upstairs—glass breaking, a thump as of someone landing on the floor. Mother didn't seem to notice it, and Abree too felt it could almost be ignored; the noise seemed to coincide so perfectly with the mood of the moment. There had, after all, been an invasion into their lives. Why would it not make an audible disruption in their home?

But Mother turned now to the open door, the dimness of the hallway, and then back again. The noise had not been imaginary, no matter how neatly it dovetailed into the present situation. Mrs. Rogers was downstairs in the kitchen. The sound was from far above, the servants' quarters at the front. It told of violence and disruption. Someone had entered the house.

Abree caught her breath and stood. There was a groan, vast and primeval, beyond the house, beyond London perhaps—thunder. Mother and Abree moved together protectively, their fingers almost touching. There came a banging sound from upstairs. Someone had thrown open a door.

"We should ring for Mrs. Rogers," said Abree's mother.

"We should call the police," said Abree.

Mother nodded. But neither of them moved.

22. JENNY O'CONNELL

JENNY HAD THROWN THE DOOR open deliberately, but the noise shocked her, made her freeze. She had needed to get to the point of no return. The confrontation must happen; there could be no slinking away this time, no obedience, no humility, no false pride.

She remembered the Silverton munitions explosion four years ago. She'd been halfway down the street on her way home. The violence had been not only startling, but unjust. Violence was always unjust, she thought. Fire, buckling steel, and deafening sound came from the human race, not the natural world. No part of nature was this angry or destructive. So, even after everything that had happened, it horrified her to be the cause of commotion in her former employer's house.

The thunder had groaned deeply a few moments before, both restful and mighty, like a snoring giant. She felt as though the storm was on her side, and she'd thrown open the door to show her allegiance to the night.

She waited for the din of vibrating wood to die away into a kind of silence—a thick silence, compromised only of the hum and hiss of rushing blood. Hiding was no good now anyway. She was breathless, anxious for a reaction, impatient for some response from downstairs.

Her old bedroom and landing were dark save for a scattering blue from the street lamps entering through the broken window. But she'd been in darkness in the square long enough, and her

accustomed eyes could make out the curve of the little bannister, the threadbare, grey carpet on the stairs. The blood from
her wrist fell with a *splat* onto the bare boards just inside the
bedroom door. She had cut herself climbing though the window.
She'd always wondered what a criminal was, what made such
a person tear through the membrane from law-abiding citizen
to housebreaker and thief. Now she knew. She'd turned to
crime because there had been nowhere else to turn.

They must have heard her below. Someone would come thundering up the stairs any moment, she thought. It was bound to
be Mr. Harker. Surely, they wouldn't leave that task to poor
Mrs. Rogers. Jenny could cope with either of these people much
more easily than Mrs. Harker or her daughter. Those two were
a living conspiracy. But Mrs. Rogers would understand well
enough, and Mr. Harker would likely be ashamed as well as
angry or frightened. She could use his shame. She could use
it to lever concessions from him, real ones, not vague and
meaningless reassurances. Or perhaps she was fooling herself.
Perhaps they would just call the police.

She sucked in air, then listening to the thick, hissing quiet
again. She'd had no choice, she told herself again. If she'd gone
to the door, they could have barred her entry. Now she was
inside. The ball was in their court. Despite everything, it was
exhilarating, this moment, the finality of her act, the waiting
for a response.

Since Covent Garden, since the gold of evening had spread its
wings over the stones, a special kind of zeal had been growing
in Jenny. She was rewriting an ancient story. She was retracing
the steps recorded in the pages of the most sacred books. The
donkey and the inn, the swirling sands of the desert. And she
hadn't chosen this. It had been foisted on her.

When she'd arrived at the square, it had been almost ten and
darkness had been falling. Clouds had been thickening over
the few timorous stars. She had tasted a hint of oncoming rain.
A gentleman, tall, dark, and foreign-looking had opened the

door for her. He had been with a young woman, one of Miss Abree's friends, Jenny had thought. There had been a slight smile on the man's face, and he had tipped his Derby at her with a trace of irony. Had he known she was an imposter? He and his young woman had been on their way out of the gardens. Once inside, breathing in the night, Jenny had found a bench surrounded by bushes. It was almost invisible from most of the paths. A fresh breeze had wrenched its way through the dark foliage, creating monstrous images as Jenny heard the warden's whistle. A chill had gone through her. The warden had been closing the square as she had known he would. Then she had heard the clank of iron and the rattle of a chain. She had trapped herself into action. To escape she would have had to climb over the high, pointed rails. She would have had to become intrepid. This had been what she wanted. She had already known where this night would take her. A beech tree at the front of the house had branches that reached very close to her former bedroom window.

As soon as the night had settled, Jenny had begun her climb. A taxi had moaned past as her angled feet gripped the dry bark. She had waited for a moment just a yard from the ground, heart thumping through the trunk. The smell of bark and moss had called her to a different time, as had the freshening wind. This had been neither Belgrave Square at night, nor a biblical past, but rather something distinctly from these islands, something earthy, and mythic, a place of faeries and night creatures and magical woodlands.

No one would be able to see her, she had told herself. No one would be looking. People don't see what they are not expecting to see, least of all in the dark. Voices, distant laughter had wafted over from the opposite side of the square. She'd moved again. Gasping with the effort, she had hauled herself upward. She'd left her bag below as she'd known it would snag and weigh on her, but she'd carried half a brick in the pocket of her skirts along with her money. The brick's edge had scraped against her thigh as she reached a ring of branches and pulled herself up. It was true no one would have seen her—probably. But if they had, if they had looked up into the branches and seen a young woman scaling a large tree in the green patch before one of the houses, what would they have thought? Londoners were used to ugliness and degradation. But they had their places—Whitechapel Road in the east or Villiers Street in the west. The desperate, the starving, and the lonely of this city were remarkably considerate when it came to keeping to their quarters. But there Jenny had been, a savage piece of nature, in the very place where she would have caused most alarm. All standards of normal behaviour had been suspended, and this had given her a sense of safety. She had been confident she would continue to outrun *the obvious expectations*, no matter the cost; *the obvious expectations* were hunger and shame and begging. No doubt she would be ashamed enough in time, but then, in that moment, her actions had suspended her in a bubble of infinite possibility.

Jenny had climbed more quickly as she passed the floor where the Harkers slept. There had been no lights on this level, just black spaces of glass. It had seemed that no one had retired yet. She had slipped once here, just a foot or less. But the bark had collided hard with the skin of her back. She had looked down briefly but had been unable to see the ground. This had made it easier, less fearful.

The hardest part had come when she had raised herself level to her own room. She had moved her weight carefully to the branch that bent towards her window like the gnarled finger of a forest giant. A sudden jolt to the left had made her hold on tight with both hands. Her body had rebelled; the branch hadn't moved. She'd waited for her heart to calm and then slowly lowered herself inch by inch until she was lying belly to bark like a snake. She had been safe enough as she tried to shimmy along. Although she had scraped her skin against the corky ridges, the branch had been solid. She'd been pinioned to it by her own weight. Soon, however, the brick had become bundled up in the folds of her skirt. As she had drawn nearer to the window, she had had to sit up again and untangle it from the various folds of material.

Her top half had been heavier than she wished. It had made her dizzy. She had been far from the ground and her hands had been shaking. And it had been due to the danger alone. For the first time since Covent Garden, she had felt foolish. Why was she was risking herself like this, risking an unborn child, when her real chance for defiance had come this afternoon when Mrs. Harker had dismissed her? She could have refused to leave. Wouldn't that have been easier? She could have demanded that she remain or that she be compensated properly with enough money and provisions to cover for the loss of her position and the state in which she found herself.

The brick had emerged dusty and warm from her skirts at last. The hint of a tear, a maudlin tug in her chest had warned her against regret. The past was gone, she had thought. Yes, she could have done those things. But this was her course now. There was no choice. Drawing room negotiations would certainly have favoured Mrs. Harker anyway. To assert herself, she must frighten. She must be radical. She must stay in the bubble of infinite possibility. Her fingers had curled around the brick. With a sudden lurch that took even her by surprise, she had thrown the brick with some force. The glass had given way, and so had the wooden cross support. There should have been room enough to crawl through, but she had to leap first.

In a moment, she had risked everything. Her right knee and left foot had left the branch. She had scooped through the darkness, arms reaching through the jagged mouth of the opening. Her hands had gripped the inner frame and both knees had struck the outer wall. Her shoes had skipped against the brick like the feet of a hamster on a wheel. One shoe had fallen off into the darkness. The foliage below had embraced it with a sigh. A rush of fear had carried her through. In a moment, her whole body had slumped over into the room.

It had been a messy birth. She'd cut her wrist but didn't know how badly. She'd lost her shoe and her arm was numb.

Now, established in the house and waiting, she stood on the threshold between her room and the narrow servants' corridor. The numbness of her arm began to lift and give way to a sharp pang on her wrist, where the shard had entered. She heard another *splat* as blood dropped onto the floorboard. There was still no movement, no sound from below. Yes, she thought, they were calling the police. She would have to go down to them, and soon, if they would not come up to her.

She thumped hard down the servants' upper staircase so they would be prepared. Another point of no return; there had been many of them since Covent Garden. She walked unevenly, her stocking foot slipping, through the narrow servants' corridor on the first floor, before reaching the door that would take her onto the main landing. With a loud, prolonged creak, the door opened. She went through, and it thudded closed behind her. The landing light was on. She saw the wound on her wrist properly now. It was two or three inches long and rather deep in the middle. Blood pooled around it as she watched, and one dollop, thick and congealing, dropped noiselessly onto the green-and-gold carpet.

Her mind was made up. In a few moments, she'd be walking down the main staircase, the very place where the master had first made his move. She laid her hand on the bannister, feeling the warmth of the teak. Distantly she heard the *ping* of the drawing room grandfather clock. It must be eleven o'clock. The sound, so familiar from her life as a servant, drained away her sense of exhilaration.

It had been her fault too, hadn't it? Couldn't she have stopped Mr. Harker somehow? She had been with him often enough after that first time. To any onlooker, her part in their dalliance would have seemed entirely voluntary. She was trembling suddenly, no longer defiant. But still, she told herself, the Harkers had to provide, no matter what they thought of her, no matter what she thought of herself.

The silence downstairs was unbearable. She listened hard for voices or movement, but there was none. Perhaps the place was empty. Why had she not thought of this? She felt like calling out but knew this would be the action of a coward. She was the housebreaker, after all. She shouldn't be the one to warn the occupants of her presence.

She descended a few steps but then stopped to take off her remaining shoe. She bent down to lay it on the carpet. A one-shoed avenger would look absurd. Suddenly everything about her mission seemed absurd.

Now she heard it, coming from the dining room: whispering, desperate whispering. They were not out. They'd heard her. Her knees almost buckled. The weakness made her go down another two steps.

"Who is it?" called a sudden voice—Mrs. Harker's—from the dining room. "Who's coming?" The cravenness of the words, the obvious fear, and the fact the speaker had not come to meet the danger, gave Jenny courage again. Her heart calmed. The strength came back to her limbs. Should she answer? Or should she make them wait? "We've called the police, you know." There was terror in the voice—real terror. Instinctively, Jenny didn't believe the claim.

She reached the hallway and made her way to the partly opened dining room door. All she could see was a sideboard, a decanter, and the striped blue-and-grey wallpaper. No more noise came from within. There was no point pausing, so she entered.

Standing by the table were Mrs. Harker and her daughter. They were turned into each other like two halves of a mussel shell, each gripping the hands of the other. Mrs. Harker's hand was trembling. Miss Abree's face was twisted curiously as though she were trying not to cry. Both sets of eyes were tear-rimmed with fear.

A spasm took her over Jenny. She folded in upon herself and collapsed almost to her knees. At first she didn't recognize the emotion, but then she knew, as relief swept through her in waves: it was mirth, loud and unapologetic. Through her blurred vision she saw Mrs. Harker's expression change from fear to outrage.

"How dare you?" said Mrs. Harker. Her hands were still entwined with her daughter's, but there was ice in her expression. Even this had an unfortunate effect. Jenny laughed even harder. She was afraid her bladder would open.

"I'll call Mrs. Rogers," said Miss Abree, but she moved only half a step away from her mother.

"How dare you come into this house?" said Mrs. Harker.

"Mother," said Miss Abree. "Her arm. It's bleeding."

Jenny's laugher sputtered at last into a cough. She wiped away a tear with the back of her hand, but then realized she'd used her wounded arm; she'd likely left a smear of blood on her face.

Mrs. Harker's eyes became small with distaste. "What are you doing here?" she asked.

Jenny gulped down the last of her cough. "You know why I'm here," she said, breathless. "I'm carrying your husband's child. I have nowhere else to go."

Miss Abree jolted backwards. She looked at her mother.

"How can you say such a thing?" Mrs. Harker whispered.

So she didn't know? Jenny looked at Miss Abree, whose face had turned a deep red.

"How can I say such a thing?" Jenny repeated slowly.

"How can you *say* it?" Mrs. Harker said again, and this time the emphasis was undeniable. It wasn't the fact itself that was horrifying so much as letting it out into the open. There was a gust of wind, sudden, almost human-sounding from outside and a patter of rain on glass.

Mrs. Harker shook her head and turned to the table, resting her knuckles on its surface.

Miss Abree stared at Jenny for a moment and then moved

to the bell pull. "I'll call Mrs. Rogers. We need to get your wound looked at."

She tugged at the cord and then came towards Jenny. Her approach was so unexpected that Jenny almost backed away. But Miss Abree took hold of her forearm and turned it, looking at the wound. Another sound, not thunder or rain, but a bang from the front door made all three of them turn. A set of keys jangled. Someone breathed heavily. Mr. Harker was home.

23. JONATHAN HARKER

LATER, JONATHAN WOULD WONDER that he should have returned to the one place he was sure to be found. But the decision had made itself. He had needed to go home, even if it was for a day, a week, or five minutes. He had needed to wrap himself with what was his, what was familiar: the Persian rug of the drawing room, the way it mingled eastern promise with homeliness; the faint tick of the grandfather clock metering away time; the golden swirl of light in the whiskey decanter. He even wanted to be near his family. Distant as they were as people, those two heartbeats—Mina's and Abree's—held all the comfort of long-term proximity. Being home meant all life as he knew it was not quite over.

He'd chosen his fate the moment the young orderly had opened the door. He could have stayed and explained. Van Helsing had provided him with the very story he should use. He could have stayed calm and explained. He could have told the orderly that the old professor had taken his own life, and that he had gripped the knife handle himself only in a desperate attempt to prevent the suicide. He would have been called on to repeat the story to the governor, then, likely, the police. In the end, they'd have had little option but to believe him, as there would have been no clear evidence to the contrary. But somehow this course of action had been simply beyond him. As soon as the young orderly had taken a step into the room Jonathan had merely bolted through the gap between the orderly and the cell door. He had found himself running down the corridor, back towards the vestibule with the grille. The bald man with the spectacles had looked up, only vaguely interested, as Jonathan had passed him. Perhaps this hadn't been the first time someone had flown from the place in a state of panic.

He hadn't run anywhere for years, and he had been amazed at his swiftness, surprised also by the silence of the institution around him, save for the echo of his shoes on the black-and-white tiled floor—there had been no alarm, no whistle, no yells. The taxi had still been there, patient under the wavering boughs of the ash tree. The driver must have been watching the entrance. Little puffs of smoke had appeared from the exhaust pipe; he had already put on his engine.

The orders to return home had been implied. So that was where the driver had taken him without further instructions. It had been a heavy dusk at the time, thick and glowering over the city. Jonathan's hands had been sticky with blood. Had the driver noticed?

He'd been a lawyer long enough, rubbing shoulders with criminal lawyers, to know that murderers were rarely, if ever, the smooth, cunning characters depicted in Conan Doyle's stories. They were usually reckless, foolish people whose tenuous grip on reality had snapped long enough for some desperate, drunken act to snuff out the life of another. Murder was a momentous crime committed by pathetic individuals. He had never thought he'd be one of them. He already had been. But that had been different. He'd shared the crime with Quincey Morris. And the two of them had shared it with Van Helsing and the others who had urged and supported them. More than this, the previous murder had been committed on desolate, foreign soil. He'd allowed himself to see it as a necessity of war, or at least of a colonial exploit that provided the banner of a just cause. But this was London. In the car, blood had been drying on his hands. What he'd done to Van

Helsing was instantly recognizable as murder.

A drop of rain had fallen on the windshield and then smeared down the glass as they entered the square. The moment they had come to a halt outside Jonathan's home, a thousand arrowheads had pounded the windshield together. Wipers had beat them away like bats' wings in the darkness. Jonathan had fumbled with his wallet, handing over two bloodied fives through the partition, mumbling for the driver to keep the change.

He had scooped through the darkness, taken out his key, turned it, and opened the door. It had slammed behind him, and he'd dropped the keys on the little hall stand. He'd expected—hoped perhaps—that his wife and daughter would be in bed. But as he stood in the hallway now, breathing heavily, he sensed that there was something odd about the atmosphere. There was a watchfulness about the house. He had a sense that people were listening for him. The lights were on in the hallway and, apparently, in the dining room, which was unusual at this time of the evening.

A door opened and closed somewhere below. There were footsteps, and then Mrs. Rogers appeared, crossing the end of the hallway and making for the dining room. When she saw him, she hesitated for a moment, curtsied, and then continued. Her expression contained a great deal, a kind of dread he had seen in the eyes of women whose husbands were terminally ill, a lack of pallor, a deepening of the grooves in her cheeks. In the brief instant in which their eyes had met, he felt he was implicated in this dread. Whatever her problems were, whatever was wrong in this household, he was at the very centre of it. Did they know already? Had the police already come for him? He looked down at his keys. A smear of Van Helsing's blood had dried on the metal of the key ring.

Loneliness had brought him home, but being home would not cure that loneliness. Loneliness was a vice, and it was closing in on him. Mrs. Rogers' expression had not lied. His condition was indeed terminal. He opened his hand, felt the *pat* of drying blood at the parting of skin from skin. His palm was a bloody map. Lightning flashed through the painted glass above him, a lurid halo arcing on the tiles. Twists and knots from the beech tree outside outlined themselves in the squares, a medieval woodcut from a magic lantern show. *Something wicked this way comes.* A rumble, deep and angry, shuddered through the night.

Lowered voices came from the dining room, more than one, Jonathan thought. Mrs. Rogers left the dining room the same way she had come. This time she was hurrying. She did not catch his eye or curtsy.

Jonathan moved through the hallway, making little sound. Tiles gave way to carpet. Static from the fibres prickled in his nose. This was his house, and yet it wasn't. He'd been usurped.

The idea came from nowhere, yet it was confirmed the moment he crossed over the dining room threshold. He saw three women. His daughter was kneeling, tending to some inexplicable wound on the arm of his former maid, the girl he thought to be permanently gone; the older woman, his wife, turned towards him, her dark eyes full of contempt.

A bell, rapidly sounding and urgent, was travelling through the night, coming closer by the moment. It took a moment to recognize the sound. He thought at first of a small church being shaken in the fist of an enormous child. But, of course, it was merely a siren, from a fire engine or perhaps a police van. He rubbed his bloody right hand on his trousers.

The siren approached, entering the square.

EPILOGUE. ABREE HARKER

ABREE FELT LIKE A HAWK watching its prey as she stared at Helen from her bedroom window. Autumn was in the air, even though it was still a full month away. Shadows of boughs and leaves wavered over Helen's patient form, over her satchel. There was a touch of Monet about the light; it was fleeting, constantly in motion.

Helen was the last person Abree wanted to meet, but her friend had now reached out several times, her requests culminating in this morning's phone call. Abree had been taken by surprise, especially when Helen suggested she could come to the square just outside Abree's house. Excuses had been both plentiful and plausible for the last several weeks, but they had finally run out. There had been her father—the business first with the police and then with the doctors. There had been a scramble to have him committed. It had been the easiest, quickest, and most reversible way of preventing further investigation, her father's colleagues had explained. Connected with this had been the task of arranging powers of attorney both for Mother and Abree. Then, once Father had been safely relocated to Hanwell, there had been some challenges: settling Jenny as a more or less permanent houseguest, calming mother, and managing the legal rigmarole about money and property and income, not to mention scheduling one hurried meeting with Professor Reynolds in order to explain all the delays with her studies—not that he had cared in the least. His eyes had wrinkled in a kind of smug hope that this might be a prelude to her giving up altogether.

When Helen had suggested they meet in the square just outside Abree's home, Abree had hesitated, and then she'd agreed. The real reason she had been avoiding her friend made her feel small. And she was finished with being small. If the business with Jenny and her father had taught her anything, it was that she must face the world with a modicum of honesty, a pinch of courage. Emily Davison was beyond her and always would be. Abree was no warrior, no martyr. But she could just about admit to the truth when it was staring her in her face. She could at least see the world as it was. They must look after Jenny and her child because they were responsible for them. That would have to do for now.

Abree had heard about Helen and Professor Florescu. They had been seen together more than once. They had been at the very performance of *Salome* at which Lord Godalming had died. But why shouldn't decent, hardworking, intelligent Helen be wooed by the handsome foreigner? No reason, but the idea of it pricked Abree, sent little fires of jealousy sparking inside her. Somehow it seemed unjust, at least in a folkloric kind of way. Wasn't goodness supposed to be its own reward? Helen already had that. Abree—beleaguered, moth-eaten, jealous, self-doubting—was the one who needed an admirer. She was the one who needed help in order to be good.

She moved away from the window, pulled on her cardigan, and made her way downstairs. No point in delaying now. She may as well hear what Helen wanted to tell her. Perhaps she would announce her engagement to Ivan Florescu. But somehow, Abree thought as she opened the front door, this didn't seem very likely, not the announcement part anyway. Helen was too modest to claim her friend's attention for the sole purpose of revealing information about herself. She would let the news come out naturally in conversation about something else, something that involved Abree as much as herself.

Gathering the keys, Abree left the house and crossed the road. A middle-aged woman who lived on the square walked past her briskly before she reached the gate. In the old days, before Father's problems, before maid became guest, the middle-aged woman would have nodded, smiled, or even made a comment about the weather. But the Harkers had become invisible recently. Presumably everyone knew some, or all, of the story. The *Tragic Incident* at Hanwell had been reported in the papers, and Father's name had appeared as a party helping the police. It wasn't much in itself, especially as charges were never filed, but other routes, more circuitous ones, must have filled in some of the murkier aspects of the case.

Abree locked the gate behind her, feeling foolish as she did so, especially as Helen, who turned to her now, had clearly gained entry without a key. Helen moved her satchel onto the ground and gave Abree a smile that was somewhere on the borderline between sadness and complacency.

"How are you, Abree?" she asked. The question carried far more meaning than usual.

The usual platitudes escaped Abree as she sat down. In the end she said nothing, but just twitched a smile in response. An elderly lady walked her poodle on the opposite side of the gardens. Despite the dappled sunshine and warmth, no one else was around.

"I can't imagine what it's been like," said Helen after a pause, "but"— she looked at Abree carefully for a moment, seemed to survey her face—"you seem older, stronger. Perhaps you have come into your own."

If anyone else had said this, Abree would have thought it presumptuous, but Helen's goodwill, and her respect, was obvious. She felt almost flattered.

"I have heard you have become close with Professor Florescu," Abree said. Her hands fluttered on her knee then settled again.

"In a *way*, yes," said Helen, frowning at the tufts of grass at her feet.

It seemed like an odd answer, so Abree looked at her friend until she turned to face her.

"During those times that you met Professor Florescu yourself, Abree," she said, "you might have noticed that he seemed to be circling around an awkward subject. I feel I'm in danger of doing the same."

Abree gave a short laugh. Her curiosity was becoming tinged with annoyance. "What can you mean?"

"I've become friends with him, but only friends. I'm not his target. In fact, he has no target in that sense. He thought perhaps you should know something, something your mother likely suspects already."

Abree looked at Helen steadily. Helen looked away, surveying the boughs above her head. "Before the professor took his history degrees, he was a medical student. Did he tell you? He served in the war. In France."

It seemed an odd change of direction, a delay perhaps before getting to the point. A thrush hopped across the grass and then stopped. It looked like it would take off, but then it hopped a few more times before spreading its wings.

"He met your brother, Abree. He met Quincey." Helen looked directly at Abree now, her expression rather grave. "He treated Quincey."

"Oh." Abree bowed her head. A wave had hit her. She couldn't tell its substance—grief, surprise, a curious mixture of both—but it was strong, almost overpowering. She thought she might faint.

Helen put her hand on Abree's shoulder. "I'm sorry. I'm sorry I had to tell you like this. But I thought it would be worse for you not to know."

"It's just..." Abree began. She didn't have the words. Her brother's death—the detail surrounding it—was sacred. It was a place she seldom trod, even in her imagination. And here was news of a man, one she had met, who had been within the temple itself. The game of tennis, the lolloping run, was no longer the last image of her brother. There was more. "Was he with Quincey at the end?"

"Very near, I believe. He'll tell you himself. But there is more."

Helen rooted in her satchel, pulled out a tissue, and handed it to Abree. Abree hadn't noticed she'd been crying. She pressed the tissue into her face.

"Yes?" she said.

"People in the infirmary commented on how similar they looked, Quincey and Ivan, the professor. Quincey was well enough to talk, apparently, during those last few days. He told Ivan all about you. That's why he came to teach at King's College. He wanted to meet Quincey's sister, his mother too. But your mother was a problem."

"Why?" Abree said.

"He didn't want to force your mother to admit to something she would not be ready to admit to."

Abree felt a sudden chill. The sun had disappeared behind a cloud. "I don't understand. What are you saying?" The breeze circled around them.

"Somehow, the professor knew that his father was"—she paused, seemed to purse her lips—"romantically involved in London before he died. There was a mystery about it. His father was, apparently, something of a lothario in some ways. There were actually two romances with English women. One led to the other."

"What does this have to do with Quincey?" asked Abree. The gate swung open and closed again. Abree crumpled the tissue into a ball. She didn't like this circling.

Helen paused. The silence was troubled, commanding attention. She was looking down carefully. "Professor Florescu also knew, from papers and letters and such, that his father had known people called Jonathan and Mina Harker as well as an English aristocrat named Arthur Holmwood, who would become Lord Godalming. One of the women was Arthur's fiancée. She died suddenly, and the professor's father was very

Photo credit: Paul Daly

Paul Butler is the author of eleven novels, most recently *The Widow's Fire* (2017) and one non-fiction work. Butler's novels have appeared on the judges' lists of Canada Reads, the Newfoundland and Labrador Book Awards shortlists, and he was on the Relit Longlist for three consecutive years. Between 2003 and 2008, he won in the annual Government of Newfoundland and Labrador Arts and Letters Awards four times and was subsequently invited to be first literary representative and then chair on the Arts and Letters committee. Butler has written extensively for national newspapers and magazines over the years including features for *Canada's History* (formerly *The Beaver*), book reviews for *The Globe and Mail* and pieces for *Canadian Geographic*. As a writing coach his roster of clients includes several prize-winning novelists. Butler blogs on subjects literary and filmic with a special interest in topics gothic and supernatural. His website is www.paulbutlernovelist.wordpress.com.

ACKNOWLEDGEMENTS

I am profoundly grateful to everyone at Inanna Publications for saying yes to this novel and for their enthusiasm in publishing and promoting progressive and feminist books and authors. A special thanks to Inanna's editor-in-chief Luciana Ricciutelli for the editorial insight, boundless energy, and focus. The editing process was a joy because of Luciana. Also sincere thanks to Renée Knapp, Publicist and Marketing Manager who works so efficiently to get Inanna books out and noticed in the world. Thanks to Val Fullard for another of her lovely covers. I was lucky to have two first-rate novelists, Leslie Vryenhoek and Trudy Morgan-Cole, agree to read drafts long before publication with a view to endorsements. I am thankful for their kind words and also some excellent editing suggestions.

I feel very privileged to live in an uber-supportive home with my wife, author Maura Hanrahan, and daughter, Jemma Butler, and I am thankful, as always, for them.

The medical term is syndactyly…"

"I know the medical term." Abree closed her fist over the ball of tissue. "What am I supposed to do with this information?" She was surprised at the family pride stirring up inside her. She wanted to protect her mother, her father too. Adulterer. Cuckold. The words were an invasion.

Helen looked at her with pity. "They worked it out for themselves in the infirmary. It's a kind of kinship, Abree," she said softly. "The professor is Quincey's half-brother. It was enough to make him search for you."

Following Helen's glance, Abree turned towards the garden entrance. The professor was there, just inside the gate, his Derby in his hand. "He'll only come in if you're ready for him, Abree."

Abree pushed her tissue into the pocket of her skirt, feeling the chill again. Now, she could see a shadow of Quincey in the man from Wallachia. She could see her brother in his eager-to-please watchfulness, in the way his feet moved against the ground. This was no time for denial. There had been enough of that.

Abree took a breath, turned back to Helen, and nodded.

suspicious about this."

Lucy again. A murder of crows clustered around the base of a tree on the opposite side of the square. Abree thought of her mother, remembering her outburst: *I let them murder her.* Nothing had been said between them about it since. There had been a real murder that same night, or at least a death. Van Helsing's. There had been so much going on, urgent tasks had sounded like gunfire around their ears: Jenny with child, Father's commitment, lawyers, banks. She had barely had time to come back to it, but the questions remained: what had happened to her parents all those years ago? What had they done?

"Professor Florescu also became suspicious regarding his father's death. At one time, he thought it was a kind of revenge."

"Revenge?" echoed Abree. One of the crows cawed loudly and took to flight. "You mean my parents and their friends?" Abree almost laughed at the idea, but she was beginning to feel uneasy. How could she really laugh at anything now?

"He realizes now this was a mad kind of suspicion," Helen said. "He's really very vulnerable, you know, even though he seems so confident, so able. It's an orphan's disease, the outward appearance of confidence, the uncertainty within."

Abree glanced at her friend again. This kindness and insight were typical of Helen, but the familiarity with which she spoke of the professor seemed to contradict the claim that there was nothing romantic going on between them.

"But what about Quincey?" Abree asked. She didn't really want to talk about her brother's death and the professor's proximity to it; she didn't want to go back into that sacred place, not in the open while crows gathered and she felt so raw. But she knew she must. It was coming anyway.

"Quincey had webbed feet," said Helen.

Abree shook her head and frowned.

"So does Ivan." Helen let the silence work. One of the crows took to wing. The others watched as it flapped in a rough circle. "The professor inherited the condition from his father.